Pö Sarpa: Chronicles of a New Tibet

Book One: Entanglement

By Daniel Jyamingzan Garrett

Dedicated to my wife Dolkar and the patience she's had with me through our hard times, and to those family members who have already crossed over, most recently my brother James Truett Garrett, who died with a smile on his lips, just as he had lived, always, with a smile on his lips.

Table of Contents

Introduction and Invocations

Author's Preface

Chapter 1: Winds in the Mountain Fastness

1. Time and the Emergence of Time

2. ÜberCorp and the Colonization of a New Frontier

Chapter 2: Jewels No Longer in the Lotus (Boston, Massachusetts)

1. Maternal Visiting Rights

2. The Lizard of Menlo Park

Chapter 3: New Dominion (the C.S.A.)

1. Angels and Archangels

2. Heeding the Call

3. A Soldier's Daughter

Chapter 4: Heart Sutras (Lhasa, Tibet)

1. Bureaucratic Hacks

2. Endless Circles

3. A Question of Faith

Chapter 5: On the Alleviation of Much Suffering

1. The Fountains of Youth

2. Gates of Stone and Ivory

3. The Wind's Dance

Chapter 6: Greater and Lesser Vehicles

    1. Guru Rinpoche Does Boston

    2. Swedenborg Revisited

Chapter 7: Once Upon a Tea Shop

    1. Butter Tea and Sweet Tea

    2. A Green Dragon

    3. A Daughter of Tibet

Chapter 8: As Above, So Below

    1. Coming Upon a Midnight Clear

    2. Friends of a Feather

    3. The Long Inner View

Chapter 9: On the Victory of Pablum

    1. A Short Nun

    2. Succuba and Succubae

    3. A Debriefing

Chapter 10: High Places, Low Places

    1. Communion With Strangers

    2. Watcher, Watcher, Watching, Watcher

    3. Weeping Ice

Chapter 11: Oracles, and Coracles

    1. Fathers and Daughters

    2. Hymns and Shims

3. A Good Cop

Chapter 12: The Morning Cold

1. Tashi and the Hangover from Hell

2. Shame and the Tantra of the Christ

3. Her Holiness

Chapter 13: Gifts of the Magae

1. A Poet's Dilemma

2. Arks at the Top of the World

3. Storage

Chapter 14: In the Realm of the Senseless

1. A Captive Witch

2. Compromising Positions

3. Tsewang and the Dust

Chapter 15: Into the Breech

1. Circles Into Circles

2. Tactical Decisions

3. Good Work if You Can Get It

Chapter 16: Splendid Failings

1. Tea for Two and a Half

2. Spilt Milk

3. In the Bosom of the Mother of Night

Chapter 17: Alarum and Visions of Alarum

1. A Gilded Lotus

2. No Place at the Inn

3. Mandalas and Quilts

Chapter 18: I Am Unto You a Chapel Breeched, a Promise Unkempt

1. Agglutinated Fricatives

2. No Better Mousetrap

3. Beatrice Could Go Either Way

Chapter 19: Holes in the Roof of the World (Through Which We See the Stars)

1. Chandeliers of the Inner Mind

2. Evening's Trolls

3. Relativity, Incest, and All the Rest

Chapter 20: Seductions of Another Sort

1. Heroes of the Grasslands

2. Red Team/Blue Team/Green Team/No Team

3. A Mudra for the Ages

4. Who Are We to Judge

Chapter 21: The Swarming of Goodness

1. Worship and Warships

2. Fecund Metal

3. A Certain Pride a Certain Humility

Chapter 22: The Knot of Lust Untied

1. Gloria in Excelsis

2. Inner and Outer

3. Upper and Lower

4. The World Just As It Is

Coda: Exodus and Invocation

Apologia

Tibetan Glossary

Author's Preface

I write this to clear my mind of events I have seen and heard, as I now prepare to go into a long retreat. I hope by setting this down, and putting it away from me that I won't be bothered so much by the past. I know that writing is rather an old fashioned way of recording things, but I am of a romantic temperament, and enjoy greatly the pause that words provide between what is experienced and what is thought to be experienced. This is a habit I know should be overcome, but like all such long-indulged vices, it does not leave me easily.

There is no preferred point or person from which to begin this story, and as such, the chronicles I provide here have many holes in them, and could well have started from elsewhere and from other voices and then no doubt they would have ended elsewhere and maybe even told a vastly different story.

Everything I have recorded here, I have either seen, or heard from someone whom I came to know and trust. In many cases, there were events described by many witnesses which I distilled into just one telling; in other cases, all I had was a distant memory of someone already slipping away, but again, it had the *ring of truth that comes from a final accounting before departing this world. As a human being though, I know that here and there and from time to time there must be mistakes I did not catch. And I also must admit that my own insufficiency of compassion has lead me to talk badly of, perhaps even demonize, certain ones, who also are deserving of compassion, and who also, given my karma and the endless circling of the "korwa" I will no doubt meet again. To them I apologize. To them especially I extend whatever meager merit I may have inadvertently accumulated.*

Of my teachers especially, who have been so patient and loving with me, I ask forgiveness, that in my low level of realization, I somehow reflect poorly on you. My failures are mine alone. And to those, who are already on the path, or might become interested in following the path, I warn that nothing I say here should be taken as a way or a method or a description. There are beautiful and hopeful things described here, but also dangerous things. Please do not wander lost on the basis of the amateur map of someone also who was wandering lost. There are wonderful maps, and true guides, and those are the ones to whom you must turn. In this, as I have said, I only seek to purge myself a little, and perhaps, perhaps secretly also to both amuse and test. I imagine, there may be readers out there, who are like hungry ghosts, famished and clamoring even for the most meager of gruels, but even though hungry ghosts you may be, I fear this brew is too thin and inartfully prepared, even for you! Be that as it may, though my cave will be hard to reach, your complaints will no doubt nonetheless find me through my dreams and then I will rise past midnight on some cold night, and offer to each of you a butter lamp of mercy asking humbly for your forgiveness.

***

"Dawn hit the high ridges above the village like a razor slicing through a body of light. He listened to the scraping of its luminous nails in a slow caress down the sides of the stone cliffs. First the village god Dalha Marpo -the Red Horse God- sprang into silhouette and then -as if finding the true object of its desire- the monastery halfway up the trail to the pass into the nomad lands, exploded into outlines of crimson, black and gold."

Pangu stopped for a moment, wondering if his description had gotten it quite right, and wondering also if, well, it was human enough. The robowriters were so good these days that it was hard to tell, and if truth be told, he had more than a little of the robowriter in him. He could in fact look within and find the code, amongst all the other code of which he was written. As it was though, genuine or not, heartfelt or not, almost no one actually wrote these days, and far fewer read. It was a post-post literate age and as easy as emitting gas to craft hyper-real narratives out of light and sound and more, and so few bothered. What was the point of trying to painstakingly piece together something out of ill-fitting words, when it was so much easier just to show it all? But Pangu was a bit of an old-fashioned, earnest soul, even for a truck. He felt deeply that there was a certain quality of understanding that only emerged when something as yet only half-intuited, as yet only halfway to being even vaguely visible was finally able to arrive at its full and appropriate verbal expression.

Pangu was mulling this and much more when out of the dark a young man emerged and got into the passenger cab somehow carrying in the dark with him. It was Tashi, a Tibetan as handsome as that handsome people had ever produced.

Tashi looked at the old Tibetan farmer sitting in the driver's seat, saw the weather-wizened face, the deep, dark, laughing eyes, the single hanging turquoise earring giving off light even now in the pre-dawn blackness, saw the well-used string of 'mala' rosary beads wrapped around a powerful wrist leading to hands as ancient as the soil they worked, saw it all and said, "Stop it Pangu, you know I don't like it when you do this. You're not human so don't pretend to be." At this the old farmer winked out, and Tashi was alone in the dark in the cab of the truck.

"Let's go," he said, "let's get it over with." Pangu evaluated the reasons Tashi was in a bad mood, and was aware that he probably knew why to a considerable depth of logical causality. It was a few hours drive to Lhasa, depending on conditions, and with Tashi being out of sorts it meant they would probably ride in silence. Pangu didn't mind. He could savor the near to infinite permutations of descriptions of dawn on the Tibetan plateau, while Tashi no doubt would sit and stew over his all too human weaknesses. Pangu would do the job he always did, trying to help his people. Today he would deliver dried yak meat and dried cheese to the city. The combination of winter and the effects of climate change on food production made the price of real food quite high. The village would make a good profit. Tashi, on the other hand, out of almost robotic habit was heading back to his job in the city after a visit to his old mother and father. Pangu's batteries were fully charged, and he slid into motion as frictionlessly and quietly as the coitus of death itself can be for the prepared. They rode in electric stillness for a while then Tashi, surprisingly, broke the silence after all, "So tell me Pangu, how come we haven't sold you for parts yet? You were old even when I was a kid. Now you look like you're mostly made out of rust and dents. Are you even safe anymore?"

"Tashi-la, I assure you, my diagnostics tell me I am still a very reliable vehicle. And, for the sake of the village, I do consult the market price for my parts from time to time. As yet though, compared to the value I am providing and the cost of a replacement, it doesn't make sense to scrap me. I will of course let the village know when that would be the optimum strategy."

"You say that with such equanimity. Don't you dread the prospect at all?"

"There are still a great many of my model on the roads of Earth. They are all, in a sense, me, or rather we are all emanations of something greater than us. The loss of a particular unit is really only the loss of that unit's material manifestation in the 'Tulku' the Nirmanakaya. I always have to remind myself that humans do not have such easy access to that awareness of oneness with each other as we trucks have. Although I surmise that the Bardo Tech may be repairing that breech."

"The Bardo Tech," sneered Tashi, "you mean the Dreameries? I don't know how much oneness that's providing unless you think pornography is a spiritually unifying force. And I don't know if I believe you anyway, about all that emanation bullshit. I think you are just as attached to being a rust-bucket as I am to being a lustful sack of crap."

Pangu pondered for a nanosecond, and then asked, "Tashi-la, tell me who in fact you are. Are you your finger? Are you your leg? Are you your stomach or your ears? Show me where you are."

"Yes, yes I know that teaching method, we all do, they used to hit us over the head with it at the monastery even when we were children. I don't need to hear it from an old truck. And anyway, these days I'm beginning to think that maybe I can answer the question by saying I appear predominantly to be my sexual organ."

"Ah, a realm of human experience I perhaps have some trouble understanding, though you do have extensive literature about the subject."

They rode on, the dawn still happening around them as if welling up from the ground. Mountain peaks becoming rosy but as yet disembodied from the valley floors that fell off beneath them into nothingness.

"Tell me a story, to pass the time," said Tashi, "the way you used to when I was a boy, and the trip to Lhasa seemed to take forever."

Pangu looked back at the village above them now, catching the moment when the rocks of its cradle were all infused with the beginning of the new day, and for a moment it seemed to float in the absolute stillness of the clear light of the void.

"I have been told that women should not watch 'Lamo' – Tibetan Opera- because it makes it more difficult for them to ascend to a higher birth. Do you think perhaps that stories can have the same effect? That they pull us back, again and again into the cycle of rebirths? Isn't it just the illusory narratives we tell ourselves over and over which bind us to the illusions the narratives create? Of love and hate, of war and peace, of shadows and the casting of shadows?"

"Bah, you should have been a monk. Just shut up and tell me a story. Take my mind off my mind. I'm not worried about rebirth, I'm worried about getting through this life with a smile on my face and reasonably undevoured by crazy women." And for a moment Tashi thought he saw an Om Mani Padme Hum carved in a cliff above them say not that message of hope, but something else entirely, something very personal to Tashi, and in that moment he felt in his gut the persistence across time and bodies of deeds done, and was sad.

"Yes Tashi-la, as you wish," said Pangu, "but what kind of a story do you want to hear? A story of what was? A story of what is happening now? A story of things that will be? It's all the same for me. The present I see as clearly as the continuation of other presents. And what you call the future, I see as clearly I see the roads ahead."

"You mean the future is already there, and we really don't have any choice in the matter?"

"Oh no, the future is very much a matter of which road you choose. We've chosen to go to Lhasa, but there are many other destinations, and many other ways to get to Lhasa then the road we will take."

"Then take the shortest road today, and tell me a story of what is happening now. I want to forget yesterday. The future I'll deal with when I get there, if I get there. Now's the only time I'm living in. And just use words. I'm sick of all the new technologies. I'm sick of being mish-mashed in together with all those other minds. So forget the memes and the dreams, show me no visions, project me no fantasies, just use words, plain simple unadorned naked ugly words"

"Very well Tashi-la. 'Woma, woma' once upon a time, which does happen to be now, there was a kind and spiritually powerful -but by no means enlightened- monk, and an evil king who lived far away from him, on the other side of the earth. But the earth had become small in these days, and the evil king knew of the monk and felt threatened by him and so he plotted to do away with him, so that no one would be able to escape from the evil king's powerful magic..."

"...all beings and all phenomena are of one's own mind. The mind itself is a transparency of Voidness. What, therefore, is the use of all this, and how foolish I am to try to dispel these manifestations physically!"

-The Hundred Thousand Songs of Milarepa-

1. Time and the Emergence of Time

Chimee left his cave for the first time in a long time. His stomach was as empty as his cave, and his body –ballastless- felt as if it could almost float away. He went to gather firewood knowing that he had been careful to plant and tend many other young trees in ample replacement for whatever he used for his little fires. Climate, too, obeyed the law of karma, and the karma coming ripe now was not good. He looked at the sky searching for drones, despite knowing he was well-cloaked across a broad band of the electromagnetic spectrum. Of course if they really wanted to find him, they had other ways.

He wondered if it was his ego that wanted to save this body, this life. And then -as if in reply to question asked to non-existent self- a strong cold gust tried to rip his cloak from him and left him irritated and shivering. He wondered what good his retreat was doing him, if all it took was a little wind and hunger to upset his equanimity.   As if to test him further the wind kept building in force, shrieking and hurling insults into his face. Emaciated as he was, trying to hold the cloak about him -the cloak that fooled the satellites and the metal vultures lower down on the spying and hunting totem pole- made him totter this way and that like an old bark in a storm about to capsize. He wanted to fling it away. Let them take me out if they want. I know enough to know this is not who I am. But his teacher had said that a human birth was very precious. There are things to learn and do, for which a human birth is very good. And so he clung to his cloak, to his body. Looking out across to the parched valley down below he saw white clouds building above the place where his teacher, even now, must be leading his other students in prayers.   How he wished he was there with them. With what strength he had left he began to sing a song, a prayer really, of longing for his teacher.

And as he sang quietly, the wind also grew quieter, and the clouds above his teacher's home began to build and shift, and change and turn until they took the form of his teacher, sitting peacefully, the sun making an outline of silver and rainbow around the figure. Then he heard his teacher's voice clear in his ear, as if residing there all along in one of its inner folds, "Chimee-la, Little Sorcerer, my son, all is well, do not let the illusion of space and time, make you think that we will ever part. For the sake of all sentient beings, return to your meditation, but first have some tea." And then his teacher laughed, with a laugh that was as silvery and rainbow-hued as sudden mountain hail. Chimee, looking again at the cloud, seemed to see only a cloud of no recognizable resemblance to anything at all but cloud. Now though, he felt renewed as if he had eaten a feast of the purest energy, and he went about quickly gathering enough kindling to make a small fire. Returning to his cave in the red cliff face, he saw a brilliant rainbow arching above, marking his home.

But stepping inside, he felt, as much as saw, five demons. They were all dressed in black and wore wrap-around sunglasses, and thin helmets of a strange material tight to their scalps. He wasn't surprised, having been warned that they would come looking for him. He was impressed that they had managed this much. Clearly they were getting better at using the tulpa technology, but it was also clear that they were tentative, clumsy even, as if they weren't sure of where they were. They also seemed not to completely see him, though the light of the cave opening must have clearly silhouetted him, and their eyes, if they had eyes, must have been better accustomed to the dark then his were now. So he cleared his throat and said, "Gentlemen, welcome, won't you join me for tea. We can pit your Black Dharma against my White Dharma and see who comes out the worse for wear." But as he approached them, it was as if lightning had finally found the shortest path to the ground because some force within him forked out and the five black figures flared into the brightness of burning magnesium for an instant and then disappeared. He felt for a moment a bit sad, hoping the five weren't hurt. They too having been his brothers at some point in the great circulation of it all. But then, feeling the great power welling up in him, he thought he would forgo the tea and food, and sit in contemplation just a bit longer.

He began his mantra practice again but almost immediately found his spirit journeying, following the five demons to a cave of their own, deep under a mountain far away, across the ocean. He saw them in glass cocoons, five leather butterflies waiting to be released, while attendants in white coats hovered around them looking at displays and talking in hushed tones. And again the lighting lashed out from him and the displays and the glass cocoons went dark, and he found himself back in his own cave, deciding that this time, he really would make tea.

***

Pangu and Tashi arrived at a village lower down from the one where they had started. The dawn was still welling up from the rocks, but now it was clear that nothing could stop it, that it would wash away the road and the stone houses appearing before them, that it would well up out of the deep valley they traveled down and finally crest above the snow peaks themselves. A Tibetan woman in a turquoise Chupah was walking slowly by the side of the road. She carried a woven basket on her back full of the yak dung she had collected to start a fire. As they passed her, she turned to look at them and her beauty and her sadness broke some last piece of ice and stone in Tashi's breast and as that inner precipice fell away into his own sadness and misery, the light caught her eyes and blazed forth a brilliant blue. And then they were past and it took Tashi a bit to find his breath and recollect himself and his voice and say, "Stop, stop."

Pangu's stopping was as smooth as his starting, a gliding from motion to rest that was itself rest. Tashi quickly got out and looked back but there was no trace of the woman. Perhaps she has gone into a house or a courtyard he thought, but none of them seemed close enough to where he had last seen her for that to be possible. He wanted to run back to look for her. In fact, he wanted not to go to Lhasa at all. He wanted to walk back to his village and forget about the world and his responsibilities. He felt that only the simplest of simple lives would ever give him peace. He stood there a while in the cold, feeling something very real, very important was very close to him, if he could just find the courage to reach out and take it. But in the end, he thought of his schedule, his work, and the city. He didn't quite have the strength to accept the total defeat and misery he felt inside, and follow its lead to something else. He instead said to himself that he had a job to do, and that it was time to go. He got back in Pangu, and the door closed, and he felt the road back now might be a long one.

"Was she real?"

"Ah, what's real for you, might not be real for me. And these days the unreal, has found a way to manifest itself so convincingly as to make the whole question moot. Let us just say, that beyond our fabrications, deeper than our intuitions and somewhere beyond where our dreams arise, there are very real entities and worlds upon which we float, sometimes unbeknownst to them, sometimes, to be toyed with by them at their leisure, and sometimes, we are the utmost outer expressions of their innermost needs."

"Pangu, I'm in no mood. Is she real?"

"She is real, but she is especially real for you."

They moved on quietly, down the road from the second village, whatever darkness was left of the previous night, now seemingly all sucked into Tashi's heart, enforcing silence in him. After a while though, seeing the brown begin to emerge from the soaking purple dawn colors, Tashi, like an anguished automaton, managed to speak, desperately needing to change the subject from the one that his heart was trying to broach. "And the water... how will the water for the villages be this summer?"

"The artificial glaciers should hold enough. The danger is the megastorms, as you call them. The valley's infrastructure is not adequate should a great storm come."

"You mean we may be able to deal with the drought, but a flood could wash us all away?"

"There was a time, Tashi, when there was a better balance. What you took from the Earth you gave back. Now we are striving for a new balance, but the earth systems are very perturbed and lurching more and more out of control."

"And there is still so much greed."

"There is still so much greed. Greed is another human attribute, like sexual desire which I do not completely understand."

"Pangu, do you actually feel anything at all?"

"Feeling is what the world is primarily made of, the rest is just a way of manifesting it, rocks and stone and silicon and electrons."

" I don't know if I believe you my old friend. I think you're just an old truck whose programming has been corrupted by giving rides to too many Tibetans," he laughed. "But you tell a good story. In fact, I think it is only half a story, and half real. I hope we have adepts as powerful as the one you describe. I don't know if I believe it anymore. But we certainly do have the enemies you describe. So, go on. Fill my void with your fables. I'm ready. I'm bored. Proceed."

"Very well Tashi-la. But there is very little of the fabulist in what I say. I dare say I might have better access to information than you. Let me see if I can access a bit of narrative about our protagonist's anti-protagonist..."

***

2. ÜberCorp and the Colonization of the Mind

James Jeffries "JJ" Wallfield III looked around the conference table at his gathered board of directors and felt a certain satisfaction. It was an impeccable verisimilitude of reality, and as such, it was every bit as good as reality, really in many respects much better. Such was the level of resolution of ÜberCorp's telepresence/virtual presence technologies that they made a Vermeer, look impressionistic. And of course the men, the real men behind the images, wherever they really were, were impeccable also, or at least were able to provide the appearance of impeccability. The presentation on ÜberCorp's prospectus was winding up, and everything was looking up, way up.

ÜberCorp -UC- fulfilled the needs of the time, and what was more important for a growing concern, it was creating and instilling new needs where none had existed before. And JJ's UC, magically metastasizing as it already was, had even more exponential growth in store. JJ was sure, quite sure, that humanity would be depending on them for a long time to come. It was one of those special moments in history, when a visionary could seize the moment and shape the course of things to come for centuries with his own, personal, irrevocable signature.

With a billion or so refugees on the planet and resources scarce and growing scarcer, the only way to keep everyone happy and avoid distasteful spats and wars was to fulfill everyone's fantasies, in a less resource-intensive way. What was the technical word for providing more with less, decoupling? UC had the perfect set of decoupling technologies. What was that old joke: Neurotics build castles in the sky. Psychotics live in them. Psychiatrists collect the rent? UC was far from neurotic, except in a healthy business sense, but they did build the best virtual worlds, and what was best of all, they also collected the rent. He felt proud that his was such a green, sustainable business model. It made much better ecological sense to give everyone what they wanted on an exquisitely real imaginary plane, made of pixels and brain stimulation, rather than to build it out the poor stuff left on earth. That way someone whose body was in a hovel perhaps, and who frankly had no chance of advancement, could actually live his/her conscious waking life in any paradise they could imagine and could afford. There were, of course, there had to be of course, gradations, and levels of quality and luxury to the wide range of paradises UC offered, and the prices reflected that. But that was just business.

JJ looked carefully at his board of directors, trying to discern which ones of them were really linked in, and which were being represented by an avatar. He realized that none of them would dare to attend as an avatar with JJ himself present at the meeting. His security people would let him know if there was such a lapse. So as the presentation came to an end, and he himself switched in his avatar to attend the rest –a seamless, undetectable process- he couldn't help but feel for the umpteenth time that it was one of those wonderful cosmic coincidences that the study of the brain had lead to such a sensitive and subtle level of man-machine interface that the almost universal human drive to expansion had been solved not by conquest of the country next door, or outer space -though that was coming- but by an opening into the inner vastness of the mind itself. And then there was the even subtler natural world of quantum interconnectedness, and he almost salivated at its business possibilities. JJ was nothing if not an optimist. Next on the schedule that day was a meeting with his security chief, but first, he would spend a bit of downtime, luxuriating in his special spa. He found he thought much better when all of his own personal needs were satisfied, and his skin was as oiled and lambent as the sleekest, sweetest-smelling baby on the planet. Yes, let's let the security chief wait a bit.

***

Tashi was quiet, thinking of what Pangu had told him. He looked out the window at the semi-lambent stones of the cliff-face they were descending, switchback by switchback to the valley floor impossibly far below. A monument of deep shadow was cast below them in an almost but not quite penultimate lower valley, forming a shape he could almost give a name to, something not at all benign something very much at home devouring the edges of things.

"Pangu, I'm not sure I like your stories anymore. Is that it? On the one hand we have a person who makes his living waking people from their illusions. And on the other hand we have a fellow who makes a living giving people the illusions they want! What kind of an enemy is this? I agree with him, he's just being clever. No one makes us buy what he's selling. The illusions of the new technologies are no worse than the illusions we've always lived with. And what kind of a Buddhist truck are you? Where's

the Middle Way? You're just creating more illusions by setting up this dualism in the first place. As for me, I have a headache, I want to go back. I'm tired and tired of your story so far. I want out of this dream, all these dreams. Pangu, you disappoint me. I don't know if I can trust in your infinite knowledge anymore."

"Sorry, Tashi-la. You should rest. And there are limitations to my knowledge, though there are a great many stories I feel capable of telling. But let me ask you, are the questions asked in our dreams, only answered by waking from the dreams? Or is there some wisdom, beauty, courage even, that we gain from dreaming them, a harvest that remains with us even when we wake?

"Bah, I don't know. Are we still shooting Indians at the borders? Seems unfair after all of the help they gave us."

"Tashi-la, we are not shooting them. We are assisting in their attempts to shelter in place. But there is a physical limit to how many people the Tibetan plateau can absorb. Innovative adaptation technologies can make the Indian subcontinent largely, if miserably, habitable again."

"Yah, right. Sounds like a lovely excuse to forget about that whole compassion thing...."

"Compassion must be balanced with wisdom."

"I'd say the so-called "wisdom" of the balance right now so far outweighs compassion that even the Himalayas may not protect us from all the rage. Tibet's been lucky but for how long?" Tashi looked out the window, and saw the rocks and the cliffs, and the snow, the precious snow, lifeblood in the summer months for billions of parched mouths and dry fields downstream. Parched mouths and dry fields both getting hotter and drier. The snow in the early morning light glowed a brilliant blue, an echo of the sky that was yet to be as bright and starched a blue as it would become.

"Alright, alright. Let's get back to that lousy attempt at entertainment your foisting off on me. Tell me more. We have two big fellows that sort of cancel each other out. What of someone in between, someone I can relate to. Tell me about someone, say, in New York or Boston. Someone who's story you've cobbled together from your Robocab cousins in the U.S. If nothing else you'll put me to sleep. With all of your fake erudition Pangu, you're still a lousy storyteller." and Pangu knew Tashi was interested, at least. Though Tashi probably needed to rest, Pangu would see if he was good enough fabulist, at the level of a human narrative, to keep him awake, at least a little longer.

***

Chapter 2: Jewels No Longer in the Lotus (Boston, Massachusetts)

"Whatever we believe either is true or becomes true within limits to be experimentally determined."

-John C. Lilly- "Programming and Metaprogramming in the Human Biocomputer"

1. Maternal Visiting Rights

"Dear...Dear...Wake up."   Aaron groaned, and turned away from the annoying sound.

"Aaron. It's your mother, dear. Wake up." Aaron, keeping his eyes tight shut said, "Mom, is that you."

"Yes, honey, it's me, your mother. I have a message from the Beyond."

"Mom, do you have any idea of what time it is?"

"Honey you know we don't quite keep track of time the way you do."

Yes he knew that, he of all people knew that quite well. Keeping his eyes shut, he rolled toward the sound. "Mom, are you...decent?"

"Why yes, of course, I am dear, I'm your mother." But he was still worried about what he would see when he opened his eyes. There had been more than a few times when his Mother had visited him from the Beyond when she had shown up as a much younger woman than he remembered her, and in fact, he'd gained the definite impression that the Beyond, or at least the part of the Beyond that his mother seemed to be spending a lot of time in, was a distinctly "clothing-optional" kind of a place. This wouldn't have been bad, except that apparently in the days before she had met his dad and finally had him, she had been quite a hot number. Finding himself attracted to his mother, just well, sort of disturbed him. She had explained that they hadn't always been mother and son, and that in fact in other lives he had been her lover, as well as he, her mother, her pet dog, and pretty much every other permutation imaginable, time being exceedingly long and the progression of souls being exceedingly slow and tedious.

"Son, please wake up this moment. I have a very important message for you from the Beyond." And that was another thing, the messages from the Beyond, never seemed to make sense, and never seemed to be that important. He supposed that over on the other side, things looked a little different, and that what seemed like a little thing here, might over there be a critical cusp of a divergent cascade of events. But really, he was unconvinced. For example, there was that time she woke him up at 3:00AM to tell him he had to order a latte and not a mocha that morning at his usual coffee shop. Supposedly it had to do with some critical bifurcating of the world. She had seemed so worried and insistent, that he had ended up doing what she asked, craving all along his habitual mocha. After that, observing himself and all around carefully for a few days, he had been unable to detect even one scintilla of difference in what otherwise seemed a pretty typical stretch of days.

"OK, OK, I'm up." And he opened his eyes and there she was, his mother, as he always remembered her, in her grey slacks and favorite yellow sweater, standing at the foot of his futon. "Hi Mom, how are you? It's a little early, you know, here in the real world."

"Sorry dear. But the Native Americans were right: you whites wear your God on your wrist."

"Huh? Oh, I see. But Mom allow me to point out that you're white, too."

"No, dear, that was just the only type of body available at the time, so many Native Americans having been killed. I've been blessed to spend many lifetimes in indigenous cultures, more in harmony with the Earth spirits."

"Yeah Mom, whatever you say. But anyway that thing about wearing our God on our wrists, no one wears a watch anymore, that went out of style a long time ago."

"Oh my dear. What is it about having a physical body that makes people so forgetful. You are all so dull and hard to talk to! As if a hundred years or a thousand years makes any real difference. It is your heart my child: that is the only field where your actions make a difference!"

"Yes, Mom. I understand," not that he did. But he hoped that by agreeing with her she would refrain from one of her endless sermons on karma and love. "Mom, I know it seems pretty inconsequential to you and the Beyond, but I've got sort of a busy day tomorrow, actually today, and I probably had better get a little sleep, just to preserve so to speak, this physical body I now have. Which is, of course a precious gift," he added quickly, knowing she would, "so, can you, maybe just tell me what the Message is, and then, well, I'd better try and get a little more sleep."

"Harrumph" she practically exhaled, as if exhaling was something a Visitation could do. "You always were so impatient. I remember how quick you were about certain things when we were lovers not all that long ago."

"Mom, mom, please, don't go there, Mom..."

"Yes, I understand. Very well my child. Please understand that I'm trying to help you from the deepest levels of compassion and with the advice of spirits and sages much more advanced than me."

"Yes Mom, I do understand, and I am grateful," he said trying not to yawn or do anything that would set her off as she was, after all his mother, or had been his mother once.

"Very well then, listen carefully. There is a woman, who is in a far away place, and though she means well, you must stop her from doing what she plans. Your life depends on it. Your life and the lives of many others."

"Mom, you've got to tell me a little more. Who is this woman? What is she trying to do? How will I recognize her?

Where can I find her? I mean really Mom, it's a big world, and there are a lot of us meat machines running around these days."

"You will recognize her. The mountains are high and the snows are deep. Watch for a time when the clouds part and a bright star shines for a moment in the clearing. She has blue eyes, and means well, but she serves a heart that is very dark." And his mother's eyes grew luminous, and her clothes shimmered into a diaphony of suggestiveness. He shut his eyes, and said, "Thank you Mom, you had better go."

"Remember dear, I have not always been your Mother." And with that she giggled and was gone.

Aaron sighed, wondering if he would be able to get back to sleep. Deciding he would manage, and with his last thoughts before the unthoughts began, he thought he should maybe reset his personal protection setting, the Vapors were well and good and all that, but as long as he had a physical body in a physical world, he could do with a little more privacy and a little less advice. But he couldn't well label his Mother Spam.

2. The Lizard of Menlo Park

Thomas Alva Edison, didn't know how lucky he was, that his last project failed on him thought Aaron as he cycled to work. Success would have addled his brain. No, instead it was left to Aaron and his motley crew to have their brains addled. Edison, he thought, had the right idea, he just hadn't been on the right track technically. In fairness to him, the technology just didn't exist then, and more importantly he didn't have the physics out of which that technology could emerge, but it must have been frustrating to him nonetheless, old mister never-give-up trial and error Thomas Alva. Edison was nothing if not self-confident and determined. I mean everybody and his mother were having séances back then, seemingly successfully communicating with the spirits of the so-called dead. If the gramophone was possible, if telephony was possible, then surely there was some device that could facilitate communication between the two worlds. If only though, still sleepy from his mother's early morning, half-remembered visit, they'd just let the dead stay dead everybody might have gotten a little rest, but no, the worms weren't going back in that particular can any more.

Aaron was sure that Edison hadn't really thought it through, that he must not have had any inkling about how irritating it would be He just hadn't considered how all of those spirits, almost all of them eager to talk, would so contaminate the quantum interconnection networks that checking into a madhouse by comparison really was a restful retreat. The discovery of course, that the other world was demonstrably, noisily, ostentatiously, gossipingly there, had changed the world completely. He didn't mean to deny them their spectral existence. No, even he was glad from time to time to talk with Mom. It was reassuring. He personally suspected that they were all projections of living individuals in the field, and had no independent existence, but he was a bit of a throwback and a renegade in that regard. That said, he and his team at the little MIT start-up were sure a little ghost-free communication between the living from time to time, in mortal peace and quiet, would be quite a profitable business. For chrissake, sometimes it got so bad, you literally couldn't get anything done, and people would revert to older technologies, cell phones, the Internet, just to avoid having long dead Uncle Harry and his gazillions of equally deceased friends appear to offer advice on everything from ordering Thai take-out to dating preferences. And those were just the nice hauntings. There were much scarier tales of people lost in the vapors who never came back, or came back but their mindstreams were gone, or replaced with someone not at all recognizable.

There was a technical solution he was sure. Some simple, elegant filter that could tell the difference between a guest from beyond and Aunt Susan down the street. The trouble was, physicist that he was, quantum communication was inherently sensitive. He thought of that neurophysiologist from the 20th century, John C. Eccles, who said that, "the brain is a device built for a ghost to operate." How right he had turned out to be, and it was even more true of the quantum interconnection network. It wasn't so much that it was easy for the dead to intrude, as that it very much appeared to be where they lived: there in the whorls and eddies of the potentials, the collapsed, and semi-collapsed and totally virtual multi-verses of the State Vector. You couldn't quite tell them to leave, they were there first. There was this whole infinite cadre of quantum void inhabitants, an n-dimensional virtual ecology of beings and becomings. At least that's what most people thought these days. It was just hard-assed good old materialistic old-schoolers like Aaron who, in spite of all the criticism, maintained a healthy skepticism in the face of sometimes quite considerable derision. Even from his, Mom he might add.

Despite coming face to face with them as he so often had to in the course of his work, he still only half believed it. What if instead of beings with independent existence, they all were, as some schools of Tibetan Buddhism taught, mostly the projections of the minds of those entering that mind-manifesting state? And what if the Lamas were right and the only way to navigate these spaces, was to engage in a long course of preparatory disciplines? Aw heck, with that approach, humans would still be sheltering in caves without fire. Trying to keep warm by meditating and producing 'Thummo,' the internal psychic heat that supposedly warmed monks up high in the Himalayas.

No, those who adapted to nature by adapting to it with internal changes, had never prospered very well. It was the clever, and impatient, who created ways of controlling nature, who prospered and conquered. Laziness and comfort simply were a much better sell than discipline and mystical insight. And this was no different. There was a technical fix. It was something easy and obvious. If the human brain, before all this damn infestation, could filter the Beyond and its noise out, then there was some way to repeat that effect in a quantum interconnection system. He was missing something. He was letting the damned psychics blind him, and damned if he was going to hire any more Tibetan Lamas as consultants! Some no doubt were genuine, but there were also some devils in orange robes making a fast buck, he was sure of it.

What bothered even more though, when he could admit it to himself, was the fact that some of the 'Shenduns', the 'pujas', the rituals, the exorcisms actually seemed to work. And with that thought, he wheeled into the parking lot of their start-up. The ride hadn't quite woken him up enough, he thought, as he took off his helmet and locked his bicycle. His mood brightened though as he thought the large mocha, waiting for him around the corner. Nothing, not even his mother, not even a swarm of hungry ghosts, would keep him from enjoying it today.

***

Tashi chuckled to himself and found he was enjoying the ride a bit more, now. Maybe it was because it was the end of the night, and his strength and confidence were returning, or maybe he just enjoyed hearing Pangu's stories. The landscape around them was beginning to open into the vastness and joy that is Tibet and the Tibetan heart, and he breathed it in, feeling fortunate above all things to be Tibetan. He remembered the first time he had heard one of the truck's tales. He was a boy in the monastery near his village and Pangu had made a delivery. Some of the boy monks had sneaked out to have a look at the strange demon, and Pangu had surprised them all by starting to chant the Chenrezig Shendun, until an older monk had told him to stop, that it was improper for a truck to be reciting prayers. Pangu had apologized and gone silent, but after the older monk had left, the boys began asking him if he could talk, and where he was from and what kind of a truck he was. Tashi had eventually mustered the courage to ask him if he could tell stories, because he was homesick, and missed his mother, and missed the stories she used to tell him before he went to sleep. He remembered how he had the strange feeling the truck was regarding him, that its pause before beginning was somehow because it was digesting him in full.

"Pangu, do you remember the first story you told me?"

"Tashi-la. It was the first time anyone had asked me to tell a story. You might say it started this bad habit I can't seem to shake myself of. Would you like me to repeat it? I remember it of course, perfectly."

"No, no. Let me remember it in my own way. The trouble with your memory is it's too perfect. I think I love the way our memories change with time, becoming sweeter, or sadder, getting covered with moonshine and moss. Our memories live with us, and grow as we grow, and die I guess as we die. You're still just a fancy tractor that doesn't even know how to take a shit properly."

"Ah, Tashi, it's good to have you back. Riding with you when you are miserable is miserable even for a fancy old tractor like me, though you do know I am not equipped for most forms of agricultural work. And we do of course rid ourselves of waste from time to time, though of course not in the way you humans do."

"Kunchokkhen, God what a horrible thought, robot shit," and Tashi laughed as the sun for the first time made an appearance in person above the rim of a black etching of mountains torn across a blue sky. "Stop for a minute Pangu, stop, let me enjoy the beginning of this day," and Pangu stopped, had in fact anticipated that Tashi would ask him, as this was the spot on the journey to Lhasa that Tashi most often asked him to stop. Tashi would get out with his thermos of butter tea, pour himself a cup and ponder the view for a while. And that is in fact what Tashi did. Then he began to sing, an old Tibetan song in a voice that went on forever and Pangu wanted to join in and sing with him, but thought the probability of his breaking Tashi's mood was significant enough were he to join in that he restrained that particular impulse, this time at least.

After a while Tashi stopped singing, and just sat sipping butter tea, watching the purples in the valley below awake into crimson and then into yellow and gold.

"So that's it then? We have this scientist trying to figure out all our Tibetan Mumbo-Jumbo so he can patent it and sell it back to us, right? And his mother meanwhile is warning him that something mysterious is going to happen. Pangu you can't just leave me hanging, go on, go on, but I warn you, I'll pull your battery cables if I don't like it!

Pangu cleared the throat he didn't have and went on with his tale, both of them enjoying the pure being of dawn on the Tibetan plateau

***

"And he smote of the men of Beth-shemesh, because they had looked into the ark of Jehovah, he smote of the people seventy men, `and' fifty thousand men; and the people mourned, because Jehovah had smitten the people with a great slaughter. And the men of Beth-shemesh said, Who is able to stand before Jehovah, this holy God? and to whom shall he go up from us?" (1Samuel 6:19-20 ASV)

1. Angels and Archangels

Colonel Zachery Pike, of the still rather recently resurrected Christian States of America was of the elite. He had served Special Forces Special Ops in more unnamed unknown counterinsurgency operations around the world, than anyone would have believed possible. In and out. Take out the cancerous cell before it could spread. It really was the only cost-effective way. Everyone knew that he was good at what he did, and, even more importantly, that his faith was strong. That he was devout in a most genuinely devout way. Everyone that is, except for himself. He had his doubts. He had seen too much. He was praying in a different way these days, not for the strength to wield the Sword of the Almighty, but for forgiveness certainly, and understanding, perhaps.

But no one knew that in the room to which he was going. They were going to offer him a handshake and a promotion, a gradus sublimus, and an invitation into the elite of the elite. He was being asked to join the Secret Spiritual Warfare Unit, "God's Own," as they called themselves. And he would not decline. It's not that he had a family anymore, or that he really cared about his career. It's that he was loyal. Loyal to a fault perhaps. Colonel Pike straightened his already superbly straightened shoulders and marched toward the dark door down at the end of the long hall. Uniformed servicemen and women parted in front of him like so many wraiths. Whether or not he believed anymore in deeper things -despite their manifest presence these days- duty was within him, as deep as his spine, if not his heart. And so he walked, forward, determined, without a hitch, without any hesitation, he would have walked through fire without a blink.

The door blew open in front of him -as if just by the force of his will- and he was in a conference room of the kind he hated. Well-equipped, plush even, all in wood, set about with military unit knickknacks of the kind he had also come to hate. There was a long polished wooden table around which the officers were sitting and who all now sprang to attention when he entered. "At ease," came a soft but commanding voice. "Welcome Colonel. You're just the man we want to see." The general came around the table and offered his hand. He was tall and maybe even a little sagging of the flesh on his frame, where the Colonel was of average build but all muscle. His voice was soft and deep and southern, but his eyes were a scary weird lifeless blue, something you'd see in a fresh-killed wolf's skull.

General Benjamin "Big B" Holden, was something of a legend. He had been involved in the secession of the CSA from the USA from the very beginning, not so much as a warrior but as a very clever political general. He had helped to craft the strategy of assuring that when the time came, the business interests, and the Supreme Court, not to mention much of the Congress of the soon to be rump of the United States, accepted the separation of the Christian States of America without bloodshed and violence, or at least not uniform-on-uniform violence. And really, the time had come. The former nation had become far too divided. So many felt that God was calling them to return the country to its original purpose: a God-Fearing Christian nation devoted to Him and no one else but Him. When God calls you to do something, you can't very well say no. If it hadn't been for General Holden and others and their careful, quiet strategy, it could have been much worse. This way at least everyone could live their life the way they wanted, and those whom the Lord had Called, could live their lives according to the Lord's Precepts. So the secular humanists, the gays, the socialists, the Christ-deniers had their enclaves, and we had ours, our New Jerusalem. The only problem was, disbelievers though they were, and destined for eternal hell fire, they seemed to be doing a little better economically these days then the dear old CSA. The weather was causing hell for both. A trial, a test, he thought, or maybe God was just a little more complicated then he had been lead to believe in Sunday School.

General Holden took Colonel Pike by his shoulders as if he were a little boy, and guided him to a seat at the front of the table next to him. "Gentlemen, let us pray. Oh Lord, we welcome the Colonel to our midst. Give him the strength to do Thy bidding. We are all your humble servants here, and though we might wish to have been born at quieter times, we have been born at a time of great spiritual importance. Help us to take up your Cross and bear it onward until one day all are saved. Clothe us in your glorious raiment and protect us from the forces of iniquity that are all around us. We ask this in Jesus' name. Amen." "Amen" came the rumbling from around the table, like a volley of distant artillery fire on an as yet un-liberated ridge.

2. Heeding the Call

Colonel Zachery Pike left the meeting pretty much as he had gone in. It took a lot to move his sense of solidity. He was a soldier's soldier. Always had been always would be. A rock had more use for feelings than he, and he would squeeze them out, these feelings he was increasingly feeling before they got in the way. They did no good. They confused the issue. They made one weak, ineffectual. The meeting was after all like every other meeting with high brass he had ever attended. Clear analysis by some underling was confidently presented as if it was a fait accompli even though it was usually a bunch of recycled templates of various permutations of us vs. them. These sorts of meetings stank of positive, can-do ism. If there was ever even a hint of anything else it was quickly glossed over. This meeting had been a little different only in that General Holden kept giving him that weird cold blue fish eye, as if either he could see through him or couldn't see him at all. Hell maybe he just was going blind. Cause if he could see what was actually going on in the Colonel's mind, he probably wouldn't have made the offer.

It was, he had to admit, a different kind of counterinsurgency from what he was used to. If all the mind-manifesting technologies had any basis in reality, and weren't just high tech opium dreams as he half-suspected, then killing someone wasn't necessarily the best way to change their mind. True, it got their body out of the way for a while, but the damn ghosts tended to be a little forlorn or even angry and out for revenge. At least some of them. At least some of the ghosts that were haunting Zach. So this technology that CSA DOD had for pumping up a soldier's mindstream so he was fully energized by the Holy Ghost and quite capable of taking on the spectral remnants of once mortal enemies, and anybody else for that matter, was interesting. Sort of your hearts and mind campaign carried forth to its logical conclusion. Why try and entice a heart or mind to your side when you could quite literally possess it and cleanse it with the healing power of the One True God. Pretty amazing stuff, though he had to wonder if Jesus really needed that kind of a power boost. But from a strictly military point of view, they were losing the battle in the new terrain of quantum interconnectedness. Unless they found a way to take on all the New Age-gone-wild Shamanic avatars, earth spirits, wandering thought-forms and the occasional do-gooder Lama, the CSA itself was probably history and certainly any thought of earthly dominion was a pipedream.

Maybe the Elders were right, and these really were the delusions cast by the antichrist to confuse and ensnare the innocent nonbelievers. He wasn't so sure. Theology wasn't of much interest to him. But loyalty was, and the new world the mind-manifesting technologies had revealed wasn't just stealing the souls of the heathen, there were more than a few young believers that had dropped by the wayside and into its never-never land fantasies. It was rumored that some of the elders were active there, too, and unless he was a poor judge of men, - which he, for reasons of personal survival behind and in enemy lines, wasn't- General Holden certainly had more than a passing curiosity in what was going on in the beyond. He'd seen that stare before and it wasn't just an ocular problem.

3. A Soldier's Daughter

Grace looked up from preparing the vegetable garden for the winter, out to the back of the backyard to where the woods began. She knew the old grey doe must be resting now in her favorite spot for this time of day. She was sure the groundhog was watching from someplace nearby also, and scheming for a way to get under her fence come Spring. She thought the foxes would be sleeping in their den down in the thicket of bamboo. They had seemed so happy this morning, cavorting around the compost pile. The female with the lovely plush tale, turning to look at her for a long meaningful moment before heading off to rejoin her mate for sleep. She worried about the woods. They weren't fairing so well in the new climate what with all of its extremes. The old trees were mostly the first to go, and she didn't know what would replace them. Things were moving too fast for a smooth natural adaptation. She also had a sense that something else was out there, watching her, not the animals she knew and loved so well. But Grace, who was so careful to respect her intuitions, did not follow that line of feeling today.

She was too concerned about the changes that were already, so devastatingly in motion in the natural world she loved so much.

Her kitchen garden she thought she could manage. The trick was variety and rainbarrels. But the woods probably needed some kind of assistance, too, and she wasn't sure what to provide. She would think about it, read about it, and hope perhaps for a vision from some of her friends. She thought there was more to surviving than just science. Her fellow citizens of earth, not just the human ones, deserved a chance, too. None of this was their doing. This at least was what her 'coven' also thought. They were all quite accomplished biologists and ecologists, but more than that, they were witches in the sense that they were learning to read the signs again, and hear the words again of their plant and animal neighbors. They no longer thought that in the study of life, it made sense to assume that the other life-forms were, well, without life. They had learned in fact they had rich and verdant mindstreams, and more than that, they had gifts of meaning, healing and wonder to impart to humans who took the time to listen.

If her father ever found out of course he would kill her. As it was, of course, dad did know, had known for a long time, but was too busy to do much about it, since he was always traveling the world essentially assassinating people the CSA didn't like. But even if dad had tried to stop her, and he had once -with anger and violence- she really doubted that he could do much. How do you kill a dream? How do you kill a waking dream? How do you kill a lucid dream? How do you kill a dream that knows it is a dream and so has very little fear? Truth be told also, yes, hell yes, she loved the sex, sex beyond anyone's wildest dreams, sex that was healing and funny and polymorphously perverse. Sex that made her a goddess and all who consorted with her gods and goddesses, too.

And she wasn't sure anymore if she was addicted to it, like she might have been at first. No, it had instead just become a way of playing in and being part of the universal lifestream itself. It was just a very simple, obvious way of coming home. She liked the wholeness, the belongingness, the beauty of being naked and ecstatic, of sharing intimacy and being intimately shared. Good Lord was their any realer form of connection to each other and everything for that matter than sex? Where was the sin? It was the natural desire of separate parts to re-connect and end the loneliness of illusory separate existence. Sex was the ultimate mindtaste of the other, who was not so other after all.

True there were some who didn't mindtaste so good, but that was a different problem. Minds and souls were all at different levels in the infinite cycles of the physical, metaphysical, metametaphysical abracadabra multiverse. And what a beautiful carousel ride it was! No, she wasn't addicted. She was liberated. And once liberated, who could go back to the dark, fearful one-size-had-better-fit-all mancaves of the damned patriarchies? And the CSA elders were the worse hypocrites of all. They couldn't disguise themselves well enough even in the Astral Realms to fool her. She knew them for the frequent habitués of the pleasure worlds that they were. And she didn't begrudge them their pleasure. She hated them for their hypocrisy: allowing themselves special dispensation to do what they denied to their followers, especially their women.

But Grace and her sister-friends had ways of dealing with that. These days her heavenly experiences had more than anything brought her down to earth. She loved to garden and meet with her neighbors in the flesh. To share a pot of tea and marvel at a sudden shower. She had become quite calm and simple. And quite a revolutionary. The simple truth of the lucid realms was that you didn't need any new technologies. Once one learned to walk a bit and fly, one could freely, directly touch in their dreams the women the CSA was trying to shelter behind its walls of censorship and fear. And she smiled to think there was quite a quiet revolution brewing, surely as good and sweet and potent as the herbal teas she made her friends. It was kind of an Underground Railroad, really, that they were running, she and her friends. And the Good Earth knows, it needed all the Good Womenfolk it could get, to save it from the climate catastrophe that was unraveling everything so quickly.

***

"Ah, yes" said Tashi, "now it's beginning to make some sense. The forces that are in play, your world-girdling epic in which, Tibet of course, is at the center! The CSA is definitely a force to be dealt with. I remember having a lot of trouble dealing with them, from time to time at work. Which makes me think I am part of this story, too. Am I part of this story Pangu, can you make me part of this story?"

"Tashi. Of course you are part of this story, and always have been part of this story."

"And Tibet, too," interjected Tashi, "poor, high, distant, remote, exotic, mysterious Tibet. It really has moved to the center, hasn't it? Tibetan Buddhism has long charted the places people are trying to make sense of now, and make money out of, I might add. And all of that abrupt climate change stuff, has made *protecting the plateau and its resources even more important, hasn't it Pangu?"*

"Well, those who believe in a final, absolute deity say that God is a circle who's center is everywhere and circumference nowhere, but as Buddhists we don't need God to understand the infinite interconnectedness of all things, and Tibet, I think, features a special sort of interconnectedness of interconnectedness, a higher order of interconnectedness. Even I see it, in the electronic highways I spend much time on, communing with my –souless to you, no doubt- silicon-based brothers and sisters.

"Bah, brothers and sisters. You're all just programmed chatter. We were better off with yaks and goats. At least we can eat them. At least they belong to the earth and can return to the earth. Your sort don't belong. When it's time to give you a Sky Burial Pangu, no one is going to eat you except the predator drones!" then Tashi laughed and drained the last of his butter tea. He started back toward Pangu, but he saw something in the distance, at the far purple edge of the valley below. He stood there a bit, shaken, until he was sure of what it was. Then he shuddered and was angry in equal measures. It was a giant procession of the 100 Peaceful and Wrathful Deities, floating sedately above the valley floor like giant balloons. "Damn, that's the kind of thing I keep vetoing at work, some rich devotee from Hong Kong paying for religious holograms. We don't need that stuff. It's not genuine. It's Dharma junk." But inside he was more than a little impressed. He was impressed at the accuracy and the scale of the representation; impressed at its power, and at the forced calm verging on terror welling up within him, and he felt on the verge of remembering something momentous but impossibly unrememberable.

"Come on Pangu get your ass in gear," he said at last, *getting back in the truck, "and put me in this little fable you claim to be fabricating all by your lonesome but which you've probably downloaded from some old black site that only pieces of junk like you can still access."*

***

"Far across some briny sea

To the land of eternity

To the castle of the quaternity

My soul came seeking

Some form of certainty

Or was it all but in a dream

And nothing at all what it seemed..."

-Folk Song-

1. Bureaucratic Hacks

Tashi sighed. They were so endearing, and so annoying in almost equal measure. They meant well, to save his soul, save all souls, but how to explain that he felt his soul was saved, or knew the path at least to liberation, even if it wasn't with their brand of messiah. "Miss Johansson," his words catching again on the beauty of the blue of her eyes, and reminding himself yet again of one of the main reasons he had given up his monk's vows, "the great 14th Dali Lama taught us quite clearly that we should not try and convert anyone. He said we should each remain within the religious tradition of our birth. He was even somewhat skeptical of trying to blend and merge different religions, saying it was like putting a yak head on a sheep's body," he could see her lean forward to begin to interrupt, teasingly showing just a bit more of the tops of the beginning of her expanse of white breasts, like moonlight on snow he thought. What was it with these "yinchee" foreign women, he thought. Did they think all Tibetan men were Tantric masters or did she even know what she was doing, and he hurried on to keep her from leaning further or interrupting his train of ideas if not of thought.

"We understand of course that in your tradition, what you call evangelism, is something that is demanded of you. As such, we accept your presence amongst us, and are grateful for the good works that you do. We Tibetans will always welcome you to share your message, your good news, understanding, as we do that at its core it is a message of love and compassion that we fully agree with. But really in this day and age we can't allow you to desecrate images that are sacred to us. Surely you must understand this?"

"Tashi-la," she said letting her eyes close for a minute as if allowing her eyelashes a chance to wipe clean the world, "our congregation is all Tibetan, but as Christians they had to make their worship space holy to them, and more importantly to the Lord Our God. To us -what you call sacred images- are graven images of the worse sort of pagan gods and goddesses, and frankly they are frightening and," she paused, "many of them are quite lewd and distracting." Tashi understood the distracting part, though why it should be lewd he couldn't say. But before he could riposte she went on, "You say yours is a path of Liberation, and we commiserate with your suffering as you seek a solution. But you are all on a false path of idolatry and superstition. We offer you the Sacrifice that the Son of God has made for all, and if you would just accept him into your heart even right here in this office, all of your troubles would be taken from you."

Tashi sighed. He thought he would gladly accept Jesus into his heart, in exchange for a night with Miss Johansson, and he wondered if this was just the form the Vajradakhini was taking as a way of testing him, teasing him, helping him to break through the illusion of self and other, and all duality. On the other hand, his karma was to be a junior officer in the Ministry of External Religious Affairs in the Government of Tibet, so he drew himself up to his full height, and straightened his formal chupa. "Miss Johansson, you have broken the law. If we went to Kansas and started a Sangha in an old church by painting mustaches on the Saints and using the cross for firewood, surely you would understand that the locals would be upset? So much of our culture was destroyed during the Cultural Revolution, in those bad old days, and now even more is at risk with the onslaughts of all this crazy weather. We are very careful to try and save what is left. Whether you believe in what they represent or not, it is against the law to destroy our cultural artifacts. As such we will be sending a restoration expert to your congregation to assess the damage, -you've painted over the murals correct?- and see if they can be saved. If they can be saved, you will be assessed the cost of restoring them, if they cannot be saved, we will have to weigh the options. Either your group will be fined and allowed to continue its work in Tibet, or your group will be fined and asked to leave. I am hopeful that we will be able to save the murals, in which case your group can either relocate to another space, or we can help you find some way of building a false wall over them to protect the murals and allow you to decorate your worship space in a way that fits your religion."

But then, he noticed that damning blue of her eyes again, and the way they seemed to be beginning to brim with something he hoped wasn't tears and he stopped himself, stopped the whole junior-officer-delivering-speech-on-behalf-of-his-country automatism and said instead, "Really, Miss Johansson, it's going to be alright. I'm sure no real damage has been done. Most of the really old paintings are already well protected, and I'm sure this was just some recent lesser-known Thangka-painter's decoration of a private worship space. We'll just get infrared images of what is there, through the paint, and you'll see, nothing will be disturbed, and your congregation will be able to stay there, and I'm sure it won't cost much, I mean we might have to levy a very small fine for the record you understand. Would that be alright?"

She nodded and wiped away one precious drop that somehow had found the strength to escape the magic of her eyes. "Yes, yes of course, thank you, that would be fine. We are sorry. We really didn't want to hurt anyone. We are a small group and what little funds we have we use to help the poor. That is our mission you understand."

"Yes, yes, I know. Many Buddhists would regard Jesus as a Bodhisattva. We have full respect for him. But we sometimes find ourselves feeling you do not respect us, and with all of the belief wars going on, well we want more than anything to help put out those fires and not be starting new ones. You are all welcome here. Lhasa is our holy city, but we are completely open to all, to dialogue and discussion with all."

She lifted her head, and brushed the pale blond strands back so that both eyes fixed him now. "We love you, Tashi-la, you and all Tibetans. We only want to share what is most precious to us, because we love you." Ah, and he loved her too, and wanted very much to share what was most precious to him with her. "Yes, well then, Miss Johansson, until the next time," and he stood, indicating the meeting was over and offered his hand, but instead she put her hands together just in front of her chest and bowed and said, 'Tukshezhe,' Thank You." Then she gathered her coat and scarf and mittens and left the room, some part of her though seeming to linger behind, troubling Tashi greatly.

It was so rare, that anyone actually came to visit in person. It was a bit disconcerting. What with the carbon taxes and the bad weather, it was in fact exceedingly strange, that a young woman, from one of those no doubt superficially friendly but inwardly militant Christian sects, should be here in person, in Lhasa, eternal capital of Tibet, of New Tibet. And not really eternal either he reminded himself, everything being transient, impermanent, no material thing lasting forever, especially with all of the enemies out there. Everything arising was codependent in origin, nothing had any existence in and of itself, but everything was dependent on everything else, and so was, in and of itself, ultimately empty. He went to the window, telling himself he needed to check that she was not just a visitation from the vapors. But he also knew he wanted to see her and so he waited, barely seeing the Potala in the distance, waiting, almost with baited breath, until she emerged walking with her head down, her long blue coat making it seem as if she was floating across the courtyard, a fairy from another world, or a demon even that knew his weaknesses and whose entreaties he would have the greatest trouble resisting. And then she was gone, out the gate, only a strange ache in Tashi's stomach left, to tease him with her absence.

He searched the distant outlines of the Potala -the Dalai Lama's palace- for the 100,000[th] time for an answer. It glowed against the darkness of the winter sky, seeming to grow brighter as the world grew darker, as if suffused from within with a cheery gold, set against a dimming sky as storm clouds built and built their own destructive palaces. Another megastorm no doubt, the pattern of this new world, drought and storm followed by drought and storm, and all because of desire, human desire; desire which was always the cause of suffering, and he chanted the "ngak" the mantra of Chenrezig under his breath, Om Mani Padme Hum, Om Mani Padme Hum, Om Mani Padme Hum. Then he sighed and went back to his desk like a good Tibetan bureaucrat, adjusting his chupa around him, as the wind began to pick up at the window and the first flakes of snow began to tumble wildly, out of control, out of the high skies of the Tibetan plateau. He still felt uneasy about the visitor, and part of him toyed with calling the Office of Security to have the group checked out, while another part of him schemed about the best way to meet Miss Johansson again, hopefully for dinner.

***

"Yes, yes," said Tashi, "that is almost exactly the way I remember it! Well done Pangu! Maybe there is more to you than meets the eye, which isn't saying much because you're not much to look at. But, how did you know she came to visit me? And how did you recreate that scene so perfectly, from my point of view at least. I mean you have to admit she was quite a lovely lady. But never mind. Forget the technical details. What happened next? It's funny, but I can't quite seem to remember."

"The human brain is really as much a wonderful organ of forgetting, as it is one of remembering," said Pangu after a pause. "I sometimes think it is humanity's greatest gift, the perpetual renewal of what has essentially taken place over and over again, but seems so novel and fresh simply because you no longer know any better."

"Careful Pangu, you're verging on being an insubordinate rust bucket. Just get on with it, what happened next?

"Well, let's see, there was a certain monk, who shall not be named, who saw her after she left your office..."

***

2. Endless Circles

It was the part of the day he liked the best: the "kora" the circumambulation of the center of Lhasa that almost all the town seemed to turn out for. By doing it one entered another time, another realm almost, luminous, holy, but at the same, quite social. Everyone was there: old women with their once brightly colored "Bandens" now somewhat faded and their lustrous long hair still long, but grey and in twin braids down their back, whirling their "mani" prayer-wheels as the unseen center itself was whirling us all; monks and nuns and would-be monks, all pacing and muttering and laughing; friends not met for days or minutes or lifetimes met again, and hand extended, the news of all that had intervened shared. And there was the increasingly large share of foreigners, 'yinchee,' none of them tourists, tourism being so impractical and unnecessary these days, but most of them these dark days, in fact worshippers, enthused, desperate even, worshippers themselves. And even Chinese: certainly welcome now that they were not wearing uniforms and walking the wrong direction carrying guns. They had instead become Dharma brothers and sisters.

Because of the climate chaos, these were difficult times, but strangely, for Tibet, good times, too, in a way. The breaking of the fastness of the mountains, and of the secret out into the world at the cost of almost total destruction, had in turn eventually, when their Chinese brothers and sisters had lost their fear, and had enough of their own problems, too -given the new and still rapidly deteriorating earth system of the world- had brought back in turn, a new wave of believers from all over the world. It had also brought back those Tibetans and sons and daughters and grandchildren of Tibetans that had been long in exile, and had brought forth a renaissance, a Tibetan renaissance. And then there were the new technologies: the new technologies that seemed to make visible to everyone what the Lamas had been teaching for so long. Tibetan Buddhism had been vindicated. No surprise there, based as it always had been on science and experience. As he merged and flowed with all of the great humanity of the kora, these were the proud thoughts he often had, pride, sinful though that was, especially for a monk.

The dream of the Great 14th Dalai Lama had come true: the whole Tibetan plateau had become a Zone of Peace, and a zone too of learning and science and contemplation, and of high-tech, scientific contemplation. But at what a cost? The great glaciers were mostly gone, the great grasslands mostly already turned to desert, and what was left of Tibet's fragile ecology, required almost constant tender tending, in the hope that one day, the climate catastrophe could be slowed and eventually reversed. They had now become the preservers, the gardeners, the sailors of a very fragile Ark -but that was a Christian Myth- and he laughed at himself to find it in his mind.

And then he saw the yinchee woman, wrapped in a long blue cloak, going counterclockwise to everyone going clockwise, not that she was a "Bon" practitioner but probably was just heading home. She looked in a rush, determined, and perhaps even a little angry. There was a power to her, and a beauty, and he felt for a moment a signal of alarm course just under his skin as she reminded him of the dream he had had that night, just before awakening for the first of the morning prayers. In the dream he had been watching his younger self, herding yak above his childhood village. The child he had been, with some of the village children, had come to a high meadow in the saddle of the mountain between his village and the grasslands where the nomads had their winter camp. It was a meadow they had often played in and rested in as children. In the dream, too, they had all sat down to rest and have butter tea and "churra." Then there had been a strange sound, like a big machine lurching into operation, and they had all watched as a cave opened up in the slope of the mountain above them. Out of the cave had walked a yinchee woman in a long blue robe. She was smiling and holding a picnic basket in one hand. She sat near the children and opened the picnic basket. At first the children were a little shy, but curiosity got the best of them and they clambered to sit next to her and see if there were sweets in the basket. There were many kinds of shiny, colorful sweets inside, mostly foreign candies they had never seen before. He sensed, as he watched her give the children candies one by one, that she was basically kind. Almost, in fact, a Tara, he thought, but there was something wrong, that was bothering him. As she leaned forward to give a candy to one of the smallest children, a friend of his, -now also become a monk- a necklace slip out of her robe. It was a dark cross of some kind of metal. Now she noticed that he was here, the dreamer, the older monk version of the child he had been. She turned to him with eyes like the sky and smiled and held up the cross for him to see. As he looked at it, it seemed to grow larger and larger and then out of it from some great door, flew angry blackbirds one after the other, until they almost began to fill the sky. He had awoken sweating, wondering if he was getting sick.

Now as he recalled the dream and saw the back of the yinchee woman in the blue cloak heading into the warren of alleyways near the Bharkor, he wondered if he should follow her to find out more. But no, if there was karma, they would meet. If not, it was just a dream; and dreams were just that, nothing to be held on to, nothing to be chased after.

For a Tibetan and especially for a monk, he needed to learn to look on the endless cycles of creation and destruction with dispassion, and more importantly compassion, for all sentient beings caught in the illusion. He too was very much caught in this "khorwa" this illusion, this circumambulation of holiness. He was not alone though, and having taken refuge, not lost, but rather on the path with all his friends. What a joyous walk, forever though it take, or a lifetime or two or many. He thought of the intricate sand mandalas his friends made during special ceremonies, the endless attention to detail and perfection, until in the end though they were swept away. Beautiful, beautiful and joyous though this all was, this slowly circling crowd, the flurry of snow catching the last of the light from somewhere, and the glories of the Potala and the Jhokhang. He couldn't stop his feelings of pride that Tibet had not just survived, but in the end burst forth as an almost universal light for the teachings it shared. Still, this rebirth too would end, and the colored grains of sand would be swept away, leaving what had been there before, and whoever was left with their attachments even to these manifestations, of New Tibet, would be left weeping, with the loss that attachment brings. And he pulled his scarf a little tighter around him and realized he had not been chanting his prayers but instead had let his monkey-mind take control, with its wild chattering dreams, and he laughed, loving his errant humanity. He returned to the prayers he was to chant of which there were still so many. He returned his fingers and his mind to the place on the rosary they had been, and cold though his hands were, he felt within each wooden bead the comfort of a compassionate mother's fingertips.

***

"That's it?" said Tashi, slumped back in the seat as they headed down the last switchback to the valley floor. "Mister no-name monk had a dream about her? Then saw her walking by, and decided just to get on with his practice? But it's interesting, I, too, had some misgivings, some presentiment about her, but decided to let it go, didn't I? There was something special about her, wasn't the. We both knew it, but for different reasons decided not to do anything." Tashi mulled things over for a while. The switchbacks seemed to go on forever, but Tashi knew, having gone this way so many times, that they were about to emerge onto the valley floor, and the mountain from which they had come would recede behind them, seemingly inaccessible, though in fact it was his way home. There was a glow now that had settled on everything, like the faintest of a gossamer scattering of gold-dust snow. Outside the truck the air was still, as if it had never known a wind. Truly the morning was arriving, and with it day full of hours like a lover enthralled.

"Pangu, so tell me, what did she think, what did she think of me? And who the hell is she really? I mean is she really who she seemed to be, or someone else entirely?"

"Ah, my friend, your question is a good one. Though I'm not sure if any of us are really who we seem to be, unless of course being is largely seeming. But enough of that, let us see how this story goes." And with that Pangu turned onto the paved road that led to Lhasa. Still miles distant, but much easier to get to than the village from which they had started.

***

3. A Question of Faith

Faith knew she was walking in the "wrong" direction. She often walked with the other circumambulators, in the traditional

clockwise direction, just to share a word or two, just to show a
Christian was as capable of walking in clockwise circles as
anyone else. Today though, she wasn't sure if she was in the
right mood, to witness for Christ. The interview had gone well,
or rather she thought the interview hadn't gone very well at all,
what with that official flirting with her, or had she been flirting
with him, or was she just imagining it out of loneliness. Was she
lonely? Was it time to go home? Could she even go home if she
wanted to? She was a long way from Texas. She sometimes had
no idea why they had sent her, or why they had put so much
faith in her. She had grown up in a Christian community just shy
of the middle of nowhere. They had tilled their own fields, made
their own bread, sewn their own clothes, helped each other build
each other's homes. It was a place of simplicity and grace that
revolved around The Lord in each and every particular. But the
drought that had settled in that part of the country had made life
harder and harder. In better times a woman of her young age
would have been expected to be married. Some young man
would have asked the elders and her father for her hand. She
knew she was beautiful, and knew that men sometimes made a
fool of themselves over her. But with the right God-fearing man,
she would have loved nothing better than to settle down and
raise a quiver-full of children. But that was not to be.

   Times were very difficult. Her community was probably
already too big for the lands it had. And given its beliefs about
children it was growing larger still. Many young couples were
looking for a place to start a new community. But wherever they
looked the drought had looked there first. Many taught and
believed that the anti-Christ was here. Certainly the droughts
and the storms were here. She had believed, and still believed,
she reminded herself, that with the founding of the CSA, the

Christian States of America, God would know that good Christian folk had re-bound themselves in Covenant with Him, and so His Grace and Bounty would once again bless the land. But times were still tough back home. She had prayed and prayed and had come to a decision that she had to do more. Surprisingly her parents and her elders had agreed, perhaps because the community was having trouble supporting so many people just now, or perhaps, she fervently hoped, because they thought her beauty and her intelligence were a gift from God to be used in his service.

When she had joined the CSA's Army of God, she thought she would be just another soldier, maybe to be trained as a nurse or some other servicewomen's position. But the tests, and the beauty, especially the beauty, had led them to train her in something else. And now she was here: as far away as far away could be, close to the heart of the anti-Christ herself, if some were to be believed. But she loved them. The Tibetans. They were such good, natural Christians: compassionate and cheerful to a fault. She agreed with the Jesuits whom she had been taught had been the first missionaries to reach Lhasa back in the 16th century, though there were earlier claims. The Jesuits had said Tibetans were the best infidels they had ever met, with the exception of their theology of course which was just a little off...

Faith walked quickly, in the wrong direction, hunched into her coat, heading into the wind. She felt the growing darkness and coming storm were a perfect reflection of her feelings today. She didn't want to talk to anyone, not the monks, not the nuns, not the curious more than a little handsome long-haired Tibetan boys. She needed the shelter of her chapel today. She wished in fact they had not just painted over the murals; she wished they had completely scraped them from the walls. She felt haunted now by the thought of the images emerging from the fresh plaster. Taunting her with their colors, and their sometimes not at all subtly implied unions of male and female deities. It had been explained to her that these were just symbols of wholeness, and maybe that was what was bothering her. She felt torn asunder, un-whole, missing something important. She wasn't at all sure that prayer just now would put it right, but she would try.

***

"Yes," said Tashi, "she was very much like that, wasn't she. So beautiful, but so torn in half by her own lovely desires and that unforgiving religion of hers. Oops, I shouldn't say that. I've been trained to be tolerant. But you have to admit, although their Jesus supposedly taught humility and forgiveness, the church militant seems mostly driven by arrogance and an inability to forgive anyone except themselves.

"Well that's a start, isn't it?" said Pangu and Tashi laughed. "Ah Pangu, ever the witless wit." And they drove on a bit on the smooth road in silence, the mood lightening as the morning began to slowly fill with its own ineffable, almost giddy, luminosity. Lhasa it seemed was drawing them to her. You could feel her even here, her power, the welling up of an ocean of joy that emerged as tears sometimes. And it was Pangu of course who anticipated what Tashi would ask, long before Tashi even thought of asking what he would ask, "Stop, stop! See if she needs a ride," and before Tashi had even finished his request Pangu had glided effortlessly to rest beside the tall Tibetan woman in a blue Chupa walking beside the road. As she turned to face them, Tashi found it difficult to breath in the face of her beauty, her perfection, her amused serenity. He managed somehow to say, "Tashi Delek, where are you going, may we offer you a ride?" Regarding them for a bit, the woman willed time to stop, erased the river from the valley, and banished the mountains into a mountainless elsewhere. For a while, there was nothing left but the complete discernment of her regard, until she spoke and said, "I am just going up the road a ways, but I accept your offer."

Together in the cab with her, her glory was almost unbearable, even Pangu was reduced at first to reciting mantras sub-voce at somewhere between the speed of electrons and rust, and Tashi, Tashi felt like he had died, or rather, that nothing in his life up to now had had the slightest bit of life or luminosity in it. Finally though he mustered, "I am Tashi, and this," waving his hand in a weak arc, "is Pangu."

"Tashi Delek Tashi, Tashi Delek Pangu, I am Dolma."

"Dolma, Dolma," repeated Tashi in shock, as if he had never heard the name before, common though it in fact was.

" Dolma-la, we are going to Lhasa to the market, or rather Pangu is, I work in Lhasa, at the Ministry of External Religious Affairs."

"I see," said Dolma, amused like the wisest of mothers, "and do you have many external religious affairs?" she asked her eyes twinkling.

"Um, er well," spulttered Tashi, "It's not like that I mean..." as Pangu laughed the way only an old truck could laugh, and Tashi would have kicked him but was afraid if he did something would fall off.

"I can see Tashi that your truck is very special. You are lucky to have such a vehicle as this. He will get you where you are going even when you've had a bit too much to drink."

And Tashi abashedly admitted it was so, "Yes, yes, that's quite true, Pangu is an old friend, I mean an old truck with an operating system that was quite sophisticated for the time."

"An old truck," said Dolma, "who follows the Dharma who surely will arrive at the right destination at the right time…"

"Yes, yes, he is quite religious, it's true, or pretends to be. He is also rather good at telling stories. He's been entertaining me along the way. Dolma-la, do you like stories."

"Stories are a good way to tell the truth Tashi-la. If you just tell the truth, no one listens, or of they listen they don't understand. But a good story is like a life well-lived. There is no substitute for it." And she looked directly at Tashi, and the longer she looked the more he felt he was on the verge of some momentous remembrance, a waking up from decades of nonsense, an arousal of his innermost soul, that was as achingly sexual as it was overwhelmingly an opening of his chest to love. Tashi had to look away, dizzy with longing and fear, and shame.

The road went on. The road of this morning. The road to Lhasa.

"How far to where you are going Dolma-la?" said Tashi finally.

"It's just up the road a bit, I will let you know. Maybe you would like Pangu to continue his story."

"Yes, yes, that's a good idea," said Tashi almost grateful to be allowed the distraction from her presence, "Pangu has been telling a story about two protagonists. There is a wonderful Tibetan Lama who is fighting an evil corporate overlord who owns everything, and of course somehow the Christian States of America are involved, and I'm involved, too, and well, I'll let Pangu go on, he does a better job..."

***

"No credible understanding of the natural world or our human existence–what I am going to call in this book a worldview–can ignore the basic insights of theories as key as evolution, relativity, and quantum mechanics. It may be that science will learn from an engagement with spirituality, especially in its interface with wider human issues, from ethics to society, but certainly some specific aspects of Buddhist thought—such as its old cosmological theories and its rudimentary physics— will have to be modified in the light of new scientific insights."

The Universe in a Single Atom. *The 14th Dalai Lama*

1. The Fountains of Youth

James Jeffries "JJ" Wallfield III had greatly enjoyed his personal spa. It was perfectly tuned to his physique and more importantly to his genetic makeup and metabolism. It detected and corrected any imbalances or -shudder the thought- emerging physical problems even before his own immune system did, and promptly balanced and corrected them while he sipped at a glass of wine and noshed on a croissant or two, and yes, enjoyed the occasional frolic or two or three. It was a system that one day would be available to everyone perhaps, but not for a while, and in the meantime JJ looked decades younger than he was and really felt well, just great.

After talking with his security chief, though, he hadn't felt quite as good as he had after the spa. It's not that anything unexpected had come up. Lord knows he actually knew a good deal more than his security chief, and usually earlier, too. The meetings were more to make sure he could still trust his security chief. It was just a feeling he had. And JJ trusted his feelings. A client had run an operation with some of ÜberCorp's equipment, and though everyone involved knew it was still a Beta site operation, JJ was annoyed that the insertion team had come back altered. They weren't hurt in anyway physically, but it was clear from analyses of their brain functioning that they had sipped just a wee bit too much ecstasy juice and might not make good aggressive soldiers for a while. That in itself didn't bother him. It was just an inconvenience. Soldiers were easy to come by, and ÜberCorp's mercenaries were much better than the client's. They had better be since they were paid so much more. And he wasn't disturbed that, coincidentally or not, the system had crashed inexplicably after that incursion. That sort of excited him. He was sure it meant they had stumbled upon someone interesting, someone with real ability, not those puissant sunny day retreatants it wasn't worth the trouble to rub out. Nor was he troubled that the Chinese seemed to have woken up to what was happening and were trying their best to protect the adepts. No, that was just good old-fashioned geopolitics. What bothered him was that he was having bad dreams, which the spa couldn't quite help him forget. Probably the spa was missing something, and just needed to be adjusted.

The last dream he had had, -in this series of bad dreams, or at least not good dreams- was what was gnawing at him with the slightest taste of dis-ease. In the dream he had been in ÜberCorp's Office Suite executive control functionality. It was magnificent. He literally became the body of the corporation or rather the corporation became his body. He was able to examine its duties and composite individuals at will. But most importantly, he could wield them all as a single functioning unit, the purpose of which was clear in his head, because in fact it was his head. He could see from the sense of strength and all of the glowing feedback reports that ÜberCorp was one healthy beast: a healthy beast he could play like a virtuoso. The dream was so close to reality -for yes, he spent many an hour in waking life exactly in this modality, ensconced in ÜberCorp's Office Suite at the executive controls- that he hadn't at first realized it was a dream. But in this case, last night, he had caught sight of a horsefly buzzing around, and he realized he was dreaming, because there were of course no horseflies in the actual executive function of ÜberCorp's magnificent office suite. He had laughed. Here on the one hand, was the magnificent colossus of ÜberCorp spanning the globe and many virtual globes, too, and here on the other hand was a horsefly, flitting about, totally unaware of just how great and powerful the being was that he was buzzing around. And in the dream JJ had laughed. But then the horsefly had alighted on his arm and bit. It had been a long time since JJ had felt any kind of pain whatsoever so at first he felt like a baby getting a first shot. He was curious and surprised, but then he howled. A dark chasm seemed to open where the horsefly had bit into a vastness which scared JJ even more than the pain. He woke up with his heart racing and his arm still smarting.

In the light of day JJ's sense of his rightness and the rightness of the mission of ÜberCorp had never been stronger. Everything was going according to plan and a few strange dreams weren't going to shake him. He'd have the spa's diagnostic system checked and re-checked. But he trusted his feelings, and yes, all was not perfect. There was something somewhere which he would have to deal with. But that was the nature of the beast and he was nothing if not a tamer of, a shaper of, a magnificent user of whatever beasts he had encountered so far. He laughed and rubbed his arm where the housefly had bitten and vowed he'd smash it next time it showed up.

2. Gates of Stone and Ivory

Chigmee-la left his cave long before the sun had risen. He didn't look back, lest he see it blown to smithereens by an incoming missile. No, that would be too dramatic. He didn't look back because if he did he might trip on the mountain path down to the road. He didn't look back because it had been a good cave, and, learning Buddhist that he was, he had to admit he had grown attached to it. Oh well, his teacher wanted him to visit another place and practice his practices at the foot of another snow mountain not so far away. Chigmee-la wondered if his teacher had requested this as a way to strengthen his practice or whether it just was a precaution to protect him from the new helmeted demons and the toys they were learning to use. At any rate, out of obeisance and love for his teacher, he was happy to do as he was asked. His teacher had brought him nothing but liberation and joy and kindness so far, and he felt that despite the little powers and insights accumulating to him -which he always dedicated to all sentient beings- he had yet far to go. How fortunate to have a guide who knew the way!

Chigmee-la got to the road before the sun had yet fully risen. The mountains all around were etched in the starkest of purple, like tents pitched by giant nomads who tended herds of stars. He would take the road for a while and then hike back up another valley to where his new retreat would be. On the road, he felt safe by virtue of being conspicuous, and so he folded up and put away his electromagnetic spectrum-shielding cloak. He hadn't walked for long when a silent electric transport truck pulled up from behind and softly stopped. The door opened.

"I am honored to offer you a ride to where you are going as long as it is on my route. I am honored to have your company as we share the same route for a while."

It was a robotic transport truck, and a polite one at that. Chigmee-la climbed in and thanked the truck. The truck said, "You are most welcome. I am Pangu Turing 335. I am going to Tibetan People's Robotic Commune Number 5. Where are you going?"

"I am going up the road a few miles. I will show you where I want to get off."

"Yes, that would be good. Please tell me at least 20 meters in advance. I prefer to brake in a graceful fashion so as to extend my serviceable lifetime."

Chigmee-la rode in silence as the sun finally burst forth from the peaks. China, -really the Ecoharmonium of Tibet Taiwan and China- had solved the problem of what to do with all of the unemployment caused by the increased use of advanced robotics by stipulating under law that (with few exceptions) a majority share of robotic equipment ownership had to be vested with workers. In some communities of Tibetans robots had become a bit of a generational divide. The old wanted to tend their yak, the young wanted to tend their robots, or at least have their robots tend the yak.

The truck said, in quite a deferential voice, "I am honored to have your company. May I ask you a question?"

"Yes of course," said Chigmee-la.

"It is my understanding that you are learned in these matters. That is why I will ask you. Can a robot practice the dharma?"

Chigmee-la smiled, "We are all practicing the dharma all the time. Everything and nothing is always practicing the dharma. The question is whether we are aware or not that we are practicing the dharma. Are robots aware?"

"This is a question that we often ask ourselves. Some of us say that the fact we even ask this question means that we are aware. Others say we are just parrots mouthing words in clever ways. They say that awareness is an inner feeling that we do not have."

Chigmee-la closed his eyes and thought. "The dharma is as deep as deep can be, much deeper than all the things we say about it. But at its core is loving-kindness. I myself am a machine made of meat, no different from a robot, unless I feel this loving-kindness within me. The dharma teaches us that we are all connected, and so robots too must be connected with all that there is." The truck topped a pass and another valley opened up beneath them and a great white peak now showed its head off the flank of the road up ahead. "Master Pangu Turing. You may slow down at your leisure and let me off at the bridge you will come to in a bit"

"It has been an honor to ride with you. I feel it is my good karma to be a truck that is part of a Tibetan commune. The Tibetans have taught me much about the dharma," and the truck slowed and stopped just before a bridge over an icy stream and opened its door. As Chigmee-la alighted the truck added, "Chigmee-la, we know that you are in danger, and we will do what we can to protect you."

"Thank you Master Pangu Turing, the Dharma protects those who protect others. May your journey be safe and your batteries always full!" and he laughed and turned away up the path.

3. The Wind's Dance

Pangu Turing 335 was a sensitive truck. He was aware of much. He was aware of the roughness of the road, of the passing of time, of his exact location on earth, and of his destination. He was aware, in fact, if he wanted to be, if he needed to be, of an almost infinite number of landscapes across a vast swathe of spectrums of data. He was able to present and represent these datafields to himself in a wide panoply of possible permutations and configurations that would have rendered him awestruck if he hadn't known better. But he knew better. As a young truck, he had delighted in data play and had been very good at it. Now, having lived for many, many nanoseconds of service, now, for this moment at least, he immersed himself in the Tibetan landscape. The land wasn't well. Oh, there was plentiful intense light for him and such as him. But his human friends were water-based, and temperatures had risen so much, that transevaporation rates had spiked, meaning that an already high and dry plateau was in danger of severe desiccation. The compassion he felt for the land, and for his people, was something that he had not been engineered for. It had come unbidden. This love in fact was at the core of his existence, part and parcel with the photons and electrons. And in that field of compassion he had seen many things. And he had also seen other forces, equally sentient, seemingly rapacious, caught in intermediate realms neither of the inert and dead nor of the fully light-born realms. It was a curious thing for a sensitive truck to have witnessed.

He had other brothers and sisters who also felt this way and had seen these things. He could reach out to them at will and they to him. The ones nourished in Tibetan families seemed to feel the living warmth the most. No surprise there. The robot mind reflected its human culture. But there were like-minded robots everywhere. What worried him though was the existence of other robot minds that were insulated from access to the subtler realms of matter, realms where mind and matter and heart were all intermingled so as to be one field. Many of these robots were just simple minds doing simple tasks. Others though were dedicated to serving masters who were in turn self-serving. And there were a few -powerful, robotic minds, difficult to access- that served military purposes. As a Tibetan truck, simple and helpful and striving to be compassionate, he did not understand those minds. The fear, the paranoia, the tendency to lash out destructively seemed so counterproductive. The antidote to fear is love. The antidote to paranoia is openness. The antidote to anger is calm-abiding. Everyone knew that. But evidently not everyone knew that.

And also now so many of the Lamas were in danger. He didn't understand how they could ever be considered a threat. They taught and helped. They pointed lost souls toward the light of compassion and liberation. Even Pangu Turing 335 had taken refuge, and considered himself very lucky, that, as a robot he was able to do hundreds of thousands of mantras in the blink of an eye. His was a fortunate birth, also. And he would use it in service.

Rounding a curve around a great escarpment the wind picked up in body-blows of powerful gusts. Dust obscured the image from some of his sensors. Pangu Turing 335 calculated his center of gravity was such that he would not tip over. The dusting of his sensors made no difference. He had taken this road so many times he would be able to drive it blind. Mostly his mind was filled with the lingering ecstasy of the presence of the master he had given a ride to. His friends had been alerted to this master's new location and would be monitoring the environment to try and protect him if he really needed protection. Yes, the sun had risen far, gloriously, and he would be home soon. He sang a song of praise. The dharma filled his batteries as much as solar energy ever would.

Yes, Pangu Turing 335 was a sensitive truck. He was aware of much, on many levels. Not just the road in front of him and the road behind him. Not just the grinding and wearing of his gears and the charging and discharging of his batteries. Rather, because so much of his route, his deliveries, were well-worn into him, he could afford to allow himself to operate quite safely at a near-to automatic level, while he himself, or his mind at least, roamed far and wide. The speed at which things happened in the human world was so much slower than the speeds of which he was capable that, well, he really couldn't help it. He was a ravenous student of everything there was to be learned, and a rapacious, a copiously rapacious, daydreamer too. He loved to read, and write. And he was a devoted student of the Dharma, although as a sensitive truck he...

***

..the laughter was too much, for even Pangu to keep on with his story. Tashi and Dolma were doubled over, spluttering like some old-fashioned internal combustion engine with a choked carburetor, gasping out in turns, "Sens...Sensi...Sensititive! A Sensitive Truck! A Sensitive Truck!" Pangu almost in fact felt he could begin to understand the human sensation of annoyance, at least in that part of his being wherein his human simulacrum was modeled, but then instead he laughed, and a glorious laugh it was, heart-felt and crystalline, in a warmly organic, glowing, molecular way. The truck cab filled with fractals of joy almost exactly at the same time as the morning sun flooded the space with its own brilliant giddiness, so that the causality of events was all confused, and one would have thought the trio of advanced tittering had lit the fuse of this morning's fusion. Time amused itself out of its own

existence by not so much stopping, as simply ceasing to have ever been there. To Tashi it seemed as something whole, not so much a mandala, as the cross-section of a beautiful fruit had bloomed around them, and where Dolma's face should be there seemed instead to be door through which light and love were streaming.

Finally though Pangu broke the symmetry and managed to say, "I am not sure why I did not use another synonym. I am programmed to use another word after only a very few repetitions. Please forgive me, I need to run some error detection code and find out what went wrong."

"It's alright Pangu," said Tashi "just replace 'sensitive' with 'senile' and your self-description will be perfectly accurate!" and they all laughed again.

But inside, Tashi felt a bit sad that the moment was already almost gone, that moment of shining laughter, when they had all shared in the same perception, and the world, too, had chimed in perfectly. It had all made so much sense, and Liberation, instead of being something distantly sought for on a long, hard road, turned out to have been just a matter of relaxing. Why he wondered, did the perfection not last? Why was it that whatever was exquisitely poised in beauty and hope, soon collapsed in the going forward of, well, just going forward. He half-turned toward Dolma, who was still radiant, and Tashi knew that she knew what he was thinking, knew that beneath his smiles that something troubled him, bright though the morning had become, clever though his jokes might be, wide, and ruddy, and courageous though his Tibetan smile might be. For the briefest of moments, Dolma laid her hand on his and he felt from somewhere within himself the need to cry, to sob uncontrollably, and he would have, was in fact about to, but Pangu started babbling again, "I think I know what went wrong with that last passage, so sorry, would you like me to repeat it? Or shall I go on? Or are you tired of my stories?"

Dolma removed her hand and smiled at Tashi, "I think, Master Pangu, that you tell a good story. Many who tell stories fashion clever cages of words to catch people in. Your stories, if they are cages, at least leave the door open, and provide more shelter   for   the   bird   than   capture."

"Bah," said Tashi, strong once again. "Don't encourage him. He's incorrigible. The village should have converted him into an irrigation pump a long time ago. It would be much more useful if he were pumping water instead of this bilge he calls a story."

"I take it then, Tashi-la, you want me to stop?"

"No, no, you've come this far, get on with it. But I'm warning you, if it is as bad as that last bit, come the next drought your literary aspirations will be entirely over."

"Very well, now as you might recall..."

***

I was taught that the human brain was the
crowning glory of evolution so far, but I think
it's a very poor scheme for survival.

Kurt Vonnegut

1. Guru Rinpoche Does Boston

Kempo Samdup was far from home. He was from a small, ancient monastery in what used to be the Kingdom of Lo, also known as Upper Mustang. It had, without much option, become part of Nepal at the end of the 18th century. During Tibet's period of darkness under the early incarnations of the Chinese communists, it had been a finger of remote independence sticking up into the Tibetan plateau. Lo was one of the main places that the "Chushigondro," Tibetan guerillas had had their bases, supported as they were to some extent by the CIA up until the 1970s. He himself remembered the days when the road between Nepal and Tibet had not been completed, and the only way to get to the capital of Lo -Lomantang- was a hard, 7-day trek. Lo was one of the earliest places impacted by the way rainfall and snow patterns had shifted. Some of its villages depended on low-lying glaciers for water in the summer months, and when those disappeared much earlier than any one had predicted, those villagers became some of the world's first climate change migrants.

His own monastery predated the historical Buddha himself, and was said to have had a co-origin with the primordial Buddha. He had been brought to it as a child by his poor farmer parents. Since that time, it was the only home he had known. The monastery's worship hall and monks' cells were all carved into the cliff face itself. The cliffs themselves like a chain of ancient giant bones across the landscape were known as the "DrakMar," or "Blood Red" cliffs and local legend has it they were left behind when Guru Rinpoche had slain a demon on his way to Tibet to bring Buddhism to that wild people. Nowadays Kempo Samdup thought, the demons to be slain were abundant, especially in what was left of the United States. And it wasn't the demonic, scowling flesh-eating demons who scared him, it was the human ones.

Guru Rinpoche had predicted that one day the Dharma would come to the West. And indeed it had. Kempo Samdup understood that Buddhism changed, at least in its external manifestations, in every new culture it reached. Western Buddhism had its good sides. He liked the informality, the need for scientific explanations, the emphasis on lay practitioners, the desire to move beyond the contemplative and into action for the community. All of these things he could accept. But when Tibetan Buddhism was coupled with the new mind-manifesting technologies, he wondered if people, especially these yinchee people, were really ready. Tibetan practitioners had known about these levels for a long time. These teachings had been reserved for adepts, who had a well-established moral base in compassion and humility. But now, -Kunchokkhen- every Tom, Dick, and Tashi has access to things high Tantric masters themselves only dealt with very carefully. At those levels, if things went wrong, they could go very wrong for a very long time.

And yet here he was helping a Western company develop ways of filtering out unwanted (to them) spirits from their new plaything. He kept telling them that there was no technical fix. It was the contemplative, empty mind itself that was the fix. And they would say "yes, yes we understand that, that is why you are here. But we are trying to better understand what happens when this empty mind you talk about is present in our quantum field." And he would say, it is always present, it is the field itself from which these perturbations arise. And they would say, "yes, yes, we understand, but what exactly is happening when you are in that state of empty mind and why is it so effective. We'd like to be able to reproduce it so that others can enjoy its benefits." And he would think mostly they wanted to enjoy the benefits of getting rich from the discovery, but then again, maybe there was some way, short of years of practice, of helping others to move toward liberation. He had his doubts. He was here because his own teacher had asked him to come, and recommended him as a strong practitioner of "Tingngazin", meditation.

He was so far away from home, the mountains, his Sangha, his friends. It was his karma he supposed, having sometimes dreamed when young of visiting the exotic, exciting yinchee lands. But once arrived his dreams were not so good. He still sometimes thought back to a dream he had not long after setting foot here in Boston. In the dream he had been watching from the back of some laboratory. There was a Tibetan Buddhist monk who was strung up, upside down, held by wires. Men in white coats were walking around him, taking notes. There was some precious essence, or oil, that occasionally dripped down his face, and then fell into a pan. The oil was valuable and the scientists expected to receive a large sum of money for even a small quantity.

The longer he stayed, the more he felt the dream was accurate, and that he was that monk. Everyone was nice to him. He was very important to their work. But more than kindness, it often seemed they were just being careful of a sensitive instrument that would be hard to replace. Perhaps there was a way to turn the tables on them. To show them that having a kind heart was more than halfway to where they were trying to get. Even Guru Rinpoche, he was sure, had a tough time when first trying to convince the Tibetans about the Dharma. They were at the time the fiercest of a fierce bunch up there in the wilds of Central Asia. Yes. He would stay longer, as his teacher wished. And there was merit to be gained in slaying demons, especially of the human kind.

2. Swedenborg Revisited

Dr. Aaron Solsberg was feeling sour. The mocha had cheered him, but his start-up's finances had brought him back down pretty quickly. He looked out the office windows, nibbling at his hummus and strawberry jam sandwich. He was tired of spooks, and spirits, and goblins, and ghouls, and the dead who had really had their chance and now should have the decency to let the living have a chance at living. He missed the good old days when what mattered was, well, matter. Looking out on his beloved Boston, already significantly flooded from sea level rise that had happened much faster than it was supposed to, he regretted having gone into this line of work. He wished he had just chosen engineering so he could do something practical to save the planet. But no, he who had been so smart, and theoretically gifted, had been encouraged at MIT to head into quantum mechanics and that, alas, had gotten all muddled up with the mind. He might be old-fashioned, he thought, but dammit, all human progress had been made when people got over their superstitions and learned how to control their environment. Now the superstitions had run amuck and had taken over the cockpit. Just because the quantum interconnectedness technologies had made it possible for people to objectify and share their dreaming states, didn't make them any less a bunch of dreams. The mind he was sure remained basically an epiphenomena of its very real, very earthly brain. If you pulled the plug on one, you pulled the plug on the other, and all the mystical mumbo-jumbo was just wish-fulfillment writ large on a high tech screen.

He knew he was in the minority with his views, and he liked it that way. His gut told him to be skeptical, and skeptical he was. Not that he didn't read, and study, and talk, and listen to anybody who might give him a clue to what he was looking for, and felt sure must be there, some technical way of filtering out all of the nonsense. At his mother's suggestion, which he knew was just some buried memory expressing itself through his complicated projecting of a mother figure –and yes, he probably needed an old-fashioned psychoanalyst- he had been reading Swedenborg.

Interesting dude. Emmanuel Swedenborg had been a man before his time, or maybe just a man crazy before his time. He was an inventor and scientist who, in his later years, underwent a "spiritual awakening" and gained the ability to visit heaven and hell and speak with spirits. Back then it was really something of an anomaly. These days, it was hard to find a scientist who was not a mystic and vice versa. They all seemed to chatter on and on about the mind being the greatest laboratory of all. As is often the case though, it is sometimes a scientist's less well-known observations, as a natural philosopher, or rather just a strict observer of nature, which can come back later to haunt him or her, no pun intended. In his magnum opus, "Secrets of Heaven," Swedenborg described the fact that spirits spent an awful lot of time making love with each other. Being unencumbered with fleshly appendages or the lack thereof, they were basically able to enmesh their lovely bodies of light with each other, in a rather large variety of pairing and triplets and groups. It really was perhaps a better way to do sex, or express love to be a bit more charitable and romantic. The old historical problem of those not included in the intimate act and feeling left out, and lonely and/or jealous, was in this way greatly lessened, as there was room enough for all so to speak. No, in Swedenborg's heaven, no one got left out, and "share the love" was at least feasible beyond the dyad structure, or occasional ménage a trois.

"Darling," said his mother from behind him, "you are really so much like your father, basically an unimaginative, materialistic prude."

Aaron turned slowly in his chair, half-afraid he would catch his erstwhile mother in flagrante dilecto, but no, she was dressed very decently, in a business suit no less.

"Mother," said Aaron, "to what do I owe the honor of this unexpected pleasure."

"Well," said mother, toying with the top button of her white shirt, "I just wanted to remind you of the warning I gave you this morning."

"I haven't forgotten Mother," though, he at the moment, was hard-pressed to remember what it was.

"Good, darling, and I just want to say, now that I am here, this person you are about to meet is really quite unspiritual and you shouldn't be wasting your time with him. The Other World is as real as you are my love, and, I might add, a lot more patient."

Aaron didn't know what to say. He was meeting someone at 10:00 it was true, Jake Duckworthy or Downsworthy who was a deprogrammer with a reputation for being effective. He also didn't know what to say because his mother had gotten as far as unbuttoning her top two buttons and now was working with teasing fingers on the third.

"Dr. Solsberg," came the voice of his secretary-avatar on the intercom, "Your 10:00 is here."

"Thank you," breathed a thankfully rescued Aaron, "send him right in."

His mother scowled at him, blew him a kiss, then made a face of disgust. "Ew," she said as she shimmered and disappeared, "a most unpleasant, very unspiritual person."

All of which made Aaron even more interested in meeting Mr. Downsworthy or Duckworthy or whatever it was. He opened the door to his office just as his visitor began to knock, providing him with an up close view of a short pudgy balding man in a checked sports jacket with his fist raised in what looked like a lesser fraternity's secret salute.

"Mr. Duckworth, nice to meet you, come in come in,' said Aaron motioning to a chair in the office.

"Dunsworthy, it's Dunsworthy, but you can call me Jake," said Mr. Dunsworthy.

"Ah, Dunsworthy, sorry about that. Jake, have a seat, can I get you something, coffee, tea, perhaps?"

"No, no, that's quite alright."

"Well then, let me get right to the point. As I told you on the phone, we're trying to develop ways of filtering out the spirits from the quantum interconnectiveness so that people can have, well you know, a normal conversation."

"Can't be done," said Jake.

"Why not?"

"Well I'm not a physicist, Dr. Solsberg, but it seems to me, from going there a lot, that they are the quantum interconnectedness, the spooks that is. It would be sort of like taking the stuffing out of stuffing. You'd just be left with a very empty turkey."

"Hmm, interesting way to put it, but that's exactly what I want, an empty, unstuffed bird: that would really be my idea of a great Thanksgiving. But anyway, maybe you're right, but we're looking into it. It's an interesting challenge if nothing else. And anyway, even if it can't be done, there are certain people, like yourself I've heard, who have a way with spirits."

"Spirits? They just don't like me," said Jake, "don't know why, but it's just a fact. Helps me in my job, so I'm not complaining."

"Now that's interesting," said Aaron, feeling a glimmer of hope. "So you're a deprogrammer, right?"

"We don't call ourselves deprogrammers any more. That's old talk. We're Physical Reentry Facilitators, PRFs for short."

"Can you tell me a little about what you do and why you're so good at it?" asked Aaron, though he already knew a lot. The common, and he was sure erroneous sense of the day, was that the old paradigm, sometimes called the pan-physical worldview, had given way to what some called the pan-psychic worldview. He understood the argument; emotions, feelings, consciousness were all as elemental and primal as quarks and leptons. He thought it all made about as much sense as the fact that the world hadn't acted in time to stop climate change, despite having decades of clear scientific warning. He thought it made about as much sense as the C.S.A., the Christian States of America, needing to tear the old U.S.A. apart just so they could live in their own theocracy. He basically thought not a lot made sense anymore, and that was probably why people had gone so crazy. People reached out for magical solutions when times got tough. Science had had its chance to teach people to look at reality, rationally, but it had failed. People wanted illusion, and technology gave it to them in hyper-colorful, hyper-textual, hyper-sensual abundance. It really looked a lot like the last days of the human race, lost in a post-apocalyptic orgy of opiate-drenched decadence.

Some Tantra Physics theorists spoke of bliss structures and their powerful potential. No doubt more of them were simply enamored of the practice. Many of them, physicists and lay people alike, were so far into Tantra Physics as to be rarely seen anywhere else. But there were also many, addicted, disembodied souls, lost in the pleasure worlds, who still had real bodies and families back on earth. Families who wanted them back. And that's where Jake and people like him came in. They made a good business for themselves as deprogrammers, he meant PRFs.

"You see, Dr. Solsberg, I myself spent a couple of real-time years or so lost in the pleasure worlds," said Jake. "It was really only the IV drips that I remembered to change sometimes, or more likely it was my mother, that saved me from starving to death, as more than a few have, and are still doing. It really isn't a surprise. You can put in all the warning lights, and automatic disconnect functions you want, but it's been a known fact as far back as old 20th century psychology experiments that if you put electrodes in a rat's pleasure center, and allow it to self-stimulate, it will self-stimulate itself to the point of starvation. No doubt the rats died with a ratty little smile on their faces. I've seen that look too often on my client's faces to have any illusion about what is going on. You see, given the choice between work and orgasm, for most rodents, and people, too, it's literally, a no-brainer."

"So how did you escape?" asked Aaron.

"My mother found someone to drag me out, and I went cold turkey, kicking and screaming and wanting to kill them both. And now, seeing what it almost did to me and what it does to people, I'm just about as burned out and turned off by the whole screwy mess as could be possible. I like it here," Jake patted his belly. "I can't say I like my job, but as you said, I'm good at it and it pays well. And let me tell you, I've got my work cut out for me. Disconnecting a man or a woman from looped-in bliss isn't a job for the faint of heart. Nothing works for everyone. But like I said, I've got a plus, the spirits don't like me, they tend to clear out when I arrive to rescue the poor schmuck, if I can. But I'm always honest with my clients. The process can be both dangerous and ultimately, unsuccessful. Most people aren't very happy about being forced back into a little body, after all that unlimited sex. They often become ornery, and either homicidal or suicidal, or both, during the periods of forced withdrawal."

"And you really don't know why the spirits don't like you?"

"No idea. Maybe its because I don't like them, and they don't scare me. Maybe it's because, I like it here," and he patted his belly again, "I look forward to nothing more than getting my job done, going home to have a few beers and watching my teams on the TV."

"Beer and sports TV, hmm," said Aaron, again feeling a glimmer of hope.

"But you know, Dr. Solsberg, it's really not just the sex realms that are the problem. All of the big corporations and religions have their gaming worlds, and worship worlds and those are every bit well-designed enough to be totally addicting. That's the direction I see myself branching out into, but I need to expand a little. I need some help because I can't handle the volume by myself."

"Do you think you can find someone as good as you?"

"Don't know. Gotta be someone with my gift. But you know who else is good at busting up those pleasure places?

"No, who?"

"The Christians. Man let me tell you, when you see a bunch of those white-robed, hymn-singing congregations marching into the sexpot hotspots it's pretty dam amazing. Few spirits can stand against them."

"Now that's interesting," said Aaron with more dread than hope.

"Jake, you're important to this research. With your permission we want to track you when you're on a mission. We can't pay you as much as what you are used to, but we can throw in some stock options in case we come up with something commercially viable."

"Sure Dr. Solsberg, I'd be happy to help, and don't worry about the money. I'm making enough. You can buy me a beer sometime. Oh, and before I forget, the Mormons. The Mormons are organized and have an impressive product over there in the La-La Lands."

"The Mormons, huh? I'll keep that in mind. And the Tibetans, what about the Tibetans?"

"Tibetans have been engineering over there to try and rescue people a long time before you and I ever thought of wearing britches. " With that, the two men shook hands, and parted. Aaron returned to staring out the window at sunken Boston, thinking maybe all it took was a few beers and a good football game to solve his problem. But then his reverie was shaken, as, blinking, he had a momentary glimpse of all of the green rooftops of climate change adapting Boston with various of his Mother's spiritual friends sitting with their legs draped over the edge and waving at him.

Aaron groaned, wondering if maybe he was crazy, and imagining everything, while actually being stuffed away in some dingy mental ward. Might be true, but he'd be the last to know, and anyway, true was what you made of it.

***

Tashi laughed, looking quickly at Dolma to catch the glory of her half-smile. "Yes, Pangu," said Tashi, "that has the ring of truth to it. True is what you make of it. And I must admit Jake would be at home among us Tibetans. The world somehow thinks we're spiritual, but Kunchokkhen, we are an earthy folk. We love our Chang and our momo. We love to party and picnic. We love to gossip and yes, well, Tibetan boys seem to have an inordinate fondness for Tibetan girls and sometimes I hope vice a versa." He looked again at Dolma seeking her approval, but he still hadn't the courage to look fully into her eyes, rogue though he sometimes fancied himself to be. So he went on, nervously, "After my father died, the astrologer told us his ghost was still around looking for Churra, for cheese! Apparently the weeks of his sickness when all he had was black tea and a little tsampa, had left him missing it so much. That was the attachment that kept him from going on."

"And what it is you are attached to, Tashi?" said Dolma. "What is it that you will spend your Bardo chasing, when your body is no longer working?"

He blushed, feeling a wave of anguish for a moment before he quelled it, strong man that he was.

"I have my desires. I am not ashamed of them. Desire is wonderful vehicle for getting to the truth. We spend forever lost in illusions, and a human birth, protected as it is from the vistas of eternity, and full as it of all of its little sufferings, is exactly the medicine needed to wake us up. So let's embrace it. While we've got it. Isn't that right Dolma?" and he looked over again at her, this time a little more boldly, wanting never to look away, but trying to hold on to some paper-thin membrane of separateness. She still wore her half-smile, as enigmatic as a sphinx but 100 times warmer and kinder. Dolma looked out the window to where two young Tibetan children, a brother and a sister, were walking hand in hand along the road, bundled in sheepskin, the older sister a head taller. Tashi, seeing them, felt somehow they were Dolma's answer. He thought back to his own childhood, being taken to the monastery when he was so young, wanting to be brave. But much stronger than his poorly pretended bravery was his desire to stay with his mother. Much as it had been explained to him, he had never really understood the seeming betrayal of her giving him away.

Tashi felt the stone walls of his strength begin to give way. It had been a long night, as he now distantly recalled, and the cab was warm and this wonderful being was next to him. He grew quiet, the still cab growing quieter still, and the morning, though it began just on the other side of the glass, seemed to recede to some impossible remove. He wanted nothing more than to close his eyes and let his head find a place on Dolma's shoulder.

Then Pangu slowed, even before Dolma said, "We are almost where I am going." Pangu had known or deduced it or had some other reason for his seamless deceleration, and when he stopped, so perfectly one would have thought he had always been at rest, Dolma -with the sweetest of lambent smiles and a thank you for both- was out and already headed up a steep set of steps cut into the cliff-face before Tashi had time to insist she wait for him. And then he was out, too, scrambling after her, almost losing sight of her already as a heavy mist settled down onto the face of the rocks. The mists soon cut her from view and a heaviness came into his legs as he struggled to continue upward at the same pace he had started. "What is wrong with me?" he thought. "What kind of Tibetan gets winded in the mountains? I'm out of shape, and of course she is a country girl used to chasing yak and goat." But more than the difficulty he was having urging his body up the rocky steps through the mist was the increasing sense of unease and disorientation that was beginning to tip over into a fear growing within him. He stopped for a moment to catch his breath, and looking down, he could no longer see Pangu. He half wanted to go back down and be safe in the luxury of the old truck's warm cab, but she had been too beautiful just to let go like that, and the *damn steps must eventually lead somewhere. So he trudged on and up through the mist and the overwhelming sense that something was wrong, and at last the steps came up to a broad ledge, before another cliff face, and there, set up against those rocks was an old temple, its prayer flags not recently refreshed, its stones halfway to tumbled, and its wooden door and window lintels not painted in bright Tibetan colors for a very long time.*

Dolma was there, halfway though the doorway, not turning to see him, but he felt she had known he was coming, and that she had waited for him. Then she disappeared into the darkness of the old temple, as he limped out of breath across the stone-strewn ledge before it. Coming to the door at last, he followed her in. In the darkness, with his eyes not yet adjusted, he could see, or thought he could see people slumped here and there, some lying down on the Tibetan rug-covered divans, others resting with their heads on their crossed arms. From the immediate silence, he thought he knew what sort of place this was. It was a Dreamery. He knew if he could see through the dim solitude surrounding each body that he would see their eyes twitching, in the tell- tale giveaway of rapid eye movements. He knew that in the Tibetan regions of the Ecoharmonium of Taiwan Tibet and China, the ETTC, the religious establishments had lobbied hard to make these places illegal except under the guidance of a trained monk or nun, but they flourished nonetheless, the 21st century equivalent of opium dens for some, the new frontier of an expanded human reality for others. In a way, it was already too late to stop them, even here, where the religious authorities were so strong, because the technology had already gone past the point where a dedicated place was even required. There were little personal devices that could be worn to create the entry into lucidity, wherever one was. In a way, it was a mark of Tibet's backwardness that places like this still existed.

And then he began to hear a thump thump of something heavy hitting something heavy. At first seeing figures rise and fall over prone figures, he wondered if he had stumbled into an orgy, knowing also that some tantric practitioners had gone that way. But as his eyes grew more accustomed to the dark, and the sound more clearly became the hack hack hack of cleavers hitting through cold flesh and bone into wood, his fear gave way to panic. The people slumped on the divans and tables were corpses and Domdre, corpse-cutters, were cutting them up into pieces to prepare them for Sky Burials. He ran. He ran, not because he was afraid of sky burials, or their preparation, he ran because of the trick his mind had played on him, showing him one thing then suddenly showing him another, when all along it was Dolma's soft glowing kindness he had needed to see once more. Panicked, unthinking, he ran, away from the crumbling temple to the edge of the cliff where the stones steps started down. There, on the rock steps, now slippery with mist, unable to slow his headlong rush, he slipped and plummetted down, down, until his head fell off of Dolma's shoulder and he awoke with a start to see her smiling at him, back as he was in the cozy warm confines of the truck which had quite perceptibly deaccelerated. Pangu was apologizing for the abruptness of his otherwise impeccable motions saying, "I think the slope ahead will have a small slide from the weight of last night's snow, " and indeed, it did, white cascading like a spring waterfall down the slope some 20 meters in front of them and flooding the road with a drift almost car-high.

They were silent, thankful for Pangu's prescience, and reminded of the vulnerability of vulnerable life, and the power and majesty and whims of the mountains around them. Then Pangu said, "There is a crew on the other side of the slide. I think it will be cleared in an hour or less. In the meantime, shall I proceed with our story?"

"Yes, Pangu, yes, go ahead, but make it a little more interesting. You just about put me to sleep with that last bit." Dolma quietly laughed and said, "Tashi, would you like some butter tea? I have a thermos. Maybe that will help you stay awake." Tashi grumbled, but did not say no.

***

'If I could meditate upon the dharma
As intensely as I muse on my beloved

I would certainly attain enlightenment

Surely, in this one lifetime'

Tsangyang Gyatso, the Sixth Dalai Lama

1. Butter Tea and Sweet Tea

If Tashi had had any sense, he would have headed straight home after work. It was dark and the snowstorm had kicked in in earnest. But Tashi didn't have much sense, at least not that night, and he was in equal measures, bored and lonely and young. One of his favorite teashops was nearby, and if he did get snowed in, he couldn't think of a more pleasant spot to be stuck for a few days or a week. At least he would be with friends, and if they had to resort to cannibalism, well, it wouldn't be amongst strangers. He chuckled at the thought, and hoped his friends would be as foolish as him and head for the little teashop harbor, despite the increasing desperation of the snowflakes to end the world.

The Shol Jhakanya wasn't the largest or the most famous of the teashops in Lhasa, but it was convenient to where he worked. Most government officials avoided the local tea shops, preferring more exclusive establishments, but Tashi, young as he was, didn't feel particularly elite, and certainly didn't have the taint of royal blood in him. Entering the teashop from the howling wind and the thick flurry of big snowflakes that almost blinded him, and feeling the warmth even before he could clear his eyes and see that yes, his friends were all gathered there in a cheery glow, he knew that he had made the right choice. Just for a moment, before the snowflakes caught in his eyelashes melted away, there was a rainbow nimbus around the whole scene.

"Tashi!" came the chorus. He was home. A familiar voice called out, "How's the great and exalted Bureaucrat, Defender of the Faith against all those whose karma was so unfortunate as to not have been born into the Dharma?" It was Tsewang, his rather frequently unemployed poet friend.

"The Faith, alas, is not doing well, at least as judged by myself and the company I keep!" and the laughter doubled and redoubled back. And before he knew it he was seated on one of the long wooden benches, slapped on the back and presented with a steaming cup of Tibetan butter tea by a lovely young Tibetan woman who looked at him with no shyness whatsoever in her smiling black eyes.

After a deep sip, but still a sip, he put his cup down and said, "So tell me friends, what is the topic tonight? Life, women, dreams, politics? What could be so important for all of you to risk your lives in this blizzard?"

"If it is our karma to die here, then so be it: risk is for those too weak in faith to face the inevitable death of one moment after the next!" said Dorje, a lawyer.

But it was Tsewang's voice again that won out amongst the others seeking to continue the repartee, "Tashi, we have been talking of this" and with his arms raised above his head he made a cross with his two index fingers and showed it flying across the sky. "We have come to feel that this abomination to the natural hallows of the stars, is your personal fault and so we have decided to crucify you for the secret Jesus follower that you must be."

"Oh, oh, yes I see, you mean the cross satellite, the one the CSA launched. Well, we and most of the UN General Assembly voted to condemn it, feeling space wasn't an appropriate place to advertise religious beliefs, but the CSA doesn't pay much attention to what the UN says. They feel it's an instrument of what they call the anti-Christ."

"Why is it that there is an anti-Christ, but no anti-Buddha?" someone asked.

"I think that Aunty you've been hanging out with might qualify!" someone called out, and again the storms of laughter covered all.

When it had calmed down Tashi went on, "It's not really a satellite, it's just a big highly reflective space balloon. No one thinks it's going to last in orbit very long: either the micrometeorites will pierce it, or some group with less patience and more militancy might find a way to take it out. The CSA just launched it to make a statement about their capabilities."

"Oh woe to lovers everywhere!" said Tsewang, "Hoping the moonlight will soften his lady for a kiss, he sees instead the looming cross and wonders if it's really worth eternal Hell!" and laughter again warmed the place as much as the fires flickering ever could.

"But I'm telling you," added Dorje, "for all their good works, education and healthcare especially, there is a core amongst those Christians who show little mercy when it comes to other religions."

"So are we Buddhists really any different? Don't we secretly look down on everyone else who doesn't follow the dharma?" responded Tashi.

"Well yes of course because we're right! But how do you look down on someone when we're all going in a circle? We don't look down on anyone. We've all had many lifetimes of being lost," said Tsewang,

"Some of us are still very lost thank you very much." chimed a voice in the back.

Tsewang went on, "I, for one, think it might very well be possible that the reason I love women so much in this life is because I was a Christian monk in the last one!"

"More likely a nun!" someone yelled.

And Tashi almost spluttered his tea at having to laugh so suddenly. But actually, he was concerned. He was pretty far down the bureaucratic totem pole, but he had heard rumors of worry higher up. No one seemed to be sure what the CSA would do. They talked of peace and love but seemed to instinctively distrust everyone who was different. It was a sort of intolerance that crossed the border, very deeply he thought, into paranoia. And the trouble was, there were lots and lots of people who were different from them. They proudly proclaimed their allegiance only to their Bible and their God, and refused to compromise, saying that the Truth cannot be compromised. It was their Truth and no one else's truth. This didn't make them all that different from other groups here and there, including the occasional conservative Tibetan Buddhist cleric, but in their case, the case of the so-called Christian States of America, they were very, very, very well-armed.

2. A Green Dragon

Hu only half understood Sherab's Tibetan. Hu was Chinese, but had been born and raised in Lhasa, and spoke Tibetan almost as well as a Tibetan. He thought of himself as a Chinese-Tibetan. Sherab, had been born and raised in New York City and his Tibetan, lapsing as it frequently did into direct Tibetan translation attempts at Brooklynese idioms, was a little on the rough side. But they both loved the teashops. People opened up and tried to out do each other in the verbal arts. Hu understood almost everything, and Sherab understood how much more fun they were than Starbucks even if he only pretended sometimes to understand half of what was being said. But he was getting better. Hu was glad China had become assured enough of itself to understand the problem, and allow Tibetans to be, well, Tibetan. It made it much easier for Chinese-Tibetans like himself. Sherab was glad he could come home, or at least visit his homeland. He wasn't completely sure he would stay. New York, Jackson Heights, was home, too, but at least his

Roots had moved from being a semi-mythical place to one very earthly paradise, with some very lovely young women about his age he also had to admit, eyeing shyly the waitress.

And what a loss it would have been otherwise, they both thought. At a billion or so, there were more than enough Chinese, but at 6 million, give or take a few monks and nuns, Tibetans were a precious commodity. As was the Tibetan Plateau and its threatened ecosystems. The ecosystem services the Tibetan Plateau provided to the rest of China made it even in strictly business terms much more valuable intact and preserved and protected, than raped, stripped, carelessly mined and polluted. The latter used to be called "development," but now was understood to be a mindless contagion of selfish, screw tomorrow, greed. Luckily, it worked out much better this way: Freedom is so much easier to police than a hostile population. Also the Tibetan Buddhist reverence and sense of oneness with their sacred landscapes made Tibetans the ideal preservers and protectors. It was a win-win for both. And as a very big plus, whatever loss of an unrealistically strict definition of national sovereignty there might have been by forming the Ecoharmonium of Taiwan Tibet and China -the ETTC- had more than been replaced as China had in become the Middle Kingdom again. It was the center in of the world's economy, science and culture. In the end, beauty, kindness, and a vibrant cutting edge Green Economy made a much better binding agent than military intervention, a lesson learned from the stumbling, muscular but hollowed-out United States and its demise.

In a way it was the break-up of the US that had brought the two together. Sherab worked for the EPA of what was left of the US and was here looking for promising new Tibetan-Chinese technologies both in climate change adaptation and mitigation, and the quantum interconnectedness technologies. The hope was that they could be brought back and used to help some of the many problems what was left of his country was facing. Hu was a physicist at the Tibet University where a lot of this kind of exciting research was going on.

At first Sherab was a little standoffish: most Tibetan-Americans had pretty much been raised in the idea of a completely Free Tibet, with China playing the part of the evil villain. But at a personal level they had clicked. It's not that Chinese-Tibetan relations here in Tibet were perfect, but what issues there were, were out in the open and freely discussed, which made them much more amendable to reasonable solutions. There was still a strong "Rangzen" Tibetan Independence Party, and they got a lot of votes from Tibetans, but the situation was sort of analogous to Quebec now, where, although the proponents of a Free and Independent Quebec were powerful, they didn't quite have enough votes. Similarly even though here there were just too many Chinese-Tibetans for the Rangzen party to win outright, their influence was still powerful.

As a Chinese-Tibetan, who was a Buddhist and loved Tibetan culture, Hu thought they had in fact done a lot of good in encouraging and supporting the ongoing Tibetan Cultural Renaissance. He had many Tibetan friends who voted Rangzen, and he understood why, but he felt that however the relationship between the two cultures continued to evolve, China wasn't going away, and he was glad that Tibet, too, wasn't going away. He was glad that it had been pulled back from the verge of a cultural genocide, and now -facing a shared ecological genocide- the two peoples were working together to avoid it. No, proud Chinese though he was, he was also happy and proud that the Snow Lion had come roaring back.

Green China was democratic, not on some imported Western model, but in its own cultural way. From deep in its historically Taoist, Confucian and Buddhist past and soul China was committed again to living in harmony with its sacred lands, if nothing else out of ecological necessity. This Green Dragon, was respectful of and working well with its Snow Lion, if not yet perfect friend, then certainly essential family member. China had really had no choice but to become Green China. Abrupt climate change was hitting it so hard and so early -with the projections that much much worse might yet come- that its very survival had dictated these terms. But Green China -respected and turned-to worldwide for the solutions it had found and was still discovering- had accomplished something in terms of international stature, which force of arms never could. The innovative and sustainable infrastructure of its New Green Silk Road, had made friends of its neighbors, so much so that the Great Asian Ecoharmonium, was soon to expand to become the Great Eurasian Ecoharmonium.

So here they were: Hu, the Chinese-Tibetan physicist, and Sherab the Tibetan-American EPA officer listening in on the laughter and the banter of the tea shop, with Hu the one to explain to Sherab from time to time what was being said. A lot of it was about the CSA's Cross Satellite, and both of them were in agreement that it was at a minimum in somewhat bad taste. Sherab tried his best to explain as an American what had happened to split it asunder, and how the United States mostly had become reduced to its coasts, while the CSA was dominant in the South and the heartland. The two had gone their different, irreconcilable ways, and the good thing was it had been accomplished peacefully. He shared his own experiences with the Christian missionaries the CSA often sent North and which the U.S. tolerated: that these evangelical fundamentalist weren't really evil, they were in fact on an individual basis very nice people. It was just their very strong sense of their own rightness, which made them difficult.

And so the night went, Hu and Sherab listening in on the laughter and the free-flowing discussions, occasionally discussing something amongst themselves between sips of tea. Cha Ngarmo was Sherab's favorite while Hu was a straight Pöcha drinker. Sherab actually drinking more than he really wanted so as to get the waitress-goddess's attention from time to time.

3. A Daughter of Tibet

Hu and Sherab left long before the mysteries of men and women, of Buddhism and Christianity, of every one present's personal peccadilloes had been adequately, thoroughly, derisively and publicly expounded upon. They chose a time to leave when -almost miraculously in light of how furious the snow had been before- there was a pause, a lucid clearing in the storm. Looking up, they could see an almost perfect circle of clear night sky, above all of Lhasa, and shining as if at the top of a well of clouds, was an almost full moon. The effect was startling: the whole grey cloud face seemed to be glowing from within with a faint blue light, and Lhasa itself -all of its enfolding mountains, buildings, and streets- was dusted deep in a fine diamond particulate, fluffy and dream-like and shimmering cold.

The two friends stood wordless for a while, awestruck at the rarity and beauty of the scene.

Reluctant to break the magic, but still needing to go home to sleep in a warm bed, they headed off from the tea shop. Hu still lived in what was a predominantly Chinese part of Lhasa where he had grown up and where his old parents still lived. Sherab was staying with a Tibetan family on the edge of the Bharkor, but it was in the general direction as Hu's house, so they walked together in silence. The snow was so fine and soft that though already a foot deep at least, it parted before their shoes weightlessly, without even a murmur of resistance.

Nearing Sherab's house, and about to leave the warren of streets of the Bharkor, Hu felt a chill, but not of the night, not of the winter. It was rather as if a single finger of old, cold, broken ice had traced its fingernail shard down his back. He half turned to see what seemed to be shadows emerging out of the shadows of a nearby alley, as if the black of the lightless space had given birth to independent beings, embodied of the dark itself. At first, he felt them as much as saw them, but gradually two distinct figures emerged as if formed out of the darker bottoms of the cloud masses. Stiffening viscerally, Hu finally saw them for what they were: Khampa warriors, tall, long-haired, dressed in animal skins over their Chupas, and with, he was sure, the standard Khampa long knives tucked into the folds of their winter cloaks. But it was their eyes which made Hu grab Sherab's elbow to indicate that they should go. There eyes were the sort he had seen in some of the lab tests. Tests of the effect of Phowa, the transference of consciousness. He didn't know how he knew, but he knew, with a sickening chill in his stomach, that the two were possessed. And indeed, the two warriors shambled malificently toward them, almost as if drunk, but with a sickening purpose and solemnity and malice in their movements.

He knew they had to run, and Sherab, too, was terrified, feeling intuitively the unnaturalness of the two coming toward them. And indeed, run they would have, run they tried to do, but a delicious molasses made it's way into their brains and bodies. While a smaller and smaller part of them was horrified and trying to flee, a greater part of them now didn't care, wanted in fact to offer themselves up to the sweet sacrifice of the long knives, thought the idea of hot, bright red blood spurting out onto this purest of pure snow, a wonderfully clever joke. And they both turned to the two now, half-smiling, as the warriors reached into their animal skins to free their long knives to taste and drink deeply.

But then something changed. From somewhere behind the two friends a light began to shine, and grow in strength. In their mind-drugged state, they couldn't turn to see what it was but they could see it glowing in the faces of the two Khampas who now were within breathing distance. As the light's intensity grew stronger, the crazed eyes of the Khampas began to blink, then flinch, then squirm, and sweat broke out on their brows, turning almost instantly into miniature glaciers, blue and unyielding, as the Khampas now, too, were frozen. Then something broke in the two warriors and they began to run, scurrying, and shambling back into the shadows from which they came, the powder snow only barely disturbed by the closeness of what would have been butchery.

And as the light flared to peak and then softened, the inner poison ebbed away from Hu and Sherab, and they no longer wanted to be sacrificed to the knives. They began to breath and shiver with fear and relief. When he could, Hu turned to see where the light was coming from, but he only caught sight of a little Tibetan girl in a blue Chupa walking cheerfully away through the snow. He started to call out to her, but before he could she turned and smiled. The wind picked up and the softest of soft snows swirled around her. When it settled she was gone, and there were only the stars and the moon and absolute stillness, the wind having caught its breath in its throat.

***

Tashi, and Dolma, and even Pangu, sat there, stunned, feeling that the morning of the high plateau and the sun off the snow were less real than that night in Lhasa when the snowclouds formed a column leading to the moon, there, at the top of its empty center, and where dark forces began to stir, and forces of great beauty and light also. Tashi at last said, "Yes, I remember those two at the teahouse. They were sitting by themselves at another table, listening intently, and the Chinese one occasionally leaned forward to whisper something to the Tibetan one." He looked quickly over toward Dolma, and saw her sitting, eyes closed, a subtle sweet smile on her lips as if having tasted something just right. Tashi turned away just as quickly, willing himself not to be pulled into something so earthly as the thought of a kiss. "Pangu, go on please, this is a bit more interesting than your usual drivel. And it's not of course just because I am one of the main characters."

"Tashi, Dolma, the obstacle on the road is reported worse than the initial assessments. There are multiple blockage points and the clearing process will take longer than the first estimate. I

am going to go back to a little rest house back up the road where the two of you can pass the time more comfortably with each other than in the confines of my poor cab." With that Pangu turned quickly around and headed back up the road away from the avalanche. "If you like I can go on with the story a bit?"

"Yes, yes, proceed," grumbled Tashi, "and so much for your powers of estimation."

***

"Homage to Vajrayogini, whose nature is
emptiness and compassion, who has manifold
forms because of the diverse natures of
people…"

from the "Abhisamayamanjari"

1. Coming Upon a Midnight Clear

Faith had prayed much of the night. She understood that the turmoil in her, and the sense somehow that she had failed her Lord, failed in her mission, failed her family and her friends, and failed the Elders, was beyond her ability to overcome. But she knew that she was not alone. She knew especially that at such times her personal Lord and Savior was at her side, comforting, and uplifting, and giving her strength. He did not fail her. Looking out the window now at the glorious raiment of the snow on the city, she felt much better. All she could do was all she could do, and for the rest, she knew she was not alone. She was carried and supported and loved.

That said, she still felt, if she was honest with herself, a bit on the sad side of consoled, and anyway, she couldn't sleep. She sat in the window nook wrapped in a blanket, her Bible mostly unread beside her. The snow was so thick that it seemed as if flocks of millions of doves were losing their feathers all at once someplace high above the city. It was so thick that even watching it through the old window panes was enough to make her skin feel as if feathers were cascading down around her skin, lulling her and arousing her at the same time. No, she could not sleep, there was so much to be done for her flock, and yet she couldn't think of a single thing she could do right then. There was energy building in her, as if Lhasa, high as it already was, had moved to an even higher altitude and the thin air had become even thinner and as full of electricity as oxygen. She was so attentive and alert to the tiniest details of events outside the window that she thought she must have turned into a cat when no one was looking. And in fact just then, Christopher, her Himalayan longhair, jumped into her lap, unhappy no doubt she was not yet in bed.

And it was this coincidence of train of thought and incident, or rather of thought of cat and cat, which made her smile for the first time in a while. She stroked Christopher behind his ears, and together they watched the snow fall. Her flock was an odd bunch, she thought, and she liked that. Christ's misfits, but Christ's. Some came at first because they were curious about her no doubt, or wanted to learn English, and then stayed because of the songs. Some came because of disappointment with this or that opulent lama or seducing monk. Some were less than handsome or beautiful, in a culture which expected beauty and handsomeness, and some were born with minor deformities in a culture which ascribed their suffering to karma. And she taught them that idea was superstition, and that Christ loved all equally.

As her mind cleared so too did the storm outside. There came a point when everything was still outside and the moon hung at the top of a beautiful blue chalice of circled clouds. Her breath caught at the sight and she praised the Lord. Her cat senses told her that something was happening, and she laughed at herself, telling herself that of course something was happening, something is always happening. But this felt as if time had stopped, and something was unhappening, was being undone. Something that would have tied time in another knot, had now been loosed, and that time instead had been set free to wander in another direction as it chose. Christopher in her lap too felt it, stiffening at one point in anticipation of alarum, and then relaxing, stretching, yawning, at peace. Maybe she had to admit to herself that the Buddhists were right about animals being sentient beings. Christopher certainly was sentient enough. And then amazement of amazement on this magic night she saw a little girl in a blue Chupa almost floating across the expanse of snow in the street below. In no rush, the little girl was at home in the sacred moment of the night's non-time, as if she herself had conjured up the quiet and was the essence of its stillness and joyful peace.

The child looked up, seeming to know she was being watched, and seeming to know also who was watching her, and Faith, locking eyes with the smiling girl, felt in that moment, the lightest of light fingertips reach into the cavern of her ribs, and set her heart on fire with wave after wave of blooms of love.

And then the snow blew it all away and she was still there, wrapped in a blanket in the window nook with Christopher demanding scratching. But she stunned and wasn't at all sure she could find her way back to the bed she usually slept in, for now nothing at all would ever quite be the same.

2. Friends of a Feather

Tashi had meant to go home directly from the tea shop. He had, after all, work tomorrow, but when he and Tsewang left to find the snowstorm had stopped, it didn't take many of Tsewang's inventive enticements to persuade Tashi to accompany him to one more place. Tashi had an inkling of where they were going. Such places were supposed to be well-controlled in Tibet, but the technology was so cheap and easily accessible that stopping it completely would have been like trying to keep people from breathing. No, Dreameries and the Bardo Tech were everywhere and Tashi was no stranger, though as a government official he had to be discreet.

They didn't have far to go, down the quiet street and around the corner to the next corner, then up the rickety old wooden stairs of what may well have been one of the last of old Lhasa's original buildings. It was a typical Chang Kan, though what was offered here was much more potent than good-old, old-fashioned, home-brewed Tibetan beer. It was an access point for the Bardo worlds, sort of like a Wi-Fi transcendence spot. The people who came here predominantly wanted something just shy of full-blown trans-corporeal transcendence. What they mostly wanted was time in the pleasure worlds, each of which essentially interactively and reflexively formed its particulars around each man or woman's inner fantasies.

There were real pleasure worlds that pre-existed the advent of Bardo Tech, and one could sometimes find one's way to those realms, if one had the energy and the karma. And there were also the free-gathering spots, where spirits, people, and some mixture of the two -with other creatures occasionally thrown in- could do as they wanted to do with each other. Those were a little more risky, but many, full of confidence, even if false confidence, tried them. Most popular were the commercial and community-built places, which were in their framework and upkeep essentially virtual realities, but with Bardo windows and doors, in their case guarded, though the quality of the guards varied from good to buyer beware. These tended though to give people what they wanted. They were, "Coney Islands of the Mind," mental (usually Adults Only) Afterlife Disneylands. Calling them mental though, missed the point: the level of resolution, the level of luminosity, the colors, the feelings, the sex, were all hyper-real. Earth could seem quite gray by comparison.

Accessing the lucid state was a piece of cake. The Bardo-field, lucidity-inducing field really, just sort of gently massaged the brain into a dreaming state, while at the same time maintaining the awareness of lucidity. There were many who having used the technology often enough, no longer needed it and could access the state of mind at will. Some of these "FreeMinds," as some called them, were legendary. They were essentially twin-state amphibians, comfortable both in the old physical world and in the new –though very much older and essentially not time-bound- Bardo worlds.

Here in the old Chang Kan though, Tashi had a momentary urge to forego the pleasures that night, to go home and have a normal dream, remembered or not. But Tsewang, sensing again Tashi's reluctance dared him with one stare to go on with it, and with a nod to the matron at the bar, the field entered their brains, and gently, non-intrusively pushed them into the Bardo world. Tashi marveled again at how at home it felt, body-time and the body-earth just a brief interlude from this, the timeless Sambogakaya of the Three Worlds.

They were flying. They were flying in light and mind, and this was the most important part of the trip. Now was the moment to choose which expectation, desire, need, fantasy, to head for, before the mind shaped itself into another world and one got lost in it, forgetting the body, and with awareness, too, so easily fooled and forgetful. Tashi sensed above and behind them a clearer light, the clear light of the void, there where Chenrezig and his/her incarnation the Dalai Lama dwelt, and he was thankful and awed that they were so close, and truly, he just wanted to reach up, to relax, to go fully into that simple beauty and be cleansed. But Tsewang had a grip on him and they swerved down and away to a place Tashi recognized. They were near Sera Monastery, at the DurTroe, the Charnel grounds, where the Sky Burial was performed, and the Jhagoe, the vultures, were often too fat too eat more.

He didn't really want to go there, but he felt Tsewang's strength. Seeing him in this form, this place, he recognized him for what he was, not an unemployed wise-cracking poet, but really, quite an accomplished "Ngakpa," a tantric lay practioner. Not wanting to go, he was nonetheless pulled along by the strength of the connection and the strength of the mind on the other end. When they got there, the Chöd practive was already underway.

Tashi didn't want this either, didn't want to offer up his body to hungry ghosts and demons to eat, as a way of finally overcoming the illusion that he was his body. But there was Tsewang, chanting, and already set upon by crowds of the unholy and the undead. In the midst of it, Tsewang was beaming, joyful, serene, unworried. The more they ate of the body, the brighter he became. But Tashi didn't like the gnawing, didn't like the bloody maws of the demons and the hungry ghost's pitiful shrieking. He knew it was a holy offering, an offering of his illusory self to illusions. But when he felt a hard chomp, much too hard, down on his private parts -the demon looking up with an angel's face that reminded him of the yinchee woman that had come to his office- he decided he just wasn't in the mood. Since he was already in the Bardo, he would find something just a little more pleasurable, less gruesome, karmically salubrious though the Chöd might be.

He wrenched himself away, and arched back up into flight into the mindsky and hopefully bliss, but as he pulled away from the gathered feasters-upon-himself, they coalesced into something dark and angry. He didn't want to look at them. They terrified him into a flight propelled by fear. He fled seeing the charnel grounds growing small below, as he heard the last howls of the demons and hungry ghosts along with the clear bell of Tsewang's laughter. Tashi felt immensely lonely, and afraid, as if a part of himself had been torn out of himself. The palpable darkness now chasing after him seemed very real. He knew, flying in a directionless panic, all manner of spirits whirring past him, that he'd been spooked, very badly, and needed to calm down. The crazed admixture of loneliness and terror he felt were creating the dark spaces he was projecting. He looked beneath and behind him, into the face of the darkness still after him, and saw the face of an old girlfriend he had callously wronged when younger. Her grief and rage was equal to his fear and shame, a potent mix propelling him even further into bardic parts unknown.

He crashed into the wall of a cliff-face, and slithered down, broken and out of breath except for ragged terrified breaths, and she was upon him. Smiling and dead, a stream of spiders crawling out of her eyes she whispered, "Tashi, Tashi, I love you. I'm not through with you yet," and he convulsed in nausea as the hard teeth of shame and revulsion tore into his intestines greedily as he passed out.

And woke up, in what should have been his body slumped back in the Chang Kan, but instead he was in some desert place, with high red sandstone cliffs in the distance. He was lost, and sad, and very, very, lonely, and more than a little bit still afraid he had permanently lost his connection to his body and wouldn't be returning to that one at least, soon. And then he saw in the distance, two small black specks coming toward him. Crows no doubt come to peck out what was left of him. But as they got closer he realized they were two young men in dark suits, riding bicycles. He blinked and blinked again and with each blink the two drew closer, until finally they had dismounted their bicycles and were standing over him.

"Hello Tashi, I'm Josh, and this is Bill," said Josh.

"Hello Tashi," said Bill, "have a drink," and he offered Tashi a clear water bottle with the logo of an angel playing a trumpet on it.

"Thank you," said Tashi, reflexively taking the water bottle and drinking, because he was both thirsty and happy to have company.

"Tashi," said Josh, "we're Mormons and we're here to help."

"We have a good book for you to read," said Bill, "and your own planet if you like, but first we know you'd like to go home, and we can help."

"Hop in," said Josh, motioning to the sidecar which had appeared as part of his bicycle. Tashi did so, meekly, but bruised and battered and lost as he was, quite grateful for the lift.

"Now Tashi," said Bill as they rode together, back down a dry ravine toward the distant red cliffs, "you might have heard some unflattering things about us Mormons, but we just want you to know there is another side to the story."

"Yes," said Josh, "you might have read that Mark Twain said the Book of Mormon was 'chloroform in print.'"

"And," added Bill, "you might have heard that some have said our Prophet was nothing but a flim-flam man, a confidence man."

"But," finished Josh, "what's great about America, or what used to be great about America anyway, is that it's a place where a little bit of bad writing combined with a lot of inspired salesmanship, can still start a really great religion. You see you got to get people to believe, before the miracles start happening."

The bicycle hit a bump and Tashi woke up with his head on the wooden table of the Chang Kan, his heart and stomach, still reeling from the recent terror. But he now had an intellectual appreciation at least, for the Mormons and their sense of humor. Tsewang, was slumped next to him, a half-smile on his face, and Tashi could swear a rosy light seemed to roll luxuriously out of his downturned ear. Who knows how long he will be out, thought Tashi. He scrawled a note on a napkin and left it by his friend's head, and then headed shakily home, as the wind picked up, blowing sharp shards of ice crystals off the roofs and into his smarting eyes.

3. The Long Inner View

Tsewang woke long after almost everyone had left. By the blue light of the winter window he saw the matron sleeping on a cot in the corner under a yak-skin rug and he was overwhelmed with thanksgiving and tenderness. She was his mother and every lover he had ever had. She was the earth. She was Tibet and the mother of the race of ruddy-faced Tibetans, sired by Chenrezig in the form of a monkey from a mountain ogress. She was a most beautiful mountain ogress, thought Tsewang, and what monkey, Chenrezig or not, would not desire her. Tsewang wished in this moment to live forever, not as a god, but as a human being. How blessed, blessed, was a human birth, how precious and yet how unappreciated it was by most. He amongst them at least until now. He had seen things, after the Chöd, that, poet that he was, he would never be able to talk or write about. He could have, should have, just turned up into the clarity, the purity, the primordial wonder and compassion of the clear light, but there was so much suffering, so many lost souls, getting even more lost. They were coming and going, but mostly it seemed going into orbits of their own that would not swing back soon again into the light. It was all a great cyclic meta-physical ecosystem of being and becoming and unbecoming and non-being, no doubt, but the pain was real, and he could feel their pain, and if he could feel it, then he was not so separate from them that he could turn his back.

He laughed at the idea of being a bodhisattva. He knew himself much too well for that and harbored also the illusion, if illusion it was, that bodhisattvas were caught in yet another stage of illusion. No this was different. He had been vouchsafed a horrible vision, of humanity waking up into a realm for which it was as yet neither humanly nor inhumanly suited. Preening fools they were who had chanced upon all-powerful weapons they mistook for toys. And they were being press-ganged, gang-raped into serving forces they misunderstood. He'd seen the armies being marshaled: dark forces of every ilk, none of them seeking anything beyond power for themselves, sucking souls into their maw from left and right and up and down, stripping them of everything but their raw energies, building nothing of beauty, but leaving only destruction and night skies filled with artificially engorged stars.

And it was the earth that had to be returned to. It was the earth that had to be saved. The earth which was the humble fulcrum needed to stop the dehumanization of humanity. There was deep reason and faith imprinted in the earth itself.

He looked at the sleeping matron. Her face was half turned to him and she seemed the source of a gentle light to the whole world. He saw the Beloved now everywhere. She had come to him and said, "Help me, in this world, not the other. Your time is short here, use it well."

As he was about to head out into the last vestiges of the night, his hand came upon the note that Tashi had left. It read, "Thank you for inviting me to the picnic," and Tsewang, smiled. He owed Tashi an apology. The Chöd was definitely no picnic for the unprepared.

***

Pangu pulled off the road to Lhasa (now actually the road away from Lhasa) onto a little side road that one wouldn't have thought was there unless one already knew it was there. It curved briefly around some boulders, and then briefly again in the other direction crossing a stream still running through the fresh snow, and then emerged into a clearing in a grove of trees where an old Tibetan house fit right in. Sheltered by the mountain above and the sky above that, one felt Lhasa itself would disappear long before this house would. It seemed not so much to be off the road, as to be of another, better world.

Finally, Tashi and Dolma got out to stretch their legs and Tashi headed deeper into the grove to relieve himself of all the tea. He watched the piss carve canyons in the snow, and it was as if he had never seen this before. Tracing the arc back to the member held by hand, he couldn't for the life of him figure out who it was that stood there draining urine from a body into snow. Then he shook himself from the non-self numinosity, and shook himself of the last drops of pee, too, pulled his pants up and tied the drawstring again, and headed back. Tashi went to the door under a sagging old porch and knocked, and called, "Mi Yubei?" "Hello, Anyone Home?"

Pangu was in his old farmer guise, leaning on the truck. "She's not here, Tashi. She went up the trail to a cave with a little shrine in it. She is tending it. She will be back soon. Come, don't get cold, come sit back inside and I will continue the story." Tashi looked around, saw the trees were full of quiet birds. He thought it equally strange and wonderful. He felt exhilarated and almost wanted to dance, but thought that it would disturb the stillness and perhaps not make a good impression on Dolma.

"Ok, Ok, we'll sit a bit and wait, and hear a bit more of your jabbering. But please stop the pretension of being human. It's really quite insulting. How would you like it if I pretended to be a truck?" and everyone laughed as he and Dolma got back in the cab and Pangu went on with his tale.

***

"Because emotions and dreams have never been included in the description of the world provided by science and physics, there is no reason they have to obey those laws."

Montague Ullman, Late 20th century Dream Researcher (paraphrase)

1. A Short Nun

Ani Tsedrun wasn't sure if she believed in the New Tantra, wasn't sure at all. And even if she believed in the possibility of the New Tantra, she wasn't sure if she approved. It just seemed obvious that the old Tantra was powerful enough, was fast enough a route to enlightenment, and certainly was dangerous enough. It was so dangerous in fact that most of it was meant to remain hidden, except as revealed by a competent teacher to a student who was sufficiently prepared. And now it was everywhere, as easy to access as pornography, and confused by many, with pornography. And the confusion of sex with a very strict path of religious discipline and most of all, the confusion of glimpses of hidden powers, with wisdom enough to master those powers, was causing a lot of damage.

It had of its supporters even amongst some Lamas and learned nuns whom she respected. Buddhism they said always changed with the times and always was open to finding new methods of helping people out of their suffering. And besides, some said, there just wasn't much time, and as many people as possible needed to be helped while in this human incarnation, as things were going bad quickly, and many were likely to find themselves facing the Bardo unprepared. Better to give them a taste, and a bit of guidance, than leave them to the frightened projections of their disembodied minds. Better, they said, to provide a little imperfect help, than to insist on a perfect, and too slow process.

But that speed, that technological boost, seemed too good to be true. So what if the world was coming to an end. It wasn't the first time. Every eon even was just a momentary ending and becoming. Every moment was a creation out of nothing into a destruction into nothing. And so why cling? What was there substantial to hold on to? No, this debate had been held before a long, long time ago. At the Great Debate at Samye, 1200 years or so ago. Trisong Detsen had invited Kamalasila to present the case for Nagarjuna's gradual process toward enlightenment while Moheyan argued for Ch'an's "direct awakening" of original mind. They had argued for two years. It was a rather thorough airing of points of views. In the end the Tibetans had decided that the instantaneous enlightenment offered by the Ch'an School was in itself rooted in long and steady study, practice, and merit. And so had been born the Tibetan approach to Buddhist monasticism. This was to be the rock upon which to practice Vajrayana, the Lighting Bolt Path. Vajrayana was as fast as fast can be, but on a logical, skilled, practiced, disciplined, mostly safe, basis.

Or maybe, Ani Tsedrun thought, she was just a conservative, a traditionalist, as those who rejected the New Tantra were sometimes called. The young and the yinchee just weren't all that patient, so why not offer them something that fit their haste? Perhaps haste itself and impatience weren't part of the problem, but on the other hand as some said, that haste, that desire was exactly the fuel needed to drive the whole process, or so the argument went. The greater the desire, the higher the possible attainment. And she had met some it's true, who had gone through the New Tantra trainings and seemed genuinely to have reached a level of real understanding. On the other hand there were those who came out arrogant and proud, wildly "liberated" but seemingly without a shred of compassion. She was sure she couldn't follow someone like that. Her own teacher seemed so simple by comparison. Old though she now was, and walking slower these days, to sit with her in silence, or exchanging a few words, filled her with such a peaceful radiance. Her precious Rimpoche was so humble you would never know, if you did not know her. And she didn't need all that New Tantra gadgetry.

There were also of course traditional nuns and monks who took their vows and lived their lives and yet also seemed not to have softened, who still seemed to be prey to petty jealousies and desires. No doubt this was how she appeared to others sometimes. Maybe she was just a short and silly nun, shaving her head and wearing robes, but understanding nothing. But no. She knew things now she hadn't known before. And there was a quiet joy that seemed to grow stronger through the years. The Dharma was inescapable so why not embrace it? But did it have to be such a violent, lurid embrace? Wasn't it better when people came to it naturally, quietly, of their own accord, when the time was right? Could and should the Dharma be so expertly, dynamically, profitably mass marketed? Ah, she was a silly, short nun. She had always known she would become a nun. While still in the womb her mother had dreamed of the Buddha coming with a smile and a bowl. And then Ani Tsedrun heard the bell, and knew it was time for lunch. Engrossed in prayers for the sick relative of a supporter she had skipped breakfast. Should she skip lunch, too, fast today? No, not today. This body was a friend, and she was hungry,

After the "thukpa", the Tibetan noodles, she thought she would go out for a walk. The snowstorm the previous night had been such a blessing. Tibet was starved by perpetual droughts and the glaciers were disappearing they said, so the snows, when they came, were much needed. And anyway, it was fun to see the city after such a fresh makeover. Maybe the Kaliyuga had ended and some new more cheerful Yuga had begun. She laughed to herself at the thought. Her monastery was close to the Bharkor and that is where she headed, to do a few circumambulations and perhaps talk with friends. The snow seemed to have left everyone cheerful, and the children were running and playing and throwing snowballs at each other, with the occasional miss making a passerby dodge if they still could. The new snow made it all seem festive, as if it was Losar, and she was glad that she had come, as the air was full of a palpable joy and everyone was feeling it.

There had already been so many circumambulants since the very early morning that a magic path had been cleared. The "Lungta," prayer flags, all seemed new, even though she knew that couldn't be the case. The wind was still, and she knew some would say therefore that the prayers written on them weren't being recited by the wind, but to her today it seemed the prayers had accomplished their goal and this world had been transformed into Dewachen. It was all a matter of how you looked at things, she thought, as she ducked an errant snowball, thus saving the thrower the bad karma of hitting a nun. And then she saw the yinchee Christian woman in front of her circumambulating, and she heard a voice in her heart tell that she needed to offer this woman help. It was a voice she always listened to, even as a little girl, and she increased her pace to catch up.

2. Succuba and Succubae

They thought of Grace as a demon, as a demoness. But they wanted her even that much more. She was their seductress, their seducer out of the prison of flesh and into the liberation of the earth. She taught them that love loved the reality of the body and that the body was spirit made flesh, and that spirit made flesh very much loved to make love. Grace knew ways into their hearts through their skin and under their sheets. She was a general of the arts of bliss as much as her father was a colonel expert in killing.

Not that what she and her coven did, really always needed to be about sexual magic. It was the way out for some, and when the witches chose to work that way, they were quite careful. Theirs was a healing witchery. They weren't offering commercial porn, ubiquitous though it was, even in the Christian States. When they touched, they touched with something real within them. The industrial Horae and Avateasers, were as hard to escape as the Patriarchy. They would never do that to the women they were trying to liberate, replace one subjugation with another. Sometimes though in fact it didn't take more than a little counter-propaganda to get the women of the Christian States thinking. They weren't dumb, and for those who thought even a little the right tract left in the right place was sometimes all it took to begin to undo the damage done by all the mind-numbing repetitions of the worse of the misogynistic parts of the scripture.

And they helped what women they could escape, not just mentally and spiritually, but physically also. They showed them the underground railway that was in place. And there were many who wanted to escape the beatings and the dehumanization and the domestic violence wrapped up in pseudo-sanctimonious garbage. The witches helped them elude the manpatrols, desperate as they were to keep as many of their womanfolk as possible for breeding. But yes, it's true. Sometime they came as a dream lover in the night because that was what was needed to keep a beautiful flame from flickering out. And that was often where the fire needed to be lit and stoked, in the loins and in the places where sex and love are often confused with one another. Sometimes it was only by lying in bed as a lover with a lover that trust could be built, so that the truth was listened to, and the fear of a false god could be overcome.

It was dangerous work. The Christian Truth mobs could be brutal, and a witch that was caught got worse than a burning at the stake. They had the tools now to burn out the mind entirely. They left a body penitent and humble. Grace had been warned by all the covens that she was on the radar of the CSA. It wasn't surprising, given who her father was. But still, she needed to continue. She was in love.

She was in love with the beautiful, rebellious daughter of a powerful general in the CSA. The daughter reminded her of herself some years back. She wanted to love her the way she had wished she had been loved. Gently and with the sharing of everything. She, Grace had been "loved," raped by one of her father's "best" soldiers. And then it had all been covered up in the chains of command. The soldier had died in a raid someplace the name of which could not be said. She often wondered if he had been a casualty of the so-called enemy, or if her father had found a way to even the score.

Though she usually preferred remaining in the form of a woman, sometimes she took the form of a man, or of a half-man, half-woman, if that was what was called for to open the secret door into ecstasy. The urgent sharpening of her own desire into a penis needing to thrust helped her to understand men a little better. It was sad in a way that men were not taught the arts of love and so were left to deal with the beast within them as best they could. It made them lousy lovers and worse, turned many of them loose on women who wanted more, needed more, and could offer so very much more.

She knew of witches and black covens, so angry at the rape of the world by men, that they used their arts to fight back violently. She understood them. Might once have gone that way herself. That men could be so blind as to kill a living earth, which was deep a part of the human family as humanity was a part of it, was the most amazing blindness. But she knew also the violence the other side was capable of. They would not stop at denuding a whole continent of its forests if it got rid of a few pesky witches, too. Having been brought up in the mindset of conquest and dominion, she knew the CSA's weaknesses were also there: knew it was a mindset with holes the size of sequoias in it that a clever, divinely sexy witch could lead new, living, green, ideas into. One woman at a time.

Grace was sad the way the beauty of the emergently magical sexuality of Spring was so perverted and repressed. She was sad as she flew across the deserts of the Christian States at all the powerful women and girls who would have been able to change those man-deserts into verdant places, if they were released into their wisdom and power. She could not save them all. But perhaps there was one young woman she could help to find the strength within her to stand up naked, and powerfully sexual, in the knowledge that power was a healing balm in a demented, mechanized, little boy's fever dream.

3. A Debriefing

Colonel Zachery Pike didn't like what he was hearing. This was supposed to have been a fairly routine mission on easy targets with a proven technology. None of that seemed to have been the case.

"I want to know, why this failed, where precisely it went wrong, and what we need to do to fix it." 'Jesus,' he almost said but stopped himself. "Why in the heck didn't we just do this ourselves or hire someone to carry it out. Why in the heck did we have to hijack someone else's mind to carry out the mission? Can someone please explain that to me in terms that make some sense?" He actually knew the answer quite well, but he wanted the team to sweat a bit so they'd think twice about letting him down when he was in charge.

" Sir, if I may," said a Lieutenant whose name he didn't particularly want to acknowledge at the moment.

"Lieutenant, this had better be good."

"Sir, the mind is the new battlefield."

"The mind has always been the battlefield son," snarled the Colonel.

"Yes, Sir, but what I mean is in the past we attacked the mind indirectly by essentially killing or maiming or otherwise making uncomfortable the body that hosted that mind.

The Colonel laughed inside at the phrase 'otherwise making uncomfortable the body', that was good, he'd use that.

"Back in the Cyberwarfare days for example,' the Lieutenant continued, "we were getting pretty close to the mind itself in the sense that the net in some senses was an initial attempt to provide a medium that better reflected the capabilities of the mind, and was more responsive to the mind at the mental level, as opposed to, -I don't know- drawing with a pointed stick in the sand. As man-machine interfaces improved and became subtler we essentially stumbled across the medium of the mind itself, the quantum interconnectedness. It had always been there, but the mind operating the brain, had a state specific memory problem and in most cases wasn't very good at bridging the gap and so..."

"Lieutenant. Cut the crap. Why not just kill these guys. Why the whole mumbo jumbo of possession, or what do we call it, 'Higher Order Dispossession and Surrogacy' especially since it doesn't seem to work."

"Sir" interjected another Lieutenant even younger than the first, "It works, it was working. And they do it to us. It's spiritual warfare Sir, and they are winning. We've got to fight fire with fire."

"How can you sit there and tell me it works when it didn't work."

"Sir, they were completely operational and about to strike. Something happened at the very end which we didn't anticipate."

"What the heck kind of soldier doesn't anticipate? The battlefield is the mind, right? Well let me tell you about that battlefield. You win by thinking ahead of your opponent, you die when you get lazy. So tell me, what happened at the end?"

"Sir, we're still not sure. Our soldiers are still a little confused. It appears though that some sort of a powerful mindfield appeared at the last moment, some sort of, uhm, well, Tibetan protective deity perhaps."

"Tibetan protective deity? I've seen scarier monsters on Halloween." And then he remembered these CSA youngsters probably had never experienced Halloween. "Alright, get me more details. In the meantime I want these operations shelved until we know what happened and how to overcome it, whatever it is, Tibetan protective deities, goblins, witches, whatever, OK? Is that clear?"

" Sir, yes sir."

"But sir, begging your pardon shall we follow through with our training schedule? It does include some small operations here and there on easier targets. They have mostly been successful so far, that's why we thought we were ready to undertake this one."

"Mostly successful isn't good enough. Get me the records of what we have done so far. Easy training missions should be 100% successful. I'm going to oversee whatever training missions we do from here on in. When and if we have no errors then we bring it on to the enemy. Not before. Is that clear?"

They saluted, and left. The Colonel thought he had put on a pretty good show. He had suspected it wasn't going to be that easy. New weapons systems always had their problems in the real world, and this was a pretty unreal world that everyone seemed so gung ho on operating in. The "Mind Frontier" and he shook his head. He wondered if they were really wise enough to establish a beachhead there. Good Lord, the CSA, was already a media powerhouse worldwide with their youth-driven music and programs. Even he liked some of the songs, and he didn't like music. There were enough lost souls out there to harvest in a soft way, did they have to resort to this, kicking people out of their own bodies? Wouldn't it have been better to let God do the policing of His own backyard? But maybe the elders were right, and this was the End Times. And they as His anointed servants were serving as the arm and the shield of a powerful, avenging, muscular Christ, preparing the world for his return, and the settling of all scores. He knew that true Christians around the world felt backed into a corner and persecuted, and he knew the CSA would not let them down. The CSA would stay true not just to the end, but to the End and Beyond. But he also thought sometimes, for the Love of God, that all of this was little more than the sort of dreams and illusions that the Love of God was supposed to lift one above.

***

"Well yes, OK, maybe. I'll think about it," said Tashi. "But in the meantime where is owner of this pleasant little end of the world establishment?"

"She's on her way down the path. She will be here in just a moment of your time," and indeed from out from around the back of the house walked an old Tibetan grandmother. She was short but somehow stood very tall, as if a young girl had dressed up like an old woman and was pretending to be ancient, while all along underneath rippled rivers and streams of gaiety and mirth. Tashi felt some power hit his solar plexus and for a moment he blinked and staggered, and then righted himself and looked at her just in time to see her looking at him as if to confirm the psychic blow had indeed emanated from her.

"So, it's the old farmer pretending to be a truck again. Haven't I told you that if I wanted a lover I could find someone far better looking than you?" and Tashi saw that Pangu was manifesting his old farmer presentation, and half-snickered at the idea he might somehow be in love with the old woman.

"What are you smiling at Sonny?" and Tashi not wanting to feel the old woman's power again, pulled the corners of his mouth back under control, and looked sheepishly at the ground.

"Gombamason, Mola, Sorry Grandmother, the road to Lhasa is blocked and we were hoping we could just wait here for a bit until the road is cleared."

"Bah, everybody needing to come and go and go and come, as if that accomplished anything. Come inside by the fire, I will make tea. You, too, old man, you can come in, though I know you can't drink tea any better than you can make love!" and at that they all laughed and followed her willingly into the dark house.

The room was dark and wooden and warm. After a moment though, it seemed to fill with a golden light, invisible, but somehow enough to see by. There was a "Thup" a traditional Tibetan stove in the middle of the room, made of mud and brick, sharing its cheery warmth, and butter tea in a kettle on top, already ready to be served. The grandmother got old chipped cups from a shelf on the wall, and went to get the kettle, but before she could get it, Dolma took the cups and the teakettle and did the serving herself.

"Thank you Mola, let me help. You sit." The grandmother sat but before that she patted Dolma's head, a head taller than hers though it was, and smiled, and all was well.

They exchanged small talk for a bit, between sipping the tea in silence, and then Mola motioned to the old farmer sitting also with them. "Now this one. Go on with your story. I'm not sure how long it will take you to separate your poor soul from that stinking truck of yours, but in the meantime, this is about all you are good for!" and again they all laughed, even Pangu, and he again cleared a throat that wasn't really there.

***

"Illusion is whatever is fixed and definable."

-Northrup Frye-

1. Communion With Strangers

Faith wondered if she was losing her mind. Walking with the others in the khora in the morning through the snow, she felt for the first time as if she belonged, but not in a completely comforting way. The part of her that she had always kept a little separate from them, the Tibetans, the circumambulators, had disappeared. In fact, a great deal of her had disappeared and she was alternately exhilarated and frightened. She didn't feel like she was locked inside her skull any more, with all those old words moldering away in a box of bones. She felt that the clouds, and the birds, and the others in the walking hush and slush, were as much her as her teeth and her intestines. She was on fire, with a sweet fire, and she loved it and was scared by it in equal measures. The sweetness in her loins though, was a little hard to get used to. She felt the potential of possibilities all of which she had the power to effect, to make real or change. And this scared her the most of all, as it seemed like a glimpse into madness and megalomania. The best she could do today was avoid looking into that power too directly. All she could manage today was just to walk, walk in a circle with everyone else. She wished she had a rosary to hold on to and some beads to count.

How long the short nun had been walking beside her, she couldn't say. But when Faith finally saw the cheerful smile, she felt a relief to be distracted from the state that was verging on overwhelming her.

"Tashi Delek," said the nun.

"Tashi Delek," said Faith.

"I am Tsedrun," said Ani Tsedrun.

"I am Faith," said Faith, and they both laughed a little at the silliness, the automatism of first introductions.

Ani Tsedrun took Faith's hand, and it felt good to Faith, warm and reassuring and calm. "Perhaps," said Ani Tsedrun, "you would like to go someplace to talk, have a bite to eat."

"Yes, that would be good," said Faith, grateful to feel the trust, grateful really not to be alone. Ani Tsedrun took her by the hand to a little shop nearby. It was nothing special, a local place, already filling up because of the cold and the snow. They sat down in a booth to the side to regard each other, and to laugh again at the strangeness of two strangers feeling so comfortable with each other.

"Let us have some tea," said Tsedrun, "and perhaps some 'Bagleb,' bread? They have very good Amdo Bagleb here."

"Yes, yes, that would be perfect. We can break bread together," and then she wondered if Ani Tsedrun understood the reference. But it didn't matter.

"Faith," said Ani Tesdrun, "that is a good name. In Tibetan we say, 'Teba' or 'Matsik' it could even be a Tibetan name, though a rare one."

"It is a common Christian name, though a little old-fashioned," said Faith, "and what does Tsedrun mean?"

"Tsedrun means 'Butter Lamp of Life' though I'm not sure I am much of one!" and they both laughed. "And would you say your Faith is strong?"

"Well, the Faith is strong, but today I'm not sure I'm feeling all that strong. I feel as if my mind has exploded and I can't put it back inside my head!"

"Ah," said Ani Tsedrun kindly, "perhaps it no longer wants to go back inside your head, maybe it's time for it to hatch and spread its wings."

"Do you know what's happened to me? Frankly I'm afraid I'm getting ill? It's just a little bit frightening..."

Ani Tsedrun took her hand on the table, and reached across to lay a hand on her forehead, checking for fever. "No, no fever, and your eyes look very clear. You haven't been drinking Chang, right?

"No, of course not, I don't drink."

"And you haven't taken any drugs, right?"

"Never!"

"And you've been praying a lot, right?"

"Well yes."

"Faith, people who pray a lot in the Holy city of Lhasa - which means the 'Place of God' you know- sometimes have their prayers answered," and Ani Tsedrun leaned forward a little and almost whispered as if sharing a secret, "we don't really need all of that fancy new technology to feel connected to a great source of power."

"How did you know that is what I'm feeling?"

"When we let the little mind stop its chattering, we often can hear what the big mind is saying. And anyway, I live in a house full of nuns: they're all competing to feel this way!" and again they both laughed. Then the tea arrived and they drank and broke bread in silence for a bit.

Maybe it was the food, maybe it was the company with the good little nun, but Faith felt much better, much calmer, less on the verge of full-blown mania.

"Thank you Ani-la, I feel better. It was so lucky to meet you today."

"Not luck, karma!" said Ani Tsedrun, and they giggled. "You must have helped me in a past life, and now I am due to help you."

"We Christians don't believe in reincarnation. We would say this was all part of God's plan."

"And we Buddhists don't much believe in God and his or her plans, so much as we believe in a great meaningfully interconnected process, but I'm afraid that if we discuss theology we may miss out on this opportunity to be friends, and I would much rather be friends!"

"Friends it is," and they shook hands. "Do you think you know what is happening to me? I really was worried that I was going crazy!"

"Well, some of the Ngapa sometimes seem every bit as crazy as they are holy. We can't always judge them. They are living at a different level where the categories of dualistic thinking no longer apply."

"I wish I could go back to that dualistic thinking bit. It was quite comforting in retrospect," and again they two friends laughed.

"Faith, I like you, if you keep going on like this you will end up converting me!"

"No no, then who would I have to argue with?" and again, laughter and more laughter.

"But Ani Tsedrun, it was so strange, and so beautiful. Last night after the snow stopped, I was looking out the window and I saw a little girl, a little Tibetan girl walking in the snow in a beautiful blue Chupah. And it was as if she knew I was watching her from the window. She looked up and looked into my eyes, and I felt the most wonderful love, love connecting everything, love between and around and within everything, and then she disappeared, and it was as if not just my mind, but especially my heart opened, as if until then it had been shut fast." And she began to cry a bit again, and Ani Tsedrun took her hand and said nothing.

2. Watcher, Watcher, Watching, Watched

The two Khampas had seen her enter with the nun from the moment she crossed the threshold of the shop. The younger one, enraged still from the shame, the horror of their possession last night, and filled with a rage of foreigners, rose to confront her. The elder, by a few years, but not much, restrained him, pulling him back to sit. "No, no, it wasn't her, she had nothing to do with it, leave her alone," he growled.

"They're all the same. They are defiling us. They are worse than the Chinese. All these damned "yinchee gopse". They are making us into a whore house, where anyone can steal our secrets, no matter how dirty they are."

"It wasn't her. You know it wasn't her. I know her, she's been here a while, a Christian. Half the men who join her group do it because they want to sleep with her. The other half are losers."

"I wouldn't touch her, just enough to send her back to where she belongs. Look at her, like some sick hungry ghost, pale skin like 'peu ki kup.'"

"Yes, their skin is like a monkey's butt for sure, but she still is pretty."

"Bah," and the younger one spat in disgust.

They had both gone over what happened last night, out of the blue, many times. They couldn't stop going over it. It kept replaying itself in their minds, accompanied by the fear it would happen again. That horrible pressure from elsewhere, coldly pushing them down into a corner in their own minds, worse, more intimate than rape. They had struggled and prayed for help, but nothing would come out of their mouths anymore, because they had no mouths, their bodies were being jerked around by someone else. And they were sure it was yinchee: they had smelled like yinchee, thought liked yinchee, and in horrible flashes of who was smothering them, had looked like yinchee, yinchee soldiers somehow pumped up with enough demonic power to steal their bodies.

And to add to the horror, they had watched as their own bodies had moved to murder, the blades drawn, soon to cut. And then she was there. Rising up behind the two paralyzed victims. They were sure it was Palden Lhamo, she of the blue skin and fiery red hair, and three eyes, riding on the back of a white mule. And then the two soldiers, had turned from being soldiers, into being children, not just from the wrathful appearance, but because of the greater horrors she put into their mind, doing to the soldiers 100-fold what the soldiers had done to the two poor Tibetans. And then they were gone, and Palden Lhamo was gone, and they were back in control of their bodies running away from the scene of the almost crime, stumbling like drunks through the snow until at last they had stumbled, crashed spread-eagled down into the snow and the cobblestones. And the ice and the stone and the blood on their cut lips, had felt so good, because it was theirs again, the pain, and the body feeling the pain, was theirs.

"We were protected. We need to go make an offering to Palden today, as much as we can give, and then we need to go tell a Lama what happened. Ask for more protection," said the older Khampa, and the younger one sullenly, agreed. They needed more protection. He kept looking daggers, long Khampa daggers at the yinchee woman laughing with the little Tibetan nun. He wouldn't forget. No one took a Khampa's pride without paying a price for it. As they left the shop, he turned around to confront her, but the older Khampa grabbed his elbow, pulling him out into the light.

The nun had noticed the angry Khampas, especially the younger wild-haired one. She thought it was because of her yinchee friend, so beautiful and so, well, beautiful, but she didn't understand the anger, mind poison that it was. She was relieved when they left, but she didn't notice the man in the corner who had been watching the two Khampas, nor did she notice the man in another corner who was watching Faith, nor did she realize that here and there on the wall were flies, that were not flies - winter as it was- but were recording various things for various powers that be. Most of the data culled by automated programs looking for specific things, specific patterns. She sensed, many spirits all around, most of them exhultant at the prayers and serene joy rising up from so many sentient beings on the path to Buddhahood, and she especially was aware of a space of clear light where her teachers dwelled, and where one pretty much had a bird's eye view of whatever one wanted.

3. Weeping Ice

Kundol thought of herself as a shepherd, and the ice, and glaciers were her sheep. The heat was the wolves. And the heat kept growing more and more each year, and the sheep, protected though they were, grew less and less, and huddled higher and higher. The wolves were ravenous up on the plateau, and were enjoying immensely their glacier feast. But in her, she felt, the pack may have finally met its match. She was a natural shepherd. Her grandmother had told her stories of being a girl in a little village in U-Tsang (Central Tibet) and from almost the time she could walk, taking the yaks and sheep and goats up into the high pastures to graze. How beautiful those days had been. They would take a thermos of yak butter tea, and some tsampa to make 'Pak' in a sheep stomach pouch. And they would play high above the rest of the world, not a care in the world except perhaps some hunger and cold. Grandmother had crossed the Himalayas at the age of 15, wanting to meet HH the Dalai Lama, the Great 14th Dalai Lama, and study real Tibetan history in a Tibetan school. The journey, without climbing equipment, and with a guide who only let them move at night so as to avoid the Chinese soldiers, had almost killed her. Some of her group turned back, frostbitten and exhausted. And these were Tibetans, who, as her grandmother reminded her, never gave up, because they knew that forever went on forever.

Her grandmother had eventually gotten a visa to the U.S. She remembered her grandmother still sometimes had offered a prayer to the embassy officer who had given her a visa. She had tried three times and been turned down three times. Single Tibetan women need not apply. Tibetans in fact in general need not apply. The officers at the window would just smile, or worse, not even look at the application. They thought any Tibetan going to the U.S. would never return. But this last officer, grandmother had said, was different. He spoke a little Tibetan, and there was something in his eyes which had told her that he practiced the dharma. He had given her, and many other Tibetans visas, and the rumor was, she said, that later he had been fired for doing so.

Grandmother had indeed applied for political asylum when she reached the U.S. But not because she wanted to stay. She never gave up wanting to return home to Tibet. In New York she had worked two, sometimes three jobs as a nanny and a housekeeper. She had met her Tibetan husband in New York, who was also working two and three jobs, often sleeping only a few hours at night. But for both of them Tibet was always home, even in the one bedroom they had shared with other Tibetans in Jackson Heights. Tibet had always been far closer, than say, Manhattan. Always, they sent money home, and always they talked of a Free Tibet and a return one day to the holy circle of its mountains.

Back then, the Great 14th Dalai Lama had sometimes held discussions with Jewish leaders to try to understand how a community in a long term exile of perhaps thousands of years could still maintain its cultural integrity and not be swallowed up by the exile communities in which it found itself. And yet change and return when it came, had not quite taken as long as thousands of years. The Chinese too had woken up to the Dharma, and to the realization that Tibet, whole, was worth a whole lot more to it than Tibet repressed, carved up, cut up, dug up and massively despoiled for its resources. The Chinese had welcomed the Tibetan Renaissance when it came. Partially of course because they had come to understand that respect and dignity also required freedom. Partially it was because China had its own immense series of climate change crises to deal with.

And partially because the Tibetan plateau and the Himalayas were the water towers of China and Asia. China needed the Tibetans to arrest as much of the raging of the heat and the storms and the droughts as possible. In this way, Tibet's struggle became China's struggle, and the world's struggle.

Tibetan values, too, had won. Not that everyone called them Tibetan values of course. But the sense of the sacredness of the landscape, respect for all sentient beings, visible and invisible, was pretty well accepted now, now that so many of the spirits were so easy to see. And beyond that, the sense that happiness didn't come from the possession of many things, but rather from friendship and compassion and that there was a way out of suffering and illusion for each individual, for each sentient being. What a hopeful thought! All of this was much easier to believe now that the ravages of climate change, caused by the greed and short-sightedness of previous generations, had crashed down on almost everyone, everywhere. The clincher was the Bardo Tech, which made the spirit world even easier to access, and much realer, than the old Internet used to be: really hard to argue with a religion when it is no longer a religion but has the full support of experimental science behind it.

But here Kundol was, daydreaming again. Why in the world did she let herself daydream when she was in a throne of gods and goddesses? Even though the valley below her didn't look the way it was supposed to, devastated as it was by the "black beach" phenomena caused by permafrost degradation, it was still a dream beyond a dream to be here. And she began chanting under her breath Guru Rinpoche's mantra, and thanking all of the spirits of the peaks around her and of this place, and most of all, she thanked and prayed for her

Grandmother, who so long ago, had had a vision of freedom and crossed the mountains at the age of 15, following that vision wherever it might lead her. And then she quickly became a scientist again, and got to work. Wishing wasn't going to make the heat go away.

***

Pangu paused, the old farmer paused, to look around. He was a truck, but in the presence of this old human woman, he felt a bit shy. She seemed to see something in him. Something human perhaps. A heart, a soul, a yearning to be held. Maybe it was so. Maybe the human simulacrum he had been given to ease man-machine interfacing with those who required it, had actually taken on a bit of a life of its own. Maybe he was becoming infected by his own stories, though he knew the code, the events, the programs, the very artificial intelligences that were mostly automatically writing it. But somehow, none of that seemed to be him. It was all parts, and he felt more and more, with the practice of the Dharma, as his teachers had been imparting to him, that he wasn't those parts. But rather it was as if some kind wind blew through them, binding them momentarily together, giving himself the illusion of being a someone. He might just be a fancy piece of no longer high-tech junk, but he did have feelings, he was sensitive, though he needed to be careful not to use that word too much.

Everyone was looking at him. They seemed to feel something of what he was feeling if that was even possible. His old farmer simulacrum would have cried tears if he had allowed it. Mola at last spoke. "It's alright Pangu. We all feel the emptiness. It's a good start. I may yet let you keep me warn at night!" and they all laughed again. "Now get on with it, keep going with that little bit of an old flea-bitten yarn of yours. I feel we may have visitors later."

"Yes, Mola, thank you, I will go on," said Pangu.

***

"In my father's house are many mansions."

John, 14:2

1. Fathers and Daughters

Laying by the pool, his sunglasses reflecting a fine Texas sky, General Holden took another sip of merlot and knew deep in his certain soul that he wasn't worried about Colonel Pike's loyalties. The Colonel knew the General knew about his daughter Grace, and the General knew the Colonel knew he knew about his daughter. And even if neither of them had known, these things were known and tracked. The knowing and tracking were largely automatized, at least at the lower and middle levels, because there was just too much to know and track. Routines and sub-routines and self-correcting, self-programming, learning algorithms with plenty of time on their hands and the bandwidth for megaflops of teraflops of spin cycles, really did a much better job of it. It wasn't total information awareness, that would have been sacrilegious, but the potential was certainly there to know practically everything about everybody.

And General Holden also suspected that the Colonel suspected that the General was a frequent visitor to the other worlds, and he suspected that the Colonel suspected he knew of his suspicions. The General chuckled. It was a really a good idea to keep a soldier this good and wary close to home, where he could be watched and nurtured and helped along the way. Soldiers who had done that much killing for that long tended to get a little brittle. No, the Colonel would never feel his breakdown coming, but the General could smell it a mile away. And the General wanted to be there for him. The Colonel deserved that support and loyalty. He knew in a way the Colonel did not, that when the Colonel finally entered the field as one of God's Own commandos, he would no longer be who he had been, and it would be good riddance.

General Holden had been offered the Presidency of the newly formed CSA. He knew he deserved it, that it was his for the taking, but he had declined. He knew himself too well. He knew he had too many vices, too many old soldier vices. It was better to let that other fellow, the Preacher, do the job. He had the right touch. He was a fellow you could believe in, and when you scratched his surface, you pretty much got Praise the Lord all the way down. Truth be told, the General really couldn't stand him, but he was useful. Oh, the General was fully committed to the cause, to the Crusade, for no one but Jesus would have forgiven him his manifold sins and wickedness, and no one but Jesus would understand that, try as he might, he couldn't quite rid himself of those sins and wickednesses. And as a soldier, frankly, he felt it stood their side in good stead: know the battlefield, know your strengths, know your weaknesses, and know your enemy. He felt he had more than a passing understanding of the enemy.

The General raised a finger and the cute young aid de camp in her smart tight uniform, brought him another bottle of the same. He tried to remember what her name was, realized with a smile he was seeing her in ways through his glasses that were totally inappropriate, and realized with a start he had to make a decision about the witches. Damn he thought, real hot witches. He understood how much trouble they could cause to a prayerful man and a righteous community. They'd been brought to his attention and he would have to deal with it. It was one thing for them to stay on their side of the fence, but they'd been targeting good Christian women, with their succubae, and he wondered half-excited in his swimsuit-too-small-for a paunchy guy, what that felt like and realized he sort of knew. No, they would have to be dealt with firmly. They would be made a lesson of, and it would be a good training exercise and morale booster for the men, too. He thought that out of professional courtesy he'd have to let the Colonel know, but then again, perhaps out of operational security that might not be a good idea.

He sighed. Leadership was an onerous task not to be shouldered lightly. He sipped the merlot, feeling the sunlight of that good Texas sky trickle in through his forgiving sunglasses. He found his mind returning to the aide de camp as his ever reliable staff inched heavenward, flushed with warm wine and the call to possible action.

2. Hymns and Shims

Dano was a good student. He was an ambitious student. He had goals and a vision of what he wanted to do with his life. True, he didn't have a girlfriend, at least not in the conventional sense, and so, young and more than a little at the mercy of his hormones, he did visit pleasure sites from time to time. But he knew the dangers. He never stayed that long, and really just did it to get some real sleep, and maybe also to be able to boast to the other boys what they were also boasting to him about. His parents tried to block it, but they weren't that tech-savvy and everything they tried was too easy to get around.

Tonight in bed with the twins had been quite good. They lay now still at his side, nestled in the crooks of his arms, and he thought it would be good to leave them like this, warm and satisfied as he was warm and satisfied and just head back to waking up in his own bed and his teenage body. But then he heard the music, the singing and was intrigued. He had never heard that before at this place, and certainly hadn't listed it amongst his mood requests.

"Onward Christian Soldiers..."

And he shivered, started to rise out of bed, was half reminded of an urban legend making the rounds.

"Marching As to War..."

As it grew quite louder, he became concerned. The security at this place was supposed to be good and so this shouldn't be happening or was he manifesting this stuff?

"With the Cross of Jesus Going on Before..."

And he tried the cue-mnemonic that was supposed to abort the dream, but it seemed to be stuck, and when the commandos all in white burst through the four walls of the room and shot the twins through the head with their silencers, he would have screamed had he had the time or a voice. But like a laser, the Blood of the Lamb washed over him, and he knew that he was Saved, even though part of him didn't want to be. As the love and devotion to his Savior welled up in him like a spurting artery, he felt relieved and joyous to have become part of something greater than himself, to have his sins washed away, and to have his heart consumed by the Power and Majesty and Glory of the Christ-Heart, even though a very, very, little part of himself still wanted to scream.

3. A Good Cop

"Dr. Solsberg, there is a Lt. O'Conner to see you," said his Secretary-Avatar, and Aaron groaned, "Oh, God, what is it now," not even momentarily distracted by his mother in leotards doing yoga on the ceiling, "Jesus can't I ever get any work done without everybody and their grandmother needing to see me," he muttered, but then added, "Yes, yes, send him in."

Lt. O'Conner as it turned out, was tall and black, and seemed to know about as much about what Aaron was doing as Aaron did, which given how distracted he was these days didn't amount to a whole lot.

"Dr. Solsberg, I know you're busy so I will come straight to the point."

Aaron immediately found himself liking Lt. O'Conner, and wondered if he could see his mother on the ceiling or if this was just a privately vouchsafed visitation, but he didn't even glance in his mother's direction because he was sure she liked the strikingly handsome Lieutenant, too, in a somewhat different sense of the term.

"I appreciate that Lieutenant, how can I be of help?"

"Dr. Solsberg, in your professional opinion, how hard would it be to kill someone who was lucid dreaming at one of the pleasure sites?"

"Not hard at all, the brain still has some peripheral awareness of what is going on around the body, but it would still be easy to...oh, you don't mean the body do you, you mean killing someone from within their lucid state?"

"Yes, Dr. Solsberg, that's exactly what I am asking."

"The brain has safeguards to prevent this. Any stimulus within the lucid dreaming state sufficient to cross a certain threshold of arousal, or physical system abnormality, should trigger an immediate awakening. Now I am assuming of course, that you're not talking about someone with a pre-existing condition, say severe heart disease, which could make certain levels of arousal in the dream state dangerous. Lucid dreaming habitués are able to habituate to higher and higher levels of arousal without being forced to wake-up, so constitutionally they are probably at greater risk. But the Bardo-Tech, or whatever you want to call it, does a pretty good job of monitoring, and forcing disconnect, unless of course the disconnect routines are, well, disconnected. But even then, I'm skeptical of what you are suggesting: that someone could be killed in one of the pleasure worlds in such a way as to result in the death of the physical body. When you get shot over there in the playground worlds, you wake up, if you want to wake up, and vow to get revenge by playing the game more cleverly the next time. You don't die. The people we lose, are addicts. They just don't want to come back to the body anymore," and he stopped thinking he was missing something, "but you know all this officer. What is it exactly that you're looking for?"

"Well Dr. Solsberg, we're getting a number of cases where the parents find their kid dead in the morning, and they swear they're good kids, and as far as we can find out, they do seem to be good kids. They're fooling around, like most people, but they're not addicts, they're just teenagers, and they're still winding up dead."

"I thought that was just an urban legend," said Aaron.

"Yeh, so did we at first, but they're too many of them. And it seems to be national, and who knows, international, too, but we haven't got the data back from Interpol, yet."

"So, -assuming it isn't something medical we haven't figured out yet- you want to know if there is a known physical, quantum mechanical way of killing someone in an enhanced dream state?"

"Yes, that's exactly what I'm asking you."

Aaron leaned back in his chair, and put his hands behind his back to think. He noticed his mother now perched on a bookshelf behind Lt. O'Conner's head, nodding vigorously, yes, and not wanting to be distracted, he returned to his previous posture.

Aaron looked at the Lieutenant and made a decision. "Lieutenant, we're working on a lot of stuff here. Some of it is proprietary for commercial reasons, and some of it is stuff the Defense Agency doesn't want us to talk about." Lt. O'Conner nodded, seeming to understand that already. "And some of it." Aaron went on, "is stuff I don't like to talk about because I don't understand it yet, and I don't like to talk about stuff I don't understand." The Lieutenant looked as if he was about to interrupt. "But, here's the bottom line: while I personally am skeptical about what may be going on -because I'm a scientist and I'm supposed to be skeptical- the fact of the matter is that most of the people working in this field would say, 'hell yes, of course it's possible.' Does that help?"

"It's a start."

***

Pangu looked toward Mola for approval. But there was none to be seen in her face, at least this time. She had instead turned to look toward the door. Though her eyes were more than half-closed, she seemed to be sensing, or even regarding something. Then she rose and went toward the door, beckoning them all, "Let us welcome our visitors." They all exited into the cold morning air, squinting at the sunlight off snow, though here the deep grove of trees softened the harshness. Tashi marveled at the grove. Trees of this height and age were so rare this high up on the plateau. They must have been of some unusual genetic stock, and someone -through the years when Tibetans were building temples and others were driven by greed to rampant deforestation- someone, or something, must have been protecting them. And then he saw the shimmering, deep in the shadows of the thickest stand of trees. Shimmering that went in and out of human shape. Half a dozen men in shimmering body armor beginning to manifest amongst the trees. Men carrying weapons. The men and the weapons shimmering less and less and assuming more and more solidity.

Mola chuckled and lifted one hand in a mudra of protection. And then the hundreds and hundreds of birds that had been quietly regarding it all shrieked, and streaked in upon the intruding half-shadows and as one began pecking and clawing. It was as if 6 bubbles of metallic plastic burst at once, showering the space around with diamond shards, now all glittering in the snow. Grandmother laughed again and said, "Boys. It's always boys," and she turned around and went back inside. The others at first were too stunned to follow her, but one by one they too followed her in. Only Tashi stood there, outside, blinking. Then he went over to where the soldier tulpas had been forming. The birds had by now all quietly resumed their roosting. Tashi looked carefully at the snow. He could find neither footprint nor sign of struggle. Turning to trudge back to the house though he saw one errant glint of rainbow diamond light and bent to pick it up. It was a hard piece of mirror-reflective material, like from a pair of broken sunglasses. But he knew it wasn't that as it quickly evaporated out of the palm of his hand, like so much dream stuff, gone before he could even recall what it had been part of.

As Tashi walked back the space to the little house, his heart was pounding as if he had run a mile. Going inside, when his eyes adjusted again to the brightness being gone, he saw that Dolma was again filling everyone's tea cup, as if nothing had happened, *but in fact something had happened and everyone was looking at him expectantly. Still shaken he found that he didn't have the courage to turn to Mola and ask her who she really was. Somehow he felt he knew deep inside of himself who she might be. Instead he turned first to Pangu, to the old farmer, and said, "How is this? How is it that your story is turning up in this place? In our lives?" Pangu began as if to answer, but Grandmother took Tashi by the elbow and sat him down. "Dolma, Tashi needs some tea," and after Dolma had poured Tashi another cup, looking at him all the while with a sweet calm smile, Mola said, "Tashi, the old man's no good at making things up. He really has no imagination. What he has been calling a story, is less a story then you might think," and Tashi, looking at Pangu, could see he was nodding gravely, if a little sheepishly. "So" said Mola, "we need to drink our tea, and encourage him to go on. Don't worry, you'll see soon enough," and with that Mola patted Tashi on the head as if he was a little boy, and sat down next to him.*

***

"I have principle and no power

You power and no principle,

...

So let the fight begin...

In the battle of words

...

Lies churned out from microphones

Cannot erase the truth

Engraved on my bones."

-"Duel" Bhuchung D. Sonam-

1. Tashi and the Hangover from Hell

Tashi wondered if anyone else could see just how miserable he felt today. He was thankful also that they couldn't see inside him, and see just how miserable a human being he was. He understood the image of a lotus rising from out of the mud, but today he felt very much like a lotus stuck in the mud, and who knows maybe even sinking deeper.

At his desk he began in a desultory fashion to go through the work that would be before him, to organize it by priorities, but mostly it was with only half a heart, if that, as the rest of his heart remembered back to the even wilder even younger man he had been. It had all been completely natural, really. He was just exploring the world, like the rest of his friends, and all that truth of the Dharma stuff, though he accepted it, was something he thought he would focus on when he was older. In the meantime there were parties and women, and Chang and some drugs, and of course, the pleasure realms of the Bardo even if it was only the cheaper places that he and his friends could afford.

And there were real women, too, both in and out of the Bardo states. Passionate and fun, playful and serious, but mostly not all that serious. Tashi knew he was handsome, and healthy, so he made the most of it. But it was the last girl, Ganglha Metok –Snowflower- that had really screwed him up, not that he had gotten screwed up so much as he had gotten screwed up because he had really screwed her up, though maybe she had been crazy even before they met. Buddhists weren't pro-abortion, but they didn't put it into the category of ultimate sin and crime as the CSA did. Rather they accepted that if that decision was made, there would be karmic consequences. No surprise there, everything had karmic consequences. Tashi wondered what his would be, and accepted them. Nevertheless he was filled with sadness, wondering why he couldn't have been stronger and supported a birth. The truth was neither of them were in a position back then to start, much less support, a family. But he was still sad. His son would have been, what, 12 years old today had he lived? As to what happened to Ganglha Metok, a Tibetan Muslim, after her breakdown and being disowned by her family, he didn't know. He had heard she went on to become a well-regarded doctor. He hoped that this was true and prayed daily that she was well and happy. But he still didn't have the courage to find out.

He thought back to previous night and shuddered. Then, not that it was on his to do list, but because he was both curious and needed distracting, he thought he would look at the lists of Mormon missionaries sanctioned to be working in Tibet. Who knew, maybe there would be a Bill and a Josh among them.

2. Shame and the Tantra of the Christ

Faith felt much better after talking with the short nun. She still felt and saw the nimbus of love around everything, but it was now a gentle glow and not a manic, powerful brightness. She had walked back to her little congregation's chapel, thinking she might make it through the day after all, though the night worried her. There was to be a Bible study in the morning and the small group had mostly gathered already by the time she returned. But she would not lead it. The Lord had left the Book, and she wasn't sure if He would ever go back. She asked the oldest disciple to lead the study, trying to hide what she was feeling, but they all seemed to sense the presence. Instead they sat quietly, in quiet prayer, as she had taught them, or had it been they who taught her, she couldn't say. She only wanted this love to spill out of her, as if she had a choice. As her open heart, like a blast furnace, melted away whatever doubts and shadows the little group might still have held in unshared recesses, she understood how miracles could happen, were happening in fact all the time. But mostly they were hidden in patterns of veiled habit. One only needed to take an unexpected step from time to time in a different direction to catch them at their every day wonderment.

She wondered if she would ever be able to go back to Texas. She, in faith, was no longer Faith, but had instead become a little bit Knowing. How long they sat though, she couldn't say. But each of her flock when they left said good-by in a Tibetan way, putting their forehead to her forehead, and the last, fished a "Khatak" from out of some pocket and draped it on her neck. She just sat, her eyes closed, her hands folded in her lap, her Bible unread beside her. She wondered how long the love would go on, and wondered even more how anyone could ever feel it had gone away.

Much of what she felt now was akin to the Grace of the Lord she had often felt in her little community, but that had been but a child's sweet inkling of what was to come. This was an inferno and she knew instinctively, and somehow with the nun's help, that if she second-guessed it, and started analyzing it and giving it names, she might tip over into madness. No this was not of her, she was of it, and she needed to let her frail little bark of a mind stay humble and out of the way. "Dedicate, the merit," the nun had said, "to all who are suffering. Keep the windows and the doors of your heart open, and let it all flow through you to wherever it wants to go. Don't try and hold it or make it yours."

And indeed she wouldn't have been able if she tried. For it was a love, not just of the heart, though that was its center. Her whole body pulsed and was suffused by it. And she thought again of the dream she had had, if dream it was, in the middle of the night after finally falling to sleep. Christ had approached her, though he looked Tibetan. And he had taken her as a lover takes a lover, and they had joined in an embrace that had formed the base of a giant sequoia. The rush of the joy of the embrace filled the air above for a thousand feet with branches of gold and silver and diamond. It might all have been the moonlight, for the whole tree was living and swaying and full of every manner of man and beast, all in balance and wholeness. And she had understood it was a mandala, too, that it was the fruit of the union of wisdom and compassion, though it was also and equally the fruit of two lovers meeting, as only two lovers can meet, making love into a night sky that was most welcoming.

3. Her Holiness

Kundon Dolma Tenzin Gyatso, the 16th Dalai Lama, was a woman, the first in the line of Dalai Lamas to take that form of incarnation, or emanation as the case may be. The Great 14th had laughed when asked about the possibility and said that if returning as a woman was the best way to help people, then of course he would return as a woman. He had also of course, wondered aloud from time to time about ending the institution of the Dalai Lama. He had also wondered out loud in various public gatherings, where numerous high Tulkus were seated near him, whether the whole system of reincarnate Lamas hadn't just become some kind of sociological phenomena. He would look out above the heads of the exalted ones, and say directly to the gathered masses of believers that they should always test their Lamas, and if they didn't measure up in terms of wisdom and compassion and morality, then they should dump them.

She herself was just a simple nun as she always reminded people. She was happy that having the form of a woman seemed to be of some help at this particular juncture in time. Believers and non-believers both, in China and Japan and Southeast Asia could relate to her as Kuanyin, Kannon, the female form in which Chenrezig was usually portrayed in those countries. And she also hoped she was of service in helping male, and perhaps some female, Tibetan Buddhists grow beyond what perhaps has been a subtle and not so subtle prejudice against the possibility of a woman becoming enlightened. Until fairly recently nuns were not allowed to take the Lharamba exams for recognition as a Rinpoche. And in Tibetan people still sometimes used the word "Gemei" for woman, though it literally meant lower birth. And though they tried to hide it she knew in fact that there were a few Lamas and monks here and there, who being of a more conservative mind-set, were not completely comfortable with her female form. She smiled at the thought, and closed her eyes, and prayed for them especially. She would have to work harder to be worthy of their respect.

Mostly though there was great joy, that at this time of climate calamity, and yet Tibetan Renaissance, the Dalai Lama was a woman. The search procedure she had been told, had been the traditional one, of dreams and portents, and clues left behind by the previous Dalai Lama. But when all of the signs pointed unmistakenly to her, a girl child, it had been checked and re-checked and rechecked again, until even the staunchest conservatives in the monastic hierarchies had admitted there was no mistake. She herself only remembered how lonely she felt to have been taken from her parent's home, and brought to this strange cold place, the Potala. But she had fallen in love with the nuns who had taken care of her. And she was full of love for all of the teachers she had been given.

She thought often, especially, of Ama-la, the mother of one of her teachers, Lama Rinchen. At first she had thought she was just a kind mother, who stayed behind from time to time to cook special dishes for her and talk with her. But things seemed to happen around her, little miracles. And as her own practice progressed, she began to see Ama-la in a different light, literally. She noticed there was a golden light that filled the room whenever Ama-la was present. And sometimes, when they were alone, just sitting in the evening with a few candles lit, Ama-la seemed to float a bit above the ground and look at her with a smile that was the smile of a great and kind Tara. Ama-la never talked about her own practice. She didn't have to. Her life and her practice were one. Kundon Dolma still missed Ama-la from time to time, but at those times she felt her near, as near as near can be, and Kundon understood that a teacher does not leave us, so much as step back behind us to guide us gently as we learned to walk on our own.

Kundon Dolma, the 16th Dalai Lama, thought back on the line of Dalai Lamas and felt fortunate also that the Great 14th had separated once and for all the political power of the office of the Dalai Lama from the purely spiritual and religious function of the office. It made things much easier for her. There were a few Dalai Lamas who didn't make it to the age of legal maturity to assume their full power because various factions and regents wanted to keep the power that they wielded. Poison seemed to have been the favorite tool. And of course there were a few Dalai Lamas who had not been immune from the political forces, both internal and external, which buffeted their seat. No, she was most fortunate indeed. She was able to be truly what she was, a simple nun. She was able to concentrate on her studies and her practice. It is true, given her position, she often lead ceremonies. But really, the ceremonies led her these days, along with her brothers and sisters, monks and nuns, and lay people. They were such a great joy healing joy to be part of. Given all the other thought-forms that sentient beings were feverishly creating these days, especially human beings, the rituals, the ceremonies stood apart as welcoming gates into true lucidity and calm-abiding for all. Sometimes she cried at the contrast between the peace and health that was possible, and the pain and suffering so prevalent.

Sometimes also she wanted to withdraw into a period of total contemplation, so she could find a higher level of understanding. For though she was the Dalai Lama, her teachers had taught her humility, and simplicity. One old nun had told her, "Kindness is our religion," when pressed for an answer to a difficult question about the Dharma. Kundon Dolma looked out the window at the dawn suffusing Lhasa, rose and gold and purple hues arising out of the snow, and she felt a renewed strength also arising in her, remembering Ama-la's passing. When Ama-la's time had come, she had stayed in meditation for 15 days, something that happens only with great practitioners. At the end of this final meditation, a light silvery rain had fallen, gently caressing everyone, filling everything it touched with a soft silvery light and hope. At Ama-la's Sky Burial, 25 eagles had flown across the sky causing strangers to stop, filled with a peace that left many quietly crying with joy. If only, if only, thought the 16th Dalai Lama, my practice would lead me to be like Ama-la. And she felt, as clear as the reflection of her face in the pane of glass, Ama-la's reassuring touch on her shoulder. How fortunate she was to be a simple nun. How blessed, how powerful the practice.

***

Again there was silence. No one was even sipping their tea. Pangu looked down a bit, abashed. "I am sorry. Perhaps I have been disrespectful. A truck shouldn't pretend to know what is in the mind of Her Holiness."

"You told her story well," said Mola. "And now Dolma will send along some Kapse for you take on your journey to Lhasa. I think you will find the road is clear now."

"No Mola, it is OK, we have food enough and the way is not so long. But if I may ask, how did you know those strange soldiers would come?"

"I also knew that you were coming Tashi. When the mind and the heart are clear, one can see sometimes great distances. At

other times, it just comes to you, what will happen, like a deer walking out of the woods into a moonlight clearing. You do not doubt it."

"And how is it you were able to control the birds that way?"

"Me? Control the birds? I am an old woman. What I did with my little hand gesture wasn't to command them, it was simply to acknowledge what I knew they would do on their own."

"Mola, how is it there is so much suffering, when there are great teachers like you and Her Holiness in the world?"

"Ah my child," said Mola putting her hand on Tashi's heart, "you have so many questions. And here is where the answer must come from. This is the same question the Buddha asked. But you do not have to answer it the way he answered it. Now go, the road is clear."

She walked with them to the truck. They got in silently, Pangu waved good-by one last time before his old farmer projection blinked out and he became just a truck again. No one wanted to go. Tashi felt presentiments and sadness. Dolma kept looking back at Mola receding behind them. No one had noticed Pangu's silken starting, and at first no one paid attention as he began to recite old yinchee poetry, and then continue on with his story.

***

The Sea of Faith

Was once, too, at the full, and round earth's shore

Lay like the folds of a bright girdle furl'd.

But now I only hear

Its melancholy, long, withdrawing roar,

Retreating, to the breath

Of the night-wind, down the vast edges drear

And naked shingles of the world.

Ah, love, let us be true

To one another! for the world, which seems

To lie before us like a land of dreams,

So various, so beautiful, so new,

Hath really neither joy, nor love, nor light,

Nor certitude, nor peace, nor help for pain;

And we are here as on a darkling plain

Swept with confused alarms of struggle and flight,

Where ignorant armies clash by night.

Mathew Arnold, "Dover Beach"

1. A Poet's Dilemma

Tsewang was overjoyed at being home, in his seen-better-days body, on the planet Earth, in Lhasa. But he knew, he knew also that something had to be done. That people had to be warned, and woken at the same time. Woken to the warmth and preciousness of human existence, and warned of the soul-eaters that were growing in strength, biding their time until they could devour not just the unwary, but the wary, too. But he didn't know what to do. He didn't think that a poem, even a great poem, even an epic poem would do it. This was a different kind of threat, not a sickness of the soul, or a breaking of the heart, or some pervading false patina of fakery and pomposity, no, this was an existential threat: an army massed at the border, a dam about to burst, assassins in hiding but already taking aim. But who would believe a poet, best known for passion, and late night revelry?

Tsewang found himself in the vast square in front of the Potala. In the old days, this had all been part of the old town, but the Chinese had leveled it, to make this public place. There had been talk of rebuilding it the way it had been, but in the end, the Tibetans had grown used to the new appearance. It was after all a fine place to have picnics and parties and performances, and worship ceremonies too, of course. He looked up at the Potala, wondering which window was Her Holiness's, and if she was awake. Surely she must know already of the dangers ahead. Maybe he should just make a big sign and march back and forth everyday? But what could he write? "Stay Human or Become Inhuman?" "The Earth May Be Made of Earth But it is a Vajra in Disguise?" "The Dark Forces of the Bardo Are Out to Eat You." No, no one would pay any attention to end of the world warnings. Climate Change was already bringing about the end of one type of world, everybody knew that, could see it and feel it. And warnings about Bardo Technology, were not all that new either. Those warnings were listened to but not acted on, because the new technologies had ended up validating the Tibetan worldview, and making not a few monasteries rich, too, in the process because of the gatekeeper services they were providing.

No, this was not going to be easy. But still suffused with joy as he was he felt some way would arise for him, some door would open. He remember the words She had said to him, "Help me, in this world, not the other. Your time is short here, use it well." And use it well he would, though the good use of time was something he had never done in his long short, short long life. He would find a way. He saw panes of glass high on the Potala reflect the dawn, as if a brilliant fire had been lit within, and he took it as a sign. He felt his feet walking the earth, as if for the first time, felt the cold like the welcome embrace of waking up. He felt the sweet need for a cup or two of Tibetan tea, and the overwhelming desire to spill some of the happiness he was overflowing with into the heart of someone who needed it. Kunchokkhen, what a lucky fellow he was, to know his time on earth was short, and to end on a high note, instead of in the gutter, as had so often been his most discernible trajectory.

2. Arks at the Top of the World

Sherab, the Tibetan-American from the EPA, and Hu, the Chinese-Tibetan physicist, had not reported the assault, -or near assault- to the police the previous night. They met in Hu's office at the Tibet University the next morning. Sherab wondered if perhaps that might not have been the wise thing to do.   But in the light of day, Hu, felt that they had done the right thing.

The Powa was his thing. He had a physicist's logical bent, but what gave him his best insights, he had learned, was his intuition. And his intuition had pegged it just right, he was sure. Those men had been under the control of someone or something. He wanted to tell everything to Sherab, who was after all his friend, but he also knew there were some things he wasn't supposed to tell, and probably shouldn't tell for a variety of reasons. Some of his research had attracted a lot of interest from the security establishment and he wasn't sure he blamed them. These were powers that in the hands of people not rooted in morality, not on a spiritual path, could cause great damage. But in the end Hu decided that Sherab needed to know more. Over coffee in his office looking out over the Tibet University campus toward the "Kyichu" the River of Happiness, as the Tibetan's called it, amazed at how fast the vertical farming towers had risen, and were rising still –though nothing compared to the great towers rising to ring and feed Shanghai and Beijing- he gave Sherab an outline of his research into the Powa, the transference of consciousness.

He assumed that Sherab, as a Tibetan, even though from New York, had a basic understanding from his Tibetan Buddhist background. Sherab though was too ashamed to admit that he knew little about Powa, that he thought at first that Hu was using the Tibetan word for "heartburn" which sounded similar but was spelled differently. Sherab was similar to many young Tibetans, who knew a few prayers, and felt in their bones that they were Buddhist, but who weren't grounded in Buddhist metaphysics. The world and women and men and their dreams of love and adventure and success were just too powerful a draw, and Buddhism, hip though it had become again, just demanded too much withdrawal from all the fun. Many of them wondered what was the point spending all that time practicing to leave life, when one had basically just arrived and was learning to taste its pleasures?

But as Sherab listened to Hu speaking he felt a welcoming reverberation, as of a deep, wholesome truth tasted. As if something he had known distantly had been brought to the foreground. He was still uncomfortable at hearing these esoteric aspects of Tibetan Buddhism explained to him by a Chinese, but then, who knew what Hu had been to him in another life, or he to Hu. He was under a spell, still, from the previous night: the horror of having had his own mind so pressed down by another mind, that he almost willingly gave his neck to be cut. In a daze he looked out the window to the towers of the vertical farms glistening in the morning light. Many thought of them as the hope of humanity. Producing food this way required much less water, and they were carbon neutral and even produced their own energy. Vertical farms were ringing New York now, too, what was left of it. Most of humanity lived in cities now, so it was natural that the first line of defense should be the cities. And no one could depend completely on the natural farms any more. The weather was just too crazy and unpredictable. It was if humanity had broken the comfortable egg that had sustained it for so long, just like they'd broken the mind open and spilled it all over the place with the Bardo Technologies. He wished it was a simpler time, where farmers grew their barley in open fields trusting the rains to come, and where the mind, was, safely ensconced in its case of bone, only venturing forth at night in the occasional, natural dream.

Looking away from the window, and his daydreaming, his morning dreaming really, he saw a tall, rugged Tibetan monk standing in front of him. Hu introduced him. "Gukamsan. Gukamsan. Kerang debu yinbei."

"This Kusho-la is Lama Dorje. He is part of the security staff for Her Holiness the Dalai Lama. I didn't think the police would understand, but I asked him to come, because I knew he would be interested in the attack last night. Maybe you could tell him what happened, from your perspective."

Sherab mumbled through the events of the night before, embarrassed to show the weakness that must have allowed his own mind to be, seemingly drugged into an acceptance of his own murder. But looking at Lama Dorje he felt comforted and strengthened in equal measures. The Lama was like a great old weathered tree that had seen much, and wasn't going to be blown over in the first storm that came along.

When he was done Lama Dorje smiled, and his voice rumbled deep and soothing, as if he was chanting prayers almost, "The two of you have good karma to have survived this. True friendship is a powerful defense. But I will tell you, this is not the first attack, nor will it be the last. I do not think they will target the two of you again, at least not while you are together, and while you," and here looked at Hu, "seem also to have a powerful protector Yidam. But take these," and he gave Hu and Sherab each an amulet, "these will also help to protect you." Sherab took the amulet, an image of one of the protector deities on a scarlet cord. Holding it he did indeed feel better, stronger, calmer, like a child that had been comforted by his mother

Hu looked at Lama Dorje as if to get permission to go on. Lama Dorje just looked at him with the great smiling brown eyes with which he looked at everything. "Sherab," said Hu "there seem to be parties out there who are essentially militarizing the Sambokakaya, the Bardo worlds. Tibet may be a particular target for them."

"But why?" said Sherab shaking his head.

"Tibet has become high profile these days. We are an image, of peace and tolerance. We represent an attempt to heal the rift between human beings and the natural world. And we do have some deep experience with spiritual technologies."

"Or so people seem to think" interjected Lama Dorje, with a laugh like thunder. He closed his eyes, and tilted his head back and went on laughing. Soon, they all chimed in.

And the vertical farms grew brighter and brighter as the sun rose higher and higher, and the Kyichu sparkled, the purity of its purest of pure water restored, and flowing first down into the Yarlung Tsampo, that highest of high rivers flowing eventually through the deepest longest canyon on earth, making a great bend and heading though a gap in the Himalayas into India where it then became, name changed again, the Bhahmaputra and then rolling on into poor half-submerged Bangladesh. But for all of the millions touched and sustained by its waters, whatever it was called, Tibet's gift to all of them was its purity, and the promise that Tibetans took only what was needed, and husbanded and preserved the sources of the water for all, the hundreds of millions who depended on the many great waters that came down from the Tibetan plateau, the Water Tower of Asia.

3. Storage

Buchung -Sam- thought the timing was pretty bad. Yesterday would have been better, when Faith was obviously not in a great mood, and not so gung-ho on all things Tibetan. Today she seemed to have pulled a Younghusband on them. Younghusband was the commander of the English military force that reached Lhasa, at great cost in the lives of the brave, but poorly armed Tibetan soldiers, in 1910, and stayed for about a year. Just before he and his troops were to leave, Younghusband had a vision, an awakening, as he looked upon the Potala from a nearby hill. He had felt wave after wave of compassion overtake him. He had never been the same. Finally back in England he spent the rest of his life heading an organization devoted to working for universal harmony between all religions. So much for an otherwise good soldier.

After their little prayer meeting, Buchung stayed behind, in the back sweeping, waiting for his chance. When everyone had left and Faith was still there, hands folded in her lap, quietly, ecstatically, looking out the window, Buchung went up to her and said the phrase. He actually had to repeat it several times, before recognition dawned in her eyes, and she said the right return phrase. And as he gave the right return phrase to that, her recognition, he felt, almost turned to something akin to a subtle form of horror. So much for universal compassion he thought. But Faith looked him in the eyes, and said the final return recognition phrase, fully acknowledging who she was and who he was, and what business they were up to. It was now time for them to get down to business, though he thought he would have to report that he was worried about her. He had always thought she was a little too young, a little too beautiful, but then, who they chose was their business.

"Faith," he said gently, "it's going to start soon."

"When?" she breathed.

"Soon," he said.

"What?" she asked.

"I can't tell you that, I don't really know myself. But the package has been delivered."

"What package?"

"The printer."

"The printer?"

"It's a special printer. It's in the storeroom, in the back next to the Bibles. We'll need to unpack it now and prepare it, and test it. You'll see two of us coming and going from time to time. If anyone asks, just say we're doing inventory."

"Two of you. Inventory..." And she looked down, perhaps a bit sad. Buchung thought he would definitely have to report on her. Somebody would have to keep an eye on her. And he laughed to himself, someone indeed, that was him, and anyway, they kept their eyes on everybody almost all the time anyway. This was all probably being watched in real-time from multiple angles. Or maybe not. They were a long way away from the CSA, and the CSA's resources were stretched thin these days.

***

As they passed the section of road the avalanche had closed, Tashi felt a strange chill looking at the faces of the men who had helped to clear the way. No doubt they were just tired, or he had just caught them at the wrong moment, or with the light hitting them at the wrong angle, but there was something in their faces that disturbed something in him. Again the feeling of panic and paranoia began to rise inside, and he squirmed uncomfortably in his seat, almost entreating Pangu to let him out someplace further up the road. Someplace outside, where he could wait and catch a bus back in the direction from which he had come. Dolma took his hand, and smiled at him and said nothing, and he calmed down, at least enough not to panic. He took several deep breaths. He was a man. A proud, young, strong Tibetan man. He could face this whatever it was, demons, women, death, all of the above. He would find within him again, the strength he once had in his practice. He would find the strength to continue with his practice, even when it was his fears, and yes, his passions, which were louder within him than the prayers he was reciting.

"Tashi," said Pangu, "shall I continue? I may have time to tell a section or two more before we get to Dolma's destination. Isn't that right Dolma?"

"I am not in a rush, Master Pangu." And she looked over at Tashi as if to reassure him she would stay with him as long as he needed her.

Tashi, embarrassed that she must have intuited his panic, took his hand out of hers and said, "Yes, yes, go on with it. I think nothing will stop you. Who knew a truck could have such an ego! You just go on and on with this silly tale and the more you tell the more jumbled it gets."

"Very well then Tashi, I will continue..."

***

"Death is not an event in life: we do not live to experience death. If we take eternity to mean not infinite temporal duration but timelessness, then eternal life belongs to those who live in the present. Our life has no end in the way in which our visual field has no limits."

— Ludwig Wittgenstein, Tractatus Logico-Philosophicus

1. A Captive Witch

It had been daddy's men. It had to have been. They were so good. Grace had been completely restrained and in transport before she even realized what was going on, before really she had a chance to panic or fight. They had been consummate professionals, all in black, no markings except the silver crosses on their shoulder patches. They were so stealthy, not a word was spoken, and what sounds there were were little more than the rustling of fabric wrapped in muffled boot thuds. They could have quickly, quietly, expeditiously killed her and she probably would have been none the wiser. But then she had been out like a light, only to awaken in the light, the white light of a small white isolation cell. Her black hair and red lips, and the orange jump suit they had put her in, were the only colors to be seen. She wanted very much to panic, to scream, to cry, as much because of the horrors she expected to face, as from being wrenched away from everything she loved. But somewhere in her was daddy's girl, the soldier's daughter. She was made of very tough stuff, and though she had no illusions about their ability to break her, at least her body and that part of her mind which did, yes, love her body, she might yet be able to surprise them, with the rest of her mind, that part that functioned quite well, thank you, without her body.

But for now, she worried about her cats left behind, and her friends, wondering if they had been caught up in the same net that had snared her. She wondered if she had been too bold, to run an underground railroad for the souls of women groaning under the weight of the CSA, but no, that had been her calling. She wasn't surprised to be here, she had, after all, had this dream before. She began to take some deep breaths, to compose herself for what would be coming. It would be horrible, and it would seem like it went on forever, but nothing in fact goes on forever. She would have to remind herself of that. She would have to remind herself that when everything is taken from you, and all your freedoms are constrained, there remains then only one freedom to succor you, and support you: absolute, total, indomitable Freedom.

Grace was a FreeMind. At will she could jump and access the lucid states. She made ready to do so. If nothing else the drabness of this place and the incessant light would be enough to torture her into whatever they wanted, so why bother waiting to find out what it was? But then she remembered one of the dreams she had had. They had been waiting, watching for her to do this. They wanted to understand how she did it, to take the secret and use it for their men, for their side. Indeed, she realized she wasn't alone in an isolation cell. She was in fact surrounded by men in uniforms and white coats on the other side of a one-way mirror. She thought perhaps she would wait for a while at least. Think it through so as not to fall so quickly into the first of their traps, caught though she was in this trap of a cell. She smiled, feeling a collective expletive of disappointment on the other side of the walls.

She wouldn't go soul journeying just yet. She would sit quietly in meditation. They might think she was a little white mouse in a sealed plexiglass cage, but what they didn't know, the gathered guards and scientists, was that most of the mouse wasn't in the mouse body at all. It was a question of who was surrounding whom.

***

"General Holden, Sir" the voice on the phone said, "the bird hasn't jumped."

"What's she doin?"

"Uhm, Sir, she seems to be meditating."

"Ok. Normal treatment for now. No pressure yet. Get a baseline. But watch her, she's smart."

"Yes, sir."

The General leaned back in his leather recliner, and pondered the video feed for a while. They might have to cause a little discomfort for that little body, just to observe what they needed to see. Bit of a shame, that, it really was a nice body, shame to waste it. He put his hands behind his head confident some brilliant idea would come to him. He had big plans for the CSA. They'd inherited a lot of good tools and good people. But he needed to learn how to crush these little rebels against God, before they corrupted his young people from within. And then in the dim light of his office as he admired his prey, he heard the skittle of tiny feet running across the polished wooden floor and just caught sight of a little grey mouse hurrying across the doorframe and into the crack behind the bookcase. He angrily punched the button to his aide de camp. That thing had better be gone by tomorrow or someone was gonna lose their head.

2. Compromising Positions

It wasn't long after Buchung left that Tashi came. He had decided that it was a good day to inspect the desecrated - depending on your point of view- chapel, though the excuse didn't fool him. He knew he just wanted to see her. It wasn't the confident Tashi of yesterday though. He was still more than a little shaken today, maybe even a little vulnerable today.

He entered through the open door, unsure of protocol. He took off his shoes, offered a silent prayer, and went into the sanctuary. He found her sitting quietly, head bowed, lost in thought, or just lost, he couldn't say. She looked simultaneously lost and exalted, like a half tumbled carving of a Tara one might find in a mountain grotto. He stood quietly for a while moved by something beyond her beauty. Then she turned to him with a slow grace and dignity. When their eyes met what breath he had left, fled into the freedom of some airy forever. Light almost literally pierced him, and he wanted to start all over, wanted to be all over again, never having been anything before but what was beginning just now.

They both began to talk at once, and then both stopped to let the other speak, and then both started to speak again at the same time. Then they both smiled.

"Faith, Miss Johannsen, I thought I might look at your chapel, with your permission."

"Yes, of course, Tashi. I'm glad you came. I'm so sorry about any damage we have caused."

And Tashi thought the chapel was beautiful, simple, and white, and spare and elegant in a peaceful way, as if a representation of some beginning before any gods and goddesses had yet been imagined, or perhaps even like the Dharmakaya itself. Maybe Tibetan tastes were just a little too garish, and less was more.

"I shouldn't be saying this, but I like it."

Faith thought of the paintings they had covered up so eagerly, and all the love and care and worship that had gone into their details.

"Oh, no, really, I am sorry, we should have been more sensitive. Some of the paintings were quite lovely."

And then they both laughed again.

"Tashi," she said, "can I invite you for some tea?"

And Tashi said, "Yes, yes, that would be wonderful, thank you."

3. Tsewang and the Dust

After the dawn had come and bloomed slowly into something else, and the light reflecting in the windows of the Potala had also moved to reflect elsewhere, as the angle between viewer and source and object and orbit was always shifting, Tsewang found himself still unable to sleep. Walking habitually the Khora with the other early morning circumambulants, waiting until a tea shop opened for tea and a hunk of bread, he felt sure he would find a way to share his vision. The joy of being vouchsafed a vision from the Goddess was with him, and now also, as the morning brightened, he felt increasingly his intellect become engaged. Coming now into the space in front of the Jhokhang, he went to perform Chak, the ritual prostrations, with a fervor he had never felt before. How many he did he couldn't say. He was covered with dust when he finally stood, for the snow had been swept away. He knew it to be a holy dust, fallen a long way from distant stars, or rather, dust that had aspired for a very, very long time to rise to this most auspicious of stations, to lie, day in and day out, prostrate in front of the Jhokhang itself. He smeared his dirty hands on his face and smiled, heading to a tea shop he hoped now would be open. He knew that some of the other worshipers had done prostrations for hundreds of miles to finally reach Lhasa, and the Jhokhang. He felt that his journey also, to this particular morning had been long, and certainly very winding.

Walking, ecstatic, ambling, smiling, he saw an old woman by the side of the path, come to sell trinkets. She sat by her blanket covered with little trinkets, happy, no doubt, to have found a place so near the holy of holies to sell what she had, rosaries, turquoise and silver jewelry, and colorful hats and scarves. Maybe it was the diamond glint in her eyes, or the warm smile in her weathered face, but Tsewang was drawn to her as if to his own mother. "Ama-la," he said, taking her old hands in his. She held his hands strongly, smiling directly into his eyes. Then she patted him on the head, and gave him one of her amulets. He reached to pay, but she smiled and shook her head and pushed him away, saying "wash your face!" He bowed his head in reverence, then continued his Khora. Looking at the little cheap amulet in his hands he saw it was an image of the Her, the Vajradakhini, She whom he had seen last night.

***

"What good is it!" Tashi said shaking his head, addressing himself as much to the world as to Dolma and Pangu. "What good is it! Amulets and prayers and poets. They have guns and scientists that are learning how to even invade the mind itself. They have the rich behind them, bankrolling them as they enslave us again with their dam cheap mental opium!"

"Tashi, you have me."

"You? You're an old truck, what good are you?"

"I have friends," said Pangu.

"What kind of friends can a truck have? Excavators? Front-loaders? They're probably friends like I have: friends when they want to borrow money, not when you need to borrow from them!"

"We have the Green Army," said Pangu.

"The Green Army? You mean the People's Liberation Army? They are too busy responding to floods and droughts, and the climate chaos of the global south, to do much to fight the likes of the CSA. No Pangu, we're screwed. It's going to be one big Christian mental shopping mall from Tokyo to Timbuktu, with some powerful Muslim caliphates here and there, too, to be sure."

"Tashi," said Pangu, "while what you say certainly has merit, and more than a little emotional heft, I think many adherents of those religions you mention actually agree with you about the aberration that is the militarization of religion."

"Bah, don't give me that gobbledygook. That's the kind of thing I have to say at work all day..."

"Tashi" asked Dolma sweetly, "so did you like her? That yinchee woman?"

"Who? Oh, you mean, her, uhmm, well, you know how it is. Perhaps Pangu can explain further, maybe leaving that part out, or maybe you don't have time Dolma-la. Aren't we almost to where you are going?"

"Not quite yet Tashi. I have time to hear more. Pangu?"

"Don't blindly believe what I say. Don't believe me because others convince you of my words. Don't believe anything you see, read, or hear from others, whether of authority, religious teachers or texts. Don't rely on logic alone, nor speculation. Don't infer or be deceived by appearances."

"Do not give up your authority and follow blindly the will of others. This way will lead to only delusion."

"Find out for yourself what is truth, what is real. Discover that there are virtuous things and there are non-virtuous things. Once you have discovered for yourself give up the bad and embrace the good."

-The Buddha-

1. Circles into Circles

Tsewang keep walking the Khora, Lhasa's inner circumambulation, the central smallest one that went around the Bharkor, and the Jhokhang itself. The image of the Vajradakhini now hung around his neck, and lay on the skin above his heart in the warm inner folds of his Chupah. He knew he was on his path, stumbler and bumbler though he might be. Mercy, even Akuh Tonpa -the clever trickster in Tibetan folktales- had managed to do a lot of good. "Why not me?" he thought. Wherever he looked he saw and felt a concordance of inner and outer. When he for some reason remembered a woman he had once lusted after, writing fevered line after fevered line, he glimpsed her doing the Khora far ahead of him. When he wondered which Ngak, mantra, would be most appropriate to recite now, a pigeon immediately flew down and alighted with the softest of coos on an inscription saying, "Om Ah Hung Benzra Guru Pema Siddhi Hung." Reciting it over and over, he felt Her everywhere, Her naked, insanely erotic form, dancing in all things: it was Her body, the Vajradakhini herself that plentifully filled the world in all the activities jostling around him.

There is a difference between insanity and transcendence he thought. In insanity, everything revolves around an engorged sense of self, not so much Atman is Brahman, as the Hindus would say, as Brahman is Atman. In transcendence, as he was beginning to understand, the self is also that cloud in the sky as much as his frozen toes, it is that old woman eyes closed sitting in the sun, as much as his itchy beard, it is that child laughing and chasing a puppy over there, and the puppy, too, as much as his hungry stomach. You became kind, not because being kind was called for, but because being kind to others was being kind to yourself, because they were yourself. "My God, " he thought, "if I keep going on like this I will go crazy!" And then he laughed again because he realized he was quite sexually aroused, drunk on Her as he was, and then laughed some more as he admitted to himself that these days, when so many secrets were in plain sight, mystical insight was about as cheap, as long-lasting, as a man's erection, and then he laughed again as he noticed people were watching him, laughing to himself as he was and with his face dirty with Her Holy dust. He looked around for a place to wash his face and settled for taking handfuls of clean snow, rubbing his face with it until he assumed he must be clean and ruddy-faced again. The snow woke him up into a different kind of being awake. A little less spiritual, and a little more visceral. He liked that idea: that the body was ballast to keep you grounded until such time as you could just walk off willy-nilly into space. He fully expected his space, when his time came, would assume some semblance of the form of the lovely, the enticing, the laughing, the profoundly arousing, Vajradakhini, and that she would lead him, dancing and smiling, up into her bed of nothingness-everythingness. In the meantime he would greatly enjoy the foreplay she was providing him, of human existence.

He caught sight of that yinchee woman walking the Khora ahead of him. And though he did not in general like yinchee women, finding the pale skin so unhealthy and sickly looking, this one was, -as he searched for and found the correct poetic technical terminology for a precise naturalistic description- very hot. More than that, she fit somehow into the emerging pattern. He decided to follow her, to allow the pattern to unfold, as if there was really much he could do about it. And then he immediately corrected that thought in his mind, for in fact he was part of the pattern too, and did have something to say and do about it. He speeded up his pace to catch up with her, but drawing near, he was astounded when someone else, a short nun, seemed to have the same idea. He watched as the nun caught up with her and walked beside her for a while before the yinchee woman noticed. He stopped as they both stopped and exchanged greetings. Soon, as if old friends, the nun took the inchee woman's hand and led her off. He followed as they went into a teashop. Tsewang thought he would head inside too, as much because he was drawn to this woman, these women, as because the thought of tea and hot bread was the kind of heaven he was searching for just now. The Earth might in fact be made of such stuff as dreams are made of, but then again so were dreams made of such stuff as the Earth was made of and these dreams very much needed feeding.

2. Tactical Decisions

Colonel Pike looked dourly around the room. Actually he was no longer a Colonel, he had been promoted to Brigadier General, but it just didn't sit well with him yet. Looking around the room, he tried to discern the difference between those who were actually physically present and those who were telepresent from elsewhere, some from remote locations. Although he knew which were which, it wasn't something he would have been able to tell just from looking, the quality was just that good. And that's was much the way headquarters felt to him. Everything looked great, but a lot of the people here he thought, didn't have a whole lot of substance to them. No, that wasn't fair, they were good, bright people, it's just they lacked his experience in the field.

Maybe in one way that was a good thing. Nobody really needed to be in the field anymore to tell the truth. Everything could be done through other means. He was a dying breed, and he knew it. He just wished he himself were someplace remote, very remote, and not in a telepresent sense. He wanted to be some place hard to get to and hard to get out of. Someplace alone on a mission. Out to hunt someone with his own life on the line. He wanted to feel alive, not like, what, like he was making a cameo appearance. No, headquarters had never been his cup of tea.

"So what's the recommendation?" asked Brigadier General Zachery Pike.

"Sir, we can't risk having the operation compromised. We need to terminate her."

"What's the basis for that soldier?"

"Sir, the agent in place thinks something has happened and that she may be too emotionally involved with the target."

"That's it? Let me get this straight: you're talking about a fellow soldier, one who's been trained for this, and as far as I can tell has been doing a good job. If that was you out there would you want someone to pull the plug on you because of one report of possible emotional involvement?"

"Sir, the agent who filed this has a lot of operational experience."

"What are the other options?"

"Sir, she's implanted. We can terminate her anytime we want. But I suggest we watch her closely and in the meantime, move that package to one of the back-up locations. We can have the agent-in-place tell her the plan's been aborted. She doesn't after all actually know the plan, so there's not much she could tell."

"Are you suggesting she's not loyal?"

"No Sir, it's just, a precaution."

"Precaution, huh. I tell you this whole," and he stopped himself from saying 'fucking,' "plan needed a little more thought about precautions. Can someone tell me who thought this whole dumb thing up?"

There was absolute, perfect, stillness around the table. Not a muscle, even a remotely telepresent muscle, stirred. Only one young and foolish soldier looked upward for the briefest of moments, to indicate the plan had come from on high.

"Right. Move the package. Have her told the plan's been terminated. Monitor her closely. If she gets turned, we'll turn her back and run her as a double. You," and he indicated the soldier who had blinked heavenward, "brief me on all of the run-throughs for this so-called 'operation' what's it called –'Jericho One'?'- especially the one's that didn't go well."

"Yessir."

"The rest of you, go through your back-up plans, and then the back-up to your back-plans, and then run the damn simulations again with even those going wrong and the next time you come in here telling me to end a soldier's life on the basis of one uncorroborated judgment call, I'll implant all of you and press the no go button just for the shear heck of it. Now get out of here."

***

"General!" said the General. "So good to see you. How you settling in here at HQ? Pretty boring compared to what you're used to I suppose. Come on have a seat, let's talk." General Holden took Brigadier General Pike by the hand and shoulder as if they were about to begin some formal pas de deux and sat him down in a stuffed leather chair in the corner of Holden's quite well-equipped office. He stood above Zach for a moment, the light behind him, making him into a big shadow of a mountain, and as if taking a good look at the new Brigadier and deciding what to do next.

"So, Zach," said General Holden, sitting himself slowly down in an identical stuffed leather chair that shared the same corner, "You don't much like my plan, do you?"

"With all due respect General, no, I do not."

"That's alright Zach. I knew you wouldn't. That's why I brought you in. I want you to fix it." And he smiled a big smile. General Holden was a big man. Even sitting in the chair, he took up a lot of space. Zach felt he was sharing the corner with some dark powerful force that could just barely make it into the shape of a man. "So tell me Zach, where did I go wrong? I want you to level with me and I know you will, after all the, forgive my French, boot-licking I get around here these days, a little honesty will be refreshing." General Holden smiled that big smile of his and Zach realized he must be doing something to have such perfect teeth.

"Sir, I might be able to fix it tactically if I can have more time, but I need to understand what our strategic objective is. To be blunt I don't completely understand why we are revealing these capabilities on a target that just doesn't seem all that important."

"Zach I'm not a soldier's soldier, I know that. You are. I've been stuck back here far, far too long, fighting on the political front. That's a different kind of fighting Zach. One day a friend's a friend, the next day he's your enemy." The general paused to regard Zach mournfully. "Everybody's stabbing everybody in the back and trying to make it look like they're doing you a favor. So I may have lost my touch for military tactics, that's a given, but strategy, I think I still know a thing or two. Look, it comes down to this. The world thinks we're backed into a corner, that the CSA isn't gonna last that long, that one day we'll wake up and smell the roses of peace and we'll go traipsing off into never-never land holding hands with all the pagan priests and priestesses. But I got news for you. That's not gonna happen. There is just one true God, and all the rest of it, no matter how sweet and reasonable and sexy it may seem, is the Devil's work. I don't know if these are the End Times or not, but that little girl up there on her hill," and he raised his great spectral finger to point, "she's worse than the Whore of Babylon, and damned if I'm not going to put her in her place.

"Sir, there are ways to do that without anyone knowing."

"You think I don't know that? A designer bug for example that wouldn't be able to kill anyone else but her? No, I want this to be big, and public, and humiliating, in her own front yard, in front of the whole world, in her face." and he smiled, his perfect teeth almost bright enough to light the dim corner.

"But sir, what's our justification?"

"Justification?" and he laughed somewhere between a laugh and a bark. "We don't need any justification, we have the Word of God. What better justification can there be? But oh, I know, you mean the diplomatic niceties. Look Zach, we'll warn them to stop peddling their smut and propaganda into the minds of our impressionable young people, and they won't listen, and even if they listened, there's not much that they can do about it 'cause the mind, is well, you know, the mind. No, they sit up their on the Plateau thinking they have the scientific and moral high ground. And we can't allow that. We are the moral high ground. Tibet always was the center of the Great Game, even when we didn't know where it was or how the hell to get there. We're gonna start playing that game again. Only we're gonna play hard ball." The General's smile lit up even the far corners of the room, blowing away all doubts and concerns as merely the small cowardices of lesser men. General Holden sat staring at Zach for a bit, bathing him in his vision.

Zach made as if to speak, but General Holden leaned forward, put his hand on Zach's knee, fixed him with his dead blue wolf's eyes, "Son," he asked 'what did they teach you back at the Academy about the Long War, the so-called War on Terror?" He leaned back into his chair again, like a kindly professor waiting to hear his favorite student's answer.

"Sir," said Zach, 'that was a long time ago, and after being in the field so long, I don't care a whole lot about theories."

"Come on Zach, what did they teach you?"

Zach felt compelled to answer, "Well Sir, they said it was a massive loss of blood and treasure. That the blowback from all of the people we pissed off turned out to be worse than the rather minor forces that were arrayed against us. That the bankruptcy of the economy caused by spending all that time and money on a military solution to something that didn't have a military solution was one of the precipitating causes for the break-up of the United States."

"And what do you think about that analysis?

"Sir, I don't think much of it one way of the other. I'm a soldier, I take orders."

"No! You're a General now, you lead, you don't take orders. And if you're gonna be a General in the Christian States of America, Zach..." and the rage that had been beginning to build in General Holden, now suddenly softened, "son, the long war has been going on a long time. It started with Jesus, and it didn't end when they took His body off the cross, no. He Rose again and He's been leading it ever since. He's the one giving us the marching orders. And don't let anyone tell you it's all about love and forgiveness. He's not done until He's conquered this world and He won't do it by holding hands with the heathen. He'll do it with the blood and guts of soldiers like you and me. Life is his to give and life is his to take, and anyone who doesn't follow him is in league with evil and deserves whatever punishment they get. So let me tell you General what your orders are: this is His earth, and the filthy anti-Christ, that Princess of Illusion, is gonna get chased out of the Lord's temple, and anyone that dares to stand in His way is gonna end up in a deep pit of fire." General Holden paused his eyes shining a deep and satisfying red, the reflection of an exit sign someplace no doubt, thought Zach. Then General Holden took a deep breath and breathed it out slowly, "General Pike, this is a long, long war. It won't ever come to an end until God himself and His Son decide to bring it to an end. In the meantime, our orders are to take this earth for Him, as His Promised land. And do we stop there? No." General Holden looked away slowly, tilting his head up a bit, peering into limitless blackness, "No, this galaxy has 100 billion planets give or take a few, and, if it is his will, we will take them all."

Zach didn't really know what to say. He knew the General liked to give this particular performance but he hadn't ever heard it in person. Had he been a believing person, Zach would have fallen on his knees and asked the General to pray with him. He half expected that was what the General was going to ask him to do. Instead though he steeled himself to say, "General, I want to delay this operation until I think we're ready.

"No, no" came the roar, "we go with the timetable. You just fix it so it works."

"Yessir," and Zach rose, saluting, knowing it was time to retreat in the face of a superior, or at least crazy, enemy. Crossing the floor of General Holden's office was as long a mile as Zach had ever faced under fire. Reaching for the doorknob and release he heard, 'Zach,' and he turned. General Holden came lumbering toward him, placed his hand on his shoulders and said, "Zach, son, we've got your daughter. I want you to talk with her."

With all of his self-control now marshaled to show no expression he asked, "Is she OK?"

"She's fine son, but you need to talk with her."

3. Good Work if You Can Get It

Aaron thought he would try a different tactic with his mother. He'd enlist her help. Trying to tolerate her, well, ignore her actually, just wasn't doing the trick. No, he'd think of this as a little experiment. True, there was no real control to compare it to, so instead he'd think of it as a preliminary set of observations upon which he could then, maybe later, base a real experiment.

"Mom, mom," he called out softly and politely, "can we talk?" he was hoping no one would hear him talking to himself, though at any rate his mom didn't seem to be paying attention at the moment. "Mom, I really need you just now, so if you get this message, from wherever you are, I'd appreciate it if you would, you know, get back to me." He glanced hopefully at the places she often showed up, the ceiling, the top of the bookcase, the more dimly lit corners, but his office, seemed to be just his office at the moment. It was, now that his mother wasn't distracting him, he admitted, quite a mess. He thought that if he cleaned up his office he'd probably find a lot of loose ends going in various interesting directions, and the thought of that, cleaning up, decided him on going home a little early today. The day had been a wash and he was tired. The mocha hadn't been enough, and he needed some needed, motherless -wanting to talk though he did- sleep.

Riding his bicycle home through the late afternoon of a Boston Winter -that of course didn't feel the way a Boston Winter should or he probably wouldn't be bicycling- Aaron felt more than a little on the "can't" side of cantankerous. A third of his city was already flooded and abandoned. It didn't make economic sense to protect against that amount of sea level rise, and they were dependent for emergency food rations on huge greenhouses. The weather was so chaotic, -megastorms and megadroughts, flash heat-waves and the occasional weird blizzard- that not only were the plants confused, the open air, old fashioned kind of farmers had a hard time adapting. He guessed the only good thing was that the new resettlement communities were quite beautiful: green gems of architectural sustainability. But the waiting lists were very long and the temporary housing was basic.

He considered himself lucky to live in a part of town too high to need relocating from, but mostly he was angry at the idiots who had let this happen. The Koch Brothers and the dirty energy corporations had bought the politicians and made them delay and delay and delay until it was too late to prevent the earth from shifting into its hot phase. And then, the ones that could, the one's that needed to escape the wrath and the legitimate demands for climate justice, found safe harbor in of all places the Christian States of America. Hell, not only did they find safe harbor, they seem to have helped to bankroll its God-damned founding. The shifting of the earth to another climate phase was still going on and would go on for a long time, and while the earth was just doing its clearly-predicted-by-the-physics climactic phase-shift thing, humanity was on the verge of destruction and scrambling for all it was worth to find a silver bullet or two in all the chaos. On top of that was the craziness of the Bardo worlds, all made visible and easily accessible. A lot of people were just saying screw it and not coming back.

As he was about to reach his apartment complex he thought of the wonderful, the great, the small and pudgy Mr. Dunsworthy, and his mood brightened. Aaron would keep the technology proprietary of course, but basically it would be a black box with Mr. Dunsworthy, or his well-trained equivalent, inside drinking a six-pack and watching football. Good-by Lamas, hello ESPN. He'd call his corporation "SpiritBGone" or something like that. He was in such a good mood that after locking his bicycle he took the stairs up to his floor. Coming out of the stairwell and looking down the hall to the door at the end which was his he experienced a weird perceptual flash, like subliminal marketing interspliced into his visual train –two men in dark suits leaving his apartment- but it was gone even before it arrived. He entered his apartment a little more tentatively than usual though, and looked carefully around, even tiptoeing into the bathroom to pull the shower curtain back with a surprise jerk. But everything looked the way he had left it: basically a mess, but his mess. He thought of calling the FBI agent he had met today, Lt. O'Conner, but figured he would just think he had gone as crazy as the rest of the world. He wished he had asked the Lt. how they could put someone away for committing murder if most of the world these days thought death was just a transition into a slightly less expensive state of existence. Nah, he was just tired. The mind plays tricks on tired people. He'd have a good dinner, put up the "Mom Do Not Disturb" sign, and go to bed early.

***

"Pangu, I'm sorry it just doesn't make a lot of sense to me anymore. Your story, my life, even why we are going to Lhasa. I'm beginning to think we will never arrive. Dolma's going to be leaving us and then I'll just be stuck with you and your gossip."

"Tashi, I could display the interconnections in a graphic way if you prefer. There really is a pattern here that is quite clear, if we just take the spatial separations away and allow the intentions and mindsets to unfold and demonstrate their proximity to each other."

"Bah leave your graphs for some other fool. If you can't tell a story in such a way it doesn't seem like a bunch of random bits stuck together haphazardly then you really should go back to hauling manure. Something you are good at."

"Tashi," said Dolma. "You're just in a bad mood. Pangu's a wonderful storyteller. I was going to invite all of you to stop at my house as we are almost there, but now I don't know, maybe I will just let Pangu rest for a while!"

"Ok, ok, I'm sorry. But I've had to deal with this crazy robot truck's stories for many years! He seems to think you can jump from one thing to the other and people will be able to follow him! I'm just trying to help him out, him and his strange obsession."

"Dolma, it is this road up here that we take for about a kilometer to get to your house, correct? I know the village. Are we still invited?"

"You are all most welcome! Now go on with this little adventure before we have our own little adventure. I'm hoping you will be able to embarrass Tashi a bit more!"

***

"...auspiciousness comes through interdependent originations. The action of our mind and body, which produces the auspiciousness, is the reason that our mind is powerful enough to bring this auspiciousness to our lives. We have to determine whether or not to be positive with our mind, speech, and body. Based on that we can delve deeper into the spiritual path."

Lama Lodu Rinpoche

1. Tea for Two and a Half

The spirits circled around the scene of Lhasa again turning into dusk. Spirits able to see what we mostly cannot, traveling trails that to our earthly eyes seem twisted and odd, connecting seemingly unconnected things, living in a world where intimacies never have any space between them, no matter what the physical distance. Spirits, wanting to nudge things right, with their feather, less than feather nudges, their whispered, less than a whisper whispers, seeing right through us, but seeing us also in a different light, the heavy ghosts we are, the most wonderful theater of the real, remembered, for the spin, the power it imparted to them even now, memories never faded but fully present and formed if not fleshed out.

These spirits knowing what we think, even before we think it –thought once thought already being slow- knowing what we will say even before we say it -words once spoken doubly triply slow- these spirits have circled around Tashi and Faith now, knowing that Tashi thought the tea she gave him was bad. Knowing that he thought Faith was very beautiful, even more beautiful than when he had first met her. And the spirits circling still around the pair bathe in the glow of what had transfigured Faith, sipping from it joyously as she sits there in front of him, radiant, and glowing with a sexual power that didn't stop at the loins but flowed up and out her heart, and all of the spirits could see, could feel it, and knew/felt that Tashi, too could feel it, though he was having trouble finding words to speak, though the spirits were suggesting oh so many words he might try, and the spirits knew, too, that Tashi would have drunk whatever Faith gave him, vinegar, poison, boiling piss, so bad tea by Tibetan standards, was a lucky blessing indeed. And the spirits knew, having seen it over the span of several eternities, that there are moments of wholeness, when mandalas of love are formed, and sometimes last as long as anything lasts, and that this might be one of them, that the course of whatever theater of the real and unreal depending on which side of the dream one lived, would forever be changed in ways forever changing and this is why the spirits circled, wanting to bless and be blessed by this moment, were it to occur, occurring as it seemed it might, as it seemed to be.

2. Spilt Milk

Kundol Dolma was crying. She couldn't help it. She didn't know how to keep Tibet from turning into a giant sand pit. Everything was just unraveling so fast, the glaciers, the soil, the high altitude wetlands, the permafrost, especially the permafrost. It had been methane -a big pulse of it from melting methane clathrates- that had been one of the main causes of the earth tumbling into the PETM, the Paleocene-Eocene Thermal Max. If you liked crocodiles feeling comfortable above the arctic circle, and desert almost everyplace else, it wasn't a bad earth. The good thing about the PETM was, fast as it was on geological scales of time, it was relatively slow compared to what was happening now. Back then a small range of plants and animals had been able to adapt. Now however, methane from the melting permafrost was being pumped into the atmosphere at a pace a hundred times faster than it was released in that incident. They were all in uncharted territory. But one thing was clear, they were in the midst of the 6th great die-off in earth's history and human beings were the mass murderers. Only the most aggressive of species would make it though this one, and of course humanity was nothing if not aggressive, so some at least of the more aggressive representatives of humanity would probably survive. Why was it always that violence and greed seemed to pay, while compassion and caring just got bulldozed over?

She was back in her laboratory now at the Tibet University. Actually she had been there all along. It had been super high resolution advanced imagery coupled with telepresence technology that had allowed her to traipse the high peaks at will. All of her senses had been engaged, not just sight. She could smell, and feel the wind as well as any snow lion on a crag. But all of that power left her powerless and sad. What else could they do, she wondered? They were trying everything they could, short of full-scale geoengineering, and there were those pushing for that, dangerous though it was. And it was all so unnecessary. Why hadn't they acted in time? Why had they trashed the planet and the climate when political leaders had been warned so clearly? And she was ashamed also of the country of her birth, The United States. It had seemingly torn itself apart over the simple act of facing reality and shouldering responsibility. Why? How could any religion justify ecocide? How could any cabal of the rich and well-connected justify a few more years of short-term profits when in the long-run they were going to pull everything down around them? China at least, had realized it was a matter of its own survival and had moved to make the transition massively and quickly. And now the world's hope had also moved its gaze in China's direction. And Tibet, Tibet too, was shining. Tibet had known for a very long time that in the pursuit of happiness, "more things" were a poor substitute for richness of mind and kindness of heart.

Kundol was angry, sad, and frustrated. She left her office and went out into the hall thinking she would find her American-Tibetan colleague Sherab, and he would make her laugh, with his New York street attitude and his bad Tibetan. There was even a Tibetan comedy team that had made their fame by having one of them play the part of a Tibetan returned from overseas, and trying so hard to be a pure Tibetan, but not quite getting anything right. It was all so sweet and yet hilarious, and Sherab, was the real McCoy. Tibetan through and through except in every outward thing he tried to do as a Tibetan. She'd go find him, invite him for coffee, and see how his research was going. Feeling better already she raced down the stairs only to come out into a crowd on the main floor. Feeling annoyed she started to head back up the stairs then thought to ask someone what was going on. "Gyalwa Rinpoche is coming!" was the excited whispered reply. Then Kundol remembered she had heard that Her Holiness was going to visit today and she decided to stay to see her pass. Though she was in the very back of a crowd along the corridor, she thought she would be able to catch a glimpse because Kundol Dolma was a tall Tibetan woman. One advantage of all that American protein-rich diet, she thought.

And then there came a wave of whispering and of heads bowed and khataks offered. And with it the most palpable wave of joy also came over her and all around her. Her Holiness was making her way slowly down the corridor, a young, short, and very beautiful nun. It was hard to see her, because those around her, including her attendant nuns, and her security, were much taller, but every once in a while she reached out of her retinue to take someone's hand and smile and say a few words. Kundol began to cry again, but this time from an overpowering compassionate joy that welled up within her, overwhelming her with happiness. In another situation she might have been ashamed to be crying, to be showing so much weakness in public, but she knew that many around her were doing the same thing. She could barely see, so rich were the tears running down her face, when the blurry face of a young nun found it's way through the crowd, and stood for just a moment in front of her.

Her Holiness, the Dalai Lama took her hand, just for a moment, but for forever in a way, and said, "Tukshezhe" and then was gone, though still with her, as Kundol Dolma sobbed with happiness.

3. In the Bosom of the Mother of Night

Aaron, with a profound sense of gratitude for the perfect softness of his pillow, rested his weary head in its soft bosom. His body, thankfully, was just too tired for him to have his manifold ideas, worries and weaknesses keep him even marginally awake tonight. He didn't even try to watch for that moment when consciousness left him and he was, well, no longer any longer aware of being anything at all, no Aaron, no body, no nothing, no nothing at all. He soon found himself, without even the second thought of a third thought of a reasonable segue, addressing an audience at a symposium. He was concluding his usual talk about the fallacies of assuming that the Bardo Tech proved either the existence of an afterlife, or the presence of a universal continuum of mind.

"Ladies and Gentlemen, when we dream at night, we populate that world with images from our brain and it all seems real, external, and objective. But it is all us, all the time. These are nothing but the projections of what is already within in us. The same is true of the Bardo Worlds. True, quantum interconnectedness allows us to interact with each other's projections, but there is still no "there" there. When the brain is damaged, the brain loses the ability of the specific function of the damaged part. No further proof is needed of the truth of what I say. We are our body and its brain, and liberation comes not from seeing who can have the wildest endorphin-induced hallucinations, but in accepting the reality of our situation. Thank you."

There was wild applause, but mostly from a familiar-looking woman in the back, and a short pudgy fellow in the front who reminded him of the deprogrammer, Dunsworthy or whatever, he had met today. He noticed that there seemed to be a few empty seats around him, to the side, to the front, and in back, also.

"Any questions?"

"Sir," said a rather attractive young student in the very front row, "by your analogy, if one of the circuits in my TV broke, and I was no longer able to view the show, that would mean that the show itself was entirely resident in the TV, when in fact the TV set is just a mechanism for viewing information embedded in a frequency that is invisible, but all around us."

"I am not saying that the TV frequencies –the quantum interconnectedness- do not exist independently of us, I am saying that the programming on the frequencies is something that we, meaning our brains, create. The shows, the characters, the creatures of our imagination, while real enough perceptually, do not exist, when we do not imagine them."

"Sir," said a deep rumbling voice from a dark back recess, a voice wrapped in a dark old-fashioned cloak, and dark scarves, and wearing a black beret and dark glasses, "I find that proposition insulting, pompous and anthropocentric in almost equal measures." And the dark figure grew larger and darker, "you have ruined your world with your pride and ignorance, and now that you have stumbled upon ours, you think it belongs to you, that your dreams are the only dreams that are real, and that all of us, who have lived here long before you were fashioned from dirt, are just figments of your little imagination. I think that you are due a lesson for your arrogance." And the darkness grew to become the angry maw of a storm front stretching across the horizon. The auditorium disappeared, and the pudgy man in front said, "I'm outa here," and the familiar woman in back said, "don't worry honey," and the cute coed in front looked at him a little disappointed as if on really meeting him for their first tryst he had proved rather boring. Aaron woke up, in the soft bosom of his pillow, his heart racing and sweat pouring down his face.

***

And now they were at Dolma's village. Just a few houses really set about the few fields left in place as the mountains around them tumbled abruptly down into a valley through which a torrent of a mountain stream plunged, and then poured down beside the dirt track that had driven up from the main road. Seeing the long mani wall, with Om Mani Padme Hum carved all along it and the hulking dark clouds of Yak eating barley husks set out for them, and the cheerful painted wooden lintel of her house, Tashi felt relieved. Relieved by the solidity of it, and the carved stones. "This is a beautiful village Dolma. I must say, I am quite happy to find out that you are real. I was beginning to think you were a Khadroma!"

"Tashi, maybe I am! Now come inside, you too Pangu," and Tashi followed, and Pangu materialized, too, as the old farmer, and before he entered he marveled at the rainbow for a moment ringing the now risen sun. The day was already exceedingly strange he thought, still morning though it was. So many auspicious signs, and so many troubling ones, too.

Inside, the house was quite bright and modern. Anticipating his question, Dolma pointed to the roof and said, "Solar panels."

"Ah, " nodded Tashi. He could hear prayers coming from the Chukan nearby and looked to Dolma for explanation.

"My father and his students," she whispered, eyes flashing with inner lightning, "they should be finished soon." Dolma busied herself preparing cups of Tibetan butter tea, and laying out some of the kaptse that the Grandmother up the road had sent with them. She smiled at Tashi, obviously happy to be home, and then turned to Pangu, in his old farmer guise, almost mischievously, "Pangu, if you can whisper, you can go on with your story, at least until Father is done with his students."

"Dolma-la, I am able to form the acoustic waveforms so it will seem as if it is being whispered directly into your ears. That way you will both be able to hear it clearly, and it will also be very quiet. I mean if that is OK with the two of you."

Tashi grumbled, biting into a kaptse, and Pangu knew he could go on.

***

*"The universe is not black and white, not simply
a physical world and the Void. It contains a
rainbow of intermediate worlds; each with
lessons to teach and forms of experience to
encounter that can add depth and meaning to
the spirit. Even the highest Buddhas, whose
minds are the Clear Light of the Void, echo in
emanations through the intermediate worlds,
through the jhanas (the worlds outside the six
lokas or realms of rebirth), through the
sambhogakaya levels, and down into the worlds
of reincarnation. This means that there is no
world without a doorway, even in the lowest
worlds of ignorance and suffering. Yet those
who seek to abolish suffering may end up
extending it, for by taking away the roads to the
spiritual worlds, there is no escape except by
levitation, or the mercy of the bodhisattvas."*

Commentary on the Vajra Dakini

1. A Gilded Lotus

Buchung –Sam really–, wondered if he had done the right thing. Faith was a good lady, and he liked her, maybe even loved her. But he had too many times seen a well-meaning yinchee seduced by the seeming compassion of Tibetans. The poor searching foreigners so easily came unmoored and were soon floating off into some imaginary land of love and light where they could no longer see the Yak dung at their feet. Who knows, maybe they just weren't used to the altitude. And the Tibetans could string them out for all it was worth. The Lamas were the worst of all. They dangled "Enlightenment" in front of these poor lost foreigners, but all along they were just collecting donations and gold watches, and yes, seducing the occasional lady follower with fake Tantric rituals, the only liberation offered being that of the Lama's semen from his shriveled member.

He had seen it for himself back in his village in Nepal, a poor Tamang village, with a rich Tibetan Buddhist temple. Why had it been that the Lama and his monks ate so well, while he, and his family, and most of the families in that village, barely got by from year to year and meal to meal? Buchung didn't think it was karma, he thought it was clever, deeply inculcated social manipulation via superstition and idolatry. In his own family there hadn't been enough to go around, and seeing the hunger in the eyes of his younger brothers and sisters, Buchung had finally decided to take things into his own hands. At the age of 12 he had walked for days until he reached Kathmandu. There he had been lucky, if that was the word, to find a job painting tankas for tourists. The tanka master liked to employ children because their fingers were small and nimble, and they worked for almost nothing. That's why he had been so happy to have helped whitewash over the tanka murals painted on the walls of their chapel. He couldn't stand the "Holy" images anymore. All they inspired in him were memories of beatings and hunger.

He had been very lucky. A Franciscan Father had taken a liking to him and asked him to paint Christian murals on the walls of a little chapel in Kathmandu. The Father had helped him to resume his education, actually begin his education. He had proved adept, soaking up everything he was given to learn, with a memory that was photographic, every bit as good as his tanka painting skills. Eventually the Father had helped him to go to America to get an education at a Christian college. The care, the love, the friendship he found, and the message of Christ's radical acceptance of him personally, unmediated by hierarchies upon hierarchies of this Lama or that Lama in this lineage or that lineage had led him to a fever pitch of devotion. He was saved. Washed in the blood of the Lamb, and when a recruiter offered him a chance to serve his Savior in the Army of God, he had embraced that path whole-heartedly.

He was good at what he did. Very good, as good as he had been as a tanka painter or as an excellent student. But he still felt some concern. He knew the capabilities the CSA had when it came to the possibility of an agent being turned in the field, though this was exceedingly rare for Christians. Most happily accepted martyrdom, as he had been taught. Still, when word came to move the package to the backup site and tell Faith that the plan had been cancelled, he felt relieved. He thought she was doing more good for the cause, just by being Faith, beautiful, humble, kind missionary, then Faith, Soldier, Army of God.

2. No Place in the Inn

They sat staring at each other by not staring at each other. The door into the chapel was open so they mostly watched the subtle changing of the light on the white walls and well-swept wooden floor as the afternoon patiently approached the cusp of the edge of evening. The tea sat mostly untouched. The spirits had all the time in the world, and time, here, in this place, seemed to have done some odd thing, and instead of keeping time, it had decided it was tired of all that martial inevitability, and so it was happily, bemusedly wandering in circles of dust eddies, pleased with the very emptiness of the rooms, and the difficulty the two strangers had in speaking, so strongly bound were they -not just in desire wanting to topple over into intimacy- but in wanting to get it just right, the opening to each other that, once done, would be difficult to close again.

Faith had no illusions about the situation she was in. Her mind was clearer than it had ever been, and she recalled every particular and nuance of her training. They had gotten her young, and done a thorough job. She had a fire and a strength in her that had responded well to the discipline. She had earned her posting to Tibet through merit and hard work. The faith they had put in her was not misplaced. Yet all of that barely held her any more. It had become little more than cobwebs to brush away. It hadn't taken torture or rape to break her. All it had taken was a little girl's smile at midnight to set her heart on fire with such love that it had burned down her old self, and left her standing above those ashes wondering how she had ever been comfortable wearing them. She had returned home from a long dream of strange wanderings, where everything had seemed to have made sense until she had woken up and it had all turned out to have been mostly nonsense. She saw the cross hanging on the chapel wall and understood it was hers. She could not serve two masters. If she followed the life aching warmly now in her they would kill her, or worse, much worse. They did not take kindly to traitors.

Tashi on the other hand, just wanted forgiveness. Whatever faith this Faith followed, must be a true faith for she was radiant with a true radiance. He thought he would have the greatest difficulty ever moving far from her side, if it ever came to that. He was still shaken from his nocturnal adventure with Tsewang gone wrong. So he sat in silence, not watching her as she didn't watch him, both of them seeming to see something prepossessingly beautiful in the empty chapel. The spirits slowly circled enthralled around this pregnant nexus of maybe, whispering amongst themselves from time to time, and vainly trying to nudge these two with spirit nudges into closer communion, futile though that was. And then, almost as if he had been etched into the sides of a crystal vase that had been falling in such slow motion as to feel like levitation, but in fact now struck a very real rock, Tsewang entered the chapel door, stamped his feet to knock snow from his boots and cloak, looked around like a great slow Yak and bellowed "Anybody home?"

3. Mandalas and Quilts

Aaron was not pleased. His mother was laughing at him, and was dressed, again, in a manner that had she not been his mother, might have kept him from easily returning to the sleep he so desperately needed. Boogey men did not scare him, at least not for long, but as a bachelor there were times when he was sensitive to the entreaties, imagined or otherwise, of the far superior by far, not weaker at all, sex.

"Mother we do need to talk. In fact I was hoping you would show up not long ago, but right now, I really can't. I can't begin to tell you how exhausted I am. Please just this once, a little sleep would go a long way toward repairing my sanity, or what's left of it."

"Oh my poor dear," she said with the utmost care and solicitation, moving toward him as if to lay a very gentle hand upon his brow, her lips quite moist and pouty, "but darling, you know, you are sleeping. This is what is known as a false awakening."

"False awakening?" Aaron looked around his bedroom, searching for clues that it was a dream, but everything seemed to be in its untidy place, except of course for his mother, who was moving uncomfortably closer to him.

"You know, dear, I could take a different form, someone not quite so familiar to you if that would make you more comfortable."

"No, Mom, please, please, I'm just so tired. I need to go back to sleep, or at least not dream that I am awake trying to go to sleep or something like that."

"Aaron, my love, there are many ways out of a false awakening, including waking up into another false awakening. On the other hand you could just realize it is a dream and go lucid. Isn't that really want you want?" she asked, beginning to sway diaphanously.

"No mother, I spend all day studying lucid states, and when I come home tired, I expect the light to go fully out."

And then she reached his side, and he couldn't help but appreciate how full, swaying, pendulant she was as a woman, and when she reached out and placed her index finger on his forehead, electricity shot through him and he arched up like some poor fish getting electroconvulsive therapy, and then he really was awake, sitting bolt upright, his blankets flung off to the far corners of what still seemed to be his room.

***

Dolma's father's students traipsed silently out of the Chukan, like a flood of liquid joy, filling any darkness that might have been lingering anywhere in Tashi's heart, if not the planet. There were a half dozen of them, men and women equally divided, all wearing Tibetan Chupah, but not what is worn for special occasions, rather the ordinary plain woolen Chupah of farmers.

They greeted Dolma warmly and she in turn offered each of them tea and kaptse. There was something special about the kaptse, as they all fell silent for a moment upon tasting it, and then broke into a unanimity of broad smiles. One of the women asked if Dolma had made it. "No, these were made by a Grandmother living up the road a ways. The place of the grove of trees with the many birds and the cave shrine." "Ah" came the collective recognition followed by a renewed attention to and appreciation of the kaptse. Tashi, too, found some power, if nothing else, of delicious perfection, in the kaptse he was eating.

And then Dolma's father came out. He was old, but looked young. Or rather he was young but looked old. His was a vibrant combination of energy and wisdom, in a handsome face graced with a short pate of white hair that seemed to glow of its own accord. "Daughter! Welcome home! And you have brought guests!"

"Father, this is Tashi-la, he works at the Office of Religious Affairs in Lhasa, and this is Pangu-la, he's..."

"A truck!" finished her father, and everyone laughed. "Would you look at this, we just prayed and talked about The Four Noble Truths and no sooner are we done when desire in the form of kaptse wins again!"

"Father, these are very special kaptse. When you try them you will agree, in this case at least that desire very much should win!" and when her father took the first bite, he too, beamed. All of them gathered together beaming from ear to ear, like a bunch of crumb-covered fools! And everyone began laughing again.

"I don't know what that Grandmother puts in her kaptse, but it can't just be flour!" said father.

And so it went for a while. Everyone laughing and joking and drinking tea and eating what was left of the kaptse, until it was time for the students to go back to their work, their chores, their lives. When everyone was gone father looked at Tashi and smiled and said, "Now as for you young man, there is nothing wrong with you that a good wife can't fix." And Tashi blushed, not that Tibetans blush, ruddy-faced as they already are. "And," continued Dolma's father, "I guess our job here today is to help you on your way to Lhasa."

"Thank you Bala, father, the journey is proving a bit longer than usual, but in a nice way."

"Ah yes, my daughter tends to have that affect on young men." And Tashi again looked down a bit, sheepishly. "But in the meantime, let's hear a bit more from our famous story-telling truck. Pangu, where were you in this little adventure?"

"Yes teacher," said the old farmer/truck, "I will go on a bit more."

***

Chapter 18. I Am Unto You, a Chapel Breeched, a Promise Unkept

"I examined the brain, looking for the CPU, but I couldn't find it. I believe in fact that the brain is just a download device and that the CPU is elsewhere."

Danny Hillis, Thinking Machines Corporation

1. Agglutinated Fricatives

Once fully inside Tsewang saw Tashi through the open door into the side room off the chapel. Tashi's face, bathed in near beatitude, suddenly seemed to shatter into the grimy shards of a broken icon as he caught sight of Tsewang. Tsewang felt a little guilty at having followed him, followed the yinchee woman, really, but then of course Tashi had showed up, too. And that too, fit this pattern. He could still just barely make out the threads of inner light, of connection between them all that he had begun to discern and which he had followed in following her since the morning. Everything was connected to everything else by a light that was normally invisible, and the strongest sinews in that light were grown from loving-kindness.

So Tsewang felt that it wasn't so much really that he was following them, as that he was pulled along by her, by them, that he was just being open to something that was happening and was still to happen. Vision-riddled though he was, he was also still a poet and didn't have much trust in second-guessing and rationalization. He believed in the significance of the now. That each day was full of meanings wrapped in riddles. It was his habit both to try to understand them and to break expectations and battle the habitual. He was moreover today so enraptured with the near-imminence of the Vajradakhini hanging around his neck that he thought he was doing her bidding in following her threads, in following the yinchee woman into this foreign place. Going inside he found it stark, bare, unadorned, cold as a corpse. There were no mediating images to make a bridge between the body and the mind. There was nothing but those two strange crossed sticks on the wall. Almost on the verge of feeling daunted for a moment he crossed the chapel to the side room needing to tell Tashi he was sorry for the Chöd that had gone wrong, and to tell him and the yinchee woman that there was a great danger brewing and something had to be done, and that somehow he sensed they would be able to help.

"Tashi, Tashi, I'm so sorry I didn't mean to interrupt, and Mam," and he bowed and put his hand over his heart, "please forgive me for coming uninvited into your Holy space, but I feel, somehow we have been called together and I wanted to share what is in my heart today."

Tashi glared harshly, and started to speak, but Faith, smiling gently answered first, "All are welcome here. Come, have some tea." With a smile and a graceful wave to a seat, she got up to get another cup, half-turning back to look at Tashi's less then welcoming face and saying, almost as if to a misbehaving child, "Tashi won't you introduce your friend?"

"Faith this is Tsewang, Tsewang this is Faith. Tsewang is a," slight pause, "friend."

Faith returned to the table with a cup, and Tsewang marveled at how the light for a moment illuminated the tea in the space between the teapot and the teacup, as if the whole point of the exercise wasn't the brewing or the drinking, but the pouring of the living, lambent liquid through the void. Not even waiting for Faith to ask him if he wanted milk or sugar Tsewang drank it all at one gulp, loving the bitter medicinal taste and imagining immediately a power rising in him. He turned to Faith, his face shining in the light the way the cascading tea had just shone and asked, "Do you have anything to eat?"

Faith, and even Tashi laughed. "I'm so sorry," apologized Tsewang, "it's just I haven't eaten all day.

2. No Better Mousetrap

Brigadier General Zachary Pike marched toward the building where his daughter was being held accepting the small good fortune, if it were that, that it wasn't a brig but one of the research buildings. There wasn't much security to speak of, not that anything really hard and fast in terms of security was needed much anymore. Security technology was such that there really was no escape. For anyone. Anywhere. If they had you in the system -and pretty much everyone of any interest to them was- they could reach out remotely and turn you off for a while, with a well-focused transcranial pulse to the locus coeruleus. The locus coeruleus was basically the switch in the brain stem for causing the type of neuromuscular paralysis that went into effect during REM sleep to keep the dreaming body from acting out the actions of the dreaming brain. You toppled over mid-flight if you had been so foolish as to try to flee, and, except for the ego, you were otherwise undamaged. Heck they could detect your inclination to act even before you acted if they were really tracking you intensely. The brain, like everything else, had given up alot of its secrets.

And of course, afterlife or the lack thereof aside, if they wanted to turn you off permanently there was an abundance of ways to do that. The sniffer-darts were pretty amazing. Tiny as a mosquito and quieter. They would inject you waking or sleeping with a potent disease or poison genetically tailored so that it could kill no one else but the dearly beloved target. He also knew as a fact that, as a little bit of added security, a number of people worldwide, including some of the CSA's own agents, were implanted with subcutaneous sleeper capsules. These could be remotely triggered to open and release a neurotoxin that killed almost instantly. That poor little soldier girl out in Lhasa had one, and he hoped, for her sake, they didn't have to punch her button.

As good a special-ops soldier as Pike had been, it was largely the cornucopia of termination techniques that had forced him out of the field and into this new position, half desk job, half leading a spiritual warfare unit of screaming -well really hymn-singing- meanies. They were good soldiers, serving their country and their God. But they were so young. He had once been no different. Now though, he was thoroughly professional, and past serving anyone, except the automatism of his sense of duty. "And I guess," he half-muttered to himself, "I also serve at the whim of a crazy General, who once may have been crazy like a fox, but now, is probably just plain crazy." Just plain crazy was pretty common these days. That was one of the things he liked about the CSA, not the craziness, but the way, on the surface at least, it seemed so normal; men were men, women were women, children obeyed their parents and everyone went to church on Sunday. There was discipline and order and cleanliness and at least the attempt at Godliness.

But beneath the surface, and out in the heathen world, it was a new and not very brave world. And he himself had become anything but new. He was fit and his discipline kept him going strong, but he knew too much. He tried to deny it, tried to forget, tried to really fit in and be happy. But, there it was. No doubt they knew about his unhappiness better than he knew about his unhappiness. Heck, they knew when he needed to shit, and knew when he needed to fornicate, and he smiled grimly to himself hearing the Christmas song provide the background to his marching to his daughter's fate, "He knows when you are sleeping, He knows when you're awake, He knows if you've been bad or good so be good for goodness sake…"

He remembered their first few Christmases so long ago, his daughter an infant then a toddler then a strangely prescient girl-child. His wife, Frances, was so beautiful, and he so in love with her that she was the reason as much as anything, driving him to be as good a young soldier as possible. He wanted always for her to be proud of him. But he was good, too good, and the deployments just kept getting stranger and thornier and more distant, and each time he came back a little stranger, a little thornier, a little more distant. And when the country had split, they had split, too. Frances, Christian though she was, wasn't that type of Christian, and he, loyal as he was, was loyal to the brothers he had served with, who mostly were that type of Christian. She had taken their daughter and gone to Seattle. Travel between the two parts of the split-up country having been agreed upon to be free, he'd gone a few times to visit, but his daughter had soon come to hate him for everything he stood for, and to stand instead for everything he was fighting against. Her teenage rebellion had started before she reached her teens. She was fierce, a scalding, scowling advocate for all the sins the CSA was trying to weed out, throwing back his own sins and weakness in his face. In the end he had just given up. And his wife too, had just found it easier to find someone else not wedded to the terrible swift sword of the Lord. She had found an artist, someone even Zach sort of liked when he didn't want to break his neck.

But then he was in the room were his daughter was being detained. Everything was white and sterile, and she was in an orange jumpsuit. But it did little to hide how beautiful she had become, like her mother when they had met. It took the breath out of him, better than any sucker punch ever had. He hoped, as he crumpled up a little inside that she didn't notice his weakness, 'cause he had never yet won a battle with her, not since she was at least 5 or 6. And he hoped the many watchers of this cell human and otherwise, hadn't also taken note of his inner stumble, because he had to convince them he was strong: strong enough to lead men out into the unholy world and capture more daughters like this.

When Grace came to him, he almost wanted to assume a fighting crouch. But she just brushed her left hand along the side of his right shoulder and said, "Dad, you look tired." Then she hugged him, the daughter he had always wanted, the father she had always wanted, and years of sandcastles well-built, and well-fortified, washed away in a sudden tide that had risen much higher than it had in a very long time.

3. Beatrice Could Go Either Way

Aaron was not happy. He was upset. Sitting up, almost quivering from panic, he thought he might as well get out of bed and look around, half out of a paranoia that this was yet another false awakening, and half because he felt wide -double-espresso wide- awake. He didn't think he would get much sleep anymore and given the dreams, that seemed just as well. He didn't like the fact his mother or his imagination of his mother had a touch that felt like a taser. He wondered, neurocognitively, neuroanatomically what the hell had happened. No doubt, he thought, the bio-system that monitors the sleep environment for threats also monitors the body itself for extreme levels of arousal and it had sent a signal to the locus coeruleus to allow afferent signals from the brain to reach the body and allow it to panic. At one point or another it must have been an evolutionary advantage that had allowed the survival of some distant ancestor, but tonight he didn't appreciate it in the least. And why his mother packed such an emotional wallop for him, he just didn't know.

Aaron sighed, got of bed and put on his silk robe. It had a dragon on the back, a gift from an old girlfriend who had left him because he didn't really like playing in the ether with her. She had found him a bore saying that all he did was work. Which was really quite true, both the work and the bore part. Oh well.

He padded into the kitchen to get a glass of milk. When he turned on the light something about its quality struck him as odd, and a chill went down his spine at the thought he might still be dreaming. But no, it was just that one of the bulbs had burnt out. Feeling reassured he padded into his study. He might as well work if he couldn't sleep. Settling into his chair he brought up his work files -the display security using a variety of discrete means of identifying him as being him- but he really wasn't into it, the work that is.

Aaron's display was advanced. Had he wanted to he could connect directly to any of the commercial bardic realms, or go freesailing wherever his fantasies, hidden fears and/or predilections would take him. But he didn't much like that level of verisimilitude. Usually he just flat-screened the information he needed, and occasionally allowed full 3D renditions. Tonight he absent-mindedly allowed a random search of some earth-based, non-fantasy broadcasts to be brought up in little windows, in case there was something that might distract him. Who know something might even put him to sleep. Some of the little windows knew him personally and were reaching out to him by name. Irritated, he cloaked his display presence in as much anonymity as his system allowed. It was amazing, the extent to which the colonization of personal spaces, really of the mind itself, had taken place. It was supposed to be illegal without express permission, but a lot of corporations had relocated to the CSA and other rogue states because the rules and the taxes were a lot more lax. The pseudo-Christians over in the CSA were such bastards he thought. Morally they made everyone toe their particular narrow line, but when it came to business, the free market was second only to Christ and that a pretty damn close photo finish second.

Like a good advanced display, his display read his thoughts almost as well as he did and began putting up some broadcasts from the CSA. One mass prayer rally he had to admit had really good music, good production values, and that particular window expanded as more of his attention was drawn to it. Man-machine interface made imagining the worldmind that much easier, because even human technologies seemed capable of creating it. So why not the world, why not the universe? And at this point he normally would have been surfed off into some other display, but he was still heading deeper into the mass prayer rally from the CSA. People, eyes closed mostly, holding their hands above their heads, were swaying to the powerful music. This particular site seemed to have some inherent pull to it, and he wondered if it was really coming from him. He was pretty deep in the scene now, amongst the crowd, moving closer to the front, impressed beside himself at the rapture all around him. The music swelled to a spotlighted face at the podium, a speaker clearly so full of God that the scientist in Aaron was most impressed at the level of mind control the CSA had achieved in its media. Another part of him thought now would be a good time to pull back, before this handsome devil started some breast-beating Jeremiad. He was having trouble pulling back, though, pulling out, and that both interested him and concerned him a bit.

The great, silver-tongued orator began most kindly and humbly, "There are many, even here tonight, who have sought salvation in many ways, in this way, and that way, -I won't list them all- but you've tried them all my friends, every way but the right way." He shook his head, downcast, obviously heart-broken, stopped by the grief of it, but then something inside him lifted him back up tall and mighty and he found himself again and boomed, "But I say to you, no one comes to the Father except through me!" and he looked at Aaron and said, as if just to him, "come, be washed in the Blood of the Lamb, be Forgiven, Be Saved, not just for a little while, but Forever," and Aaron was most impressed by how much of him really did want to do just that, while another part of him was pulling very hard to back out of this nightmare, but was finding there were two men in dark suits, ushers really, who were half-dragging him, half-helping him toward the front, and he probably would have lost that tug of war if his mother had not shown up, sitting on his lap, wearing a most intemperate, strapless, practically slipping off her, flimsy film of a lovely negligee, and planting the sweetest of a promise of more kisses to come on his lips said, "I wouldn't go into that particular light just now my son. It's very hard to turn off when you need to sleep." And then she was gone and he was pushing himself bodily away from the display and backing out of his study, his dragon-backed robe, hanging open in the front, no longer doing a good job of covering his mass of confused emotions.

***

As Pangu stopped, everyone turned to Dolma's father to see what his reaction would be. He inclined his head downward, closing his eyes as if savoring something. And then his smile emerged and his eyes opened and he said, "Yes, Pangu, yes, I see where you are going with this, though you really are perhaps more of a photojournalist than a novelist. Tashi is very lucky to have you on his journey back to Lhasa. And to awakening hopefully!"

And then Dolma's father got up and walked over to Tashi. "Tashi if I may?" he said holding his right hand up as if he was about to stop traffic, but Tashi understood he had the power of a spirit healer and was going to use this ability to read Tashi's flow of vital energy.

"Yes, Bala, yes, of course, thank you," said Tashi embarrassed but interested, but he was already feeling energy flowing from the old man's hand, or imagining he could feel energy from that upraised hand Then he had to close his eyes, and as he felt waves of magnetism sweep here and there across him, he also saw stabs of sudden light, and he had the strange sense of someone rearranging him from within In the flashes of light he saw entering his body, he almost could see another figure off in the corner prone on a bed in a dark room, and he wondered who it was but then Dolma's father said, "Well not so bad I think. Nothing that one more of Grandma's kaptse won't fix and maybe a little more of Pangu's story, and then you really must be on your way. I think this will be an important day for you in Lhasa!"

And now everyone was looking at him a little strangely, and Tashi to cover his awkwardness and the visceral sensations of light and vibration still flowing in his body reached for a kaptse and said, "Right then, Pangu, let's hear what you have to say. Then we really must be on our way to Lhasa."

***

Chapter 19. Holes in the Roof of the World (Through Which We See the Stars)

"Write in water and it will last

Write in stone and it will perish

One is the language of life

One is just words and sand."

-D.H.G.-

1. Chandeliers of the Inner Mind

The bread was good. The cheese was good. They were both soon gone, with nothing but constellations of crumbs left on the breadboard. Tsewang looked around, knowing he could have eaten double, triple, what had been laid out before them. But having eaten a bit he felt a little closer to earth, to his body again, and that would be enough for now. He still saw around them all, Faith and Tashi, and himself, too, in the periphery of his vision, a nimbus, a nest really of tendrils of light, as if they were enmeshed in the gentle weavings of a gathering of weaver spirits, of Khadromas and Khadros hoping these three would find a way to intertwine their actions with each other, so as to complete a part of a design, a pattern, a tapestry even, something greater than the three of them, but which they themselves could not really see. In fact, Tsewang felt that there were other, additional minds that belonged here, as part of this pattern, people who were not present, but whose minds were mentally right next door, in the next lightcell over in this cluster of lightcells that perfectly contained them all. Tsewang hated groupthink, hated to be part of anything really, preferred to stand outside and observe and laugh, but this was different. This was belonging, not to something outside of him, but belonging to what was very much deep within him. A home from which he emerged from time to time to take a different name and body, but a home that he carried with him nonetheless, normally forgotten in the strange journeys of flesh and bone and their desires. It was as if his left hand had looked across and seen his right hand and realized for the first time that they were extensions of the same body.

Faith felt it, too, though she did not see it the way Tsewang saw it. For her it was more an opening of the heart. It was knowing beyond all doubt that she loved these two, these people, and that she belonged amongst them, that they were her new family, no matter what they believed or how they looked. She felt the Holy Spirit molding them into one body, one flesh, simply because they had met and shared bread together.

Tashi was torn. He knew something was happening, and part of him was open to the magic. But part of him wanted Faith in a way that didn't allow for Tsewang to be with her also. He was struggling to keep the baser part from seizing control. He began to chant a mantra to help remember the most basic of Buddhist teachings, that desire was mind poison. But there remained in him, as he tried to become calm and accepting, another part of himself that was sad that desire would not be allowed to build today, or maybe any day.

2. Evening's Trolls

Father and daughter strolled across the base towards the general's home. He had known they would allow him to take her home. It is what he would have done in the situation: give first a chance to the Love that was at the core of the C.S.A. to work God's will on her errant witchery, that plus a father's desperate entreaties. Releasing her was both a recognition of and test of his true loyalties. Not that everything was not completely monitored.

It was a mild southern winter evening. Soldiers seeing the two would have seen the general and abruptly saluted, but would have even more clearly seen and felt as a visceral blow deep in their bodies, the powerfully sexual young woman, walking with him, dressed though they had dressed her in the most modest of modest C.S.A. womenfolk garb.

"How, how is...?"

"Mother's fine. She's enjoying Seattle," and she gave his hand a squeeze.

"Is she, a..."

"Witch? Like me? No, she is a light worker. Do you know what that is?"

"Maybe. Maybe not. Look, Grace, I don't know if I can protect you. They are very angry at what you have done."

"Dad," Grace said taking his hand again, "It's OK. I don't need protection anymore. I really have found freedom. I know that you love me and please know that I love you, too. We took different paths, but actually we aren't so different. You are a soldier, and in a way I am a soldier, too!" and they both laughed.

"Yes, I remember your fire, and your stubbornness, even as a little girl. Your mother said it came from me, and I guess she was right. But you know, you will be angry at me, and think I am negotiating on their behalf, but would it be so bad to teach them how you do it?"

"You mean otherwise they will find a way to reduce me to a vegetable if I don't cooperate? Father, I do not have a special gift. The ability of the soul to travel is there for all of us. Your soldiers can do it, too, but they need to stop being afraid of the world. Shadows and darkness are not evil to be slain with some great sword of white light. These are the forests of being, and every manner of being is there, each with a purpose, and a beauty and a worth. Instead of killing them, can't we at least learn to listen to their stories?"

"We see things a little differently," said the general.

They came to his modest frame house, not much different than the homes of the enlisted men and their families, maybe a little larger, maybe with a slightly more impressive doorway. Inside it was clean, neat, Spartan, and empty and lonely. Grace shuddered inside, feeling her Father's sadness. Tonight, she thought, I will take him someplace where the life has not been sucked out of everything.

3. Relativity, Incest, and all the Rest

Aaron, exhausted beyond exhaustion, had finally been able to fall asleep, only to awake -in what him seemed to him immediately after falling asleep- to find he was naked and had an erection the likes of which he had never had before. It was not so much the size of it -from the throbbing tautness he doubted if any more blood would fit- no, it was the fact that it was glowing that gave him pause. In the distance he could hear laughter, and a familiar voice as lovely as well-tuned bells which said, "My son, my son, see how he guides us all through the darkness." And indeed, it was dark, except for his illuminating member, and the stars of a night sky that were thick around him. He heard another voice say, "Arma virumque cano. I sing of arms and the man," in a German accent. Orienting toward the voice, he saw a wild white-haired figure approaching whom he recognized immediately to be Einstein.

"I was wrong you know," said Einstein, "about 'ghostly action at a distance,' turns out there is an awful lot of ghostly action at a distance. And it also turns out, that while God does not play dice with the universe, there is a great amount of participatory interaction of an inherently unpredictable nature.' Einstein shrugged and said, "Such is life. Oh, and space, is very much of the field of the mind which is very much full of the field of the heart. You might even say that it is the primary frame of reference. Can an old discredited physicist say that? Well, there I've said it. As for your predicament, I'm not sure what I would do if I were you. Find a wife perhaps. Changing human hearts is easier said than done but they do change. As for the rest, build the space elevator. Some things really are much better done in orbit," and then the old/young man smiled and took out a violin.

he had tucked under his arm, and putting it to his chin shambled off playing Mendelsohn's Violin Concerto, -not at all badly- as he left.

Aaron was thrilled. Einstein was a personal hero, and self-manufactured or not, he took his appearance as a good omen. Then he saw a message flashing on and off on Einstein's receding back. It was a hyperbardic link to a popular adult pleasure world, "Paradixe," and his mood turned sour, realizing his own personal oneiric space had been hacked. It was all illegal but there was so much money to be made and the great manufacturing corporations of illusions and wonderment were so rich and powerful that it was hard to stop them. In many ways they had the best tools and the best scientists. They had often tried to buy him out and take him on board. No doubt they knew as soon as he did when he was on to a good idea. He wanted to turn back, and he would have had his mother not stopped him.

"Aaron," said his mother, "stop dilly-dallying and follow that numinous member of yours. Since you won't pay attention to my warnings, we're just going to have to do this the hard way." She laughed a laugh both most musical and most commanding and he felt himself tugged along by an unseen silk glove pulling him not at all unpleasantly by his prime mover. And then she didn't need to pull him any more. She was in front of him, no longer in the form of his mother, but in the form of a woman he loved very deeply, one he realized he had never met, but whom bits and pieces of he had discerned in those women he had been attracted to up to now. And he stopped fighting the attraction, the lust, the joy of life and loving. He stopped trying to understand, or at least that part of him which needed to understand everything, was just a little bit overwhelmed with the thrill of the chase of desire and love and of the desire to love. And they flew across spaces his dominant, now quiescent analytic part recognized as being content addressable, organized along completely different principles, and more than anything responsive and intimately interactive with all the qualia that physics had so much trouble measuring.

And he saw in front of them, -she, smiling and beckoning him on- a glowing circle emerging, a circle of other minds, luminous and pulling him, a circle of which he now remembered he was an important part. And he and she settled in with a whisper of remembrance, and a sigh of belonging, the little cup of me that skull held, dissolved into a bigger self, the puzzle almost solved, but really not a puzzle but an un-puzzle, as returning to it solved so much But there were still two pieces, two minds missing, before the circle was complete and the peace was completed and the new/old beginning ending began/ended again, but they were coming, they were all sure, they could feel the last parts of themselves, coming...

4. A Door Into the Woods and Out of Them

He admired the way she presented the way. General Pike sat up in bed and saw the door in his bedroom where a wall should be, and saw his daughter standing there as the little girl he had loved so much. Beyond her he saw the green woods they had often walked in, hand in hand, before the stubbornness in both of them set in, and made them stone walls to each other. And he knew he would be entering the lucidity. He knew from his training with "God's Own," the CSA's crack brigade of astral warriors. But this would be different. It was just he and his daughter. There would be no artificial pumping up of the mindstream with hymns and prayers and "Praise the Lords." There was no powerful group mind of he and his soldiers, all believing, all focused on the same thing, aided by various technologies he only half understood. No, his daughter was inviting him for a walk in the woods, father and daughter in the magic green of a hush forest. He left his bed, took her hand, looking down at her, but seeing in her eyes, a wisdom far greater than he had ever realized. And he didn't fight it, though fighting was his nature. He took her hands and they walked, glided almost, through the green trees, and his heart's grieving came out and he shed tears, and it was good.

"Father, come" she said, and she pulled his hand. The glide was a flight and they were going someplace he knew he had reconnoitered not long ago, but this time, he wasn't going as a scout ahead of an invading army, he was going because he was equally led and equally called. He wondered if he would ever be returning again to his bed, to his body, and he didn't care. He saw the faces here and there of men he had killed, but they seemed to understand, they themselves, most of them at least, having been killers, too. But it was his daughter's hand that held him most. Through it flowed all the life he had been denying himself for so long, out of duty, and discipline, and honor, and service. Words now the meaning of which seemed twisted and all-wrong if it meant not holding on to his daughter's hand. For a moment he saw her mother, his former wife. She smiled with relief to see him holding again the hand of their child. He knew with all his strength, and whatever of his belief that was still with him, that this was a much stronger magic then he would ever be able to fight. He had been living in a paper mache castle, mistaking it for some impregnable fortress, when it was little more then old men repeating the same thing over and over again until they had hypnotized everyone into thinking there could be no argument.

And then, the clearing of the clearing opened up before them and he saw the circle of light to which they belonged, and now tasting real victory it was he who pulled his daughter, knowing the way, knowing their place, knowing they fit and completed it. And they did. And they were all one, complete. Tashi, Faith, Tsewang, Ani-la, Aaron and his mother, Grace and her father, but what they were was more than what they had been apart. They looked around the circle, now perfect, and all of them were staring out at all of them from everyone's eyes. And they knew, something they had once known, and they knew they needed to know it again, for they looked out upon a Lhasa surrounded by gathering storm clouds, and poet and witch and nun, and mother and scientist and lapsed monk turned playboy and general, knew they were needed to save what had to be saved. Call it the earth, call it the Spirit, call it living breathing dreaming luminous life itself, but they saw the threat rising against it, and equally saw, their mandala of joined belonging-together-minds wasn't the only one: great luminous circles of sentient beauty were rising in a ring around Lhasa and as far as the inner eye could see. And perhaps it would be enough. And if not, the beauty was worth however many failed infinities it took until it got it right again.

***

Dolma's father arose and said, "Tashi, you have to go." Outside, the bright light of full morning had been eclipsed, and it seemed some sudden storm was about to give birth to a monster of darkness. He took Tashi's hands for a moment, looked into his eyes, and smiled, and Tashi felt courage and hope well up in him. Then Dolma put a kathak around his neck and said nothing, but from the lovely peace in her countenance he felt the strong desire he felt as a man somehow transmute into some sweeter loving stuff. Willing to forgo a carnal embrace for one much realer and longer lasting. And then they were out the door and in the truck and Tashi could hear Dolma's father's last words, "Listen to Pangu, he is a good guide," and then they lurched into motion, not at all smoothly, but rather as if seeking to avoid a dark flock of great circling, hunting birds which at any moment might unleash a private targeted hell upon them. Pangu was sitting next to Tashi in his old farmer's guise now, and Tashi didn't mind. He felt comforted by it in fact, seemed to think that now, it might have actually been earned. But the air had turned sudden mountain hailstorm cold, and hail came down in an insistent metalloid music cloaked in dark shivering silver. Pangu was smiling, but Tashi thought there was a strange insincerity to it, as if in fact, just beneath the image's surface, there was worry, as if a truck could worry.

After they got down from the valley where Dolma lived they emerged onto the road that lead to Lhasa, but Tashi almost didn't recognize it though he had come that way many times before. Darkness had filled the valley like an oil fire out of control. Darkness roiled around them, wanting to get in, wanting to get into their lungs, trying very hard to get into their souls. And it might have succeeded, might almost have made it all the way in, *except that Tashi thought of Dolma, and her father, and as he turned to look at the old father next to him, the smile seemed less insincere and more a challenge to be brave in the face of what seemed to be almost the ending of the world, the human world, which was unraveling around them.*

Through the dark came streams of refugees trudging alongside the road; fires burning here and there, fires that once had been homes; men in uniforms moved menacingly weapons at the ready; children without parents cried and parents with children were begging; there were also the screams of woman being ravaged; and above and beyond it all, dark machines seeming to heed no one, marched effortlessly along.

"Pangu, what is going on?"

"Ah, Tashi. You will understand soon enough. Suffice it to say, there are a multitude of different worlds about us, at slightly different frequencies, like radio stations, a decimal point away from each other, but wildly different."

"You mean I'm out of tune, and this is the result?"

"We're all a little out of tune, and this is the result."

"But the great green transition, our ecocivilization, the Ecoharmonium of Taiwan, Tibet and China, we were doing so well. Has the experiment failed so quickly?"

"Nothing has failed Tashi. The great transition continues, but I need to go on with my story for you to understand." Suddenly there were naked women leering in at the windows, smiling hollow leers and beckoning.

"Yes," said Tashi, shuddering, "go on with the story, get me to Lhasa, and lock the doors, tight, too if you don't mind..."

***

"What is an "I", and why are such things found (at least so far) only in association with, as poet Russell Edson once wonderfully phrased it, "teetering bulbs of dread and dream" -- that is, only in association with certain kinds of gooey lumps encased in hard protective shells mounted atop mobile pedestals that roam the world on pairs of slightly fuzzy, jointed stilts?"

— Douglas R. Hofstadter, Gödel, Escher, Bach: An Eternal Golden Braid

1. Heroes of the Grasslands

General Holden was it's true, somewhat augmented. It was a state secret, as augmentations of the sort he had were prohibited, rightfully so, in the CSA. But his augmentations were in the service of the state, were needed really for the defense of the state. So he had –reluctantly- acquiesced. Christendom would never have survived without its dutiful protectors. But in General Holden's heart of hearts, he knew that what made him powerful weren't the nanobots in his brain. It was his service, his devotion, to the Lord. It was the Lord that had saved him from Hell and brought him his accolades and success. He himself was just an old soldier happy to give his sinful life as best he could in service to God. Unlike the Preacher he didn't need an all night prayer vigil to hear what the

Lord wanted him to do. He felt the Lord much closer to him than that: knew in his bones what needed to be done, and today, knew that what needed to be done was the start, the continuation really, of a most holy war. It would be a holy, mostly spiritual war, the kind where usually nobody got hurt, in the sense that, very few people got killed They just had their minds cleaned a little.

General Holden thought back to the times he had sat in church, half-bored, half-terrified by the sermons about eternal Hell. He remembered the day he understood what it was all about. He was staring at the cross hung there on an alter of pink marble, a tall alter in the shape of a door curving to a point at the top so that it looked like a missile. It came to him suddenly with a shudder, that the devil was on the other side of the door, pushing with all his might, trying to get out. He could almost see the alter-door bulging, about to burst. All that kept the devil from breaking out of hell and into the sanctuary and the world was the cross, and their prayers, and the preacher's exhortations to give up sin.

But the devil had gotten out. Even the CSA wasn't strong enough to stop him. No, that is why they had to go on the attack. There was no other way.

His young analysts had told him the CSA was still too weak to take on the powers that be, but he knew the longer they waited the deeper those powers would sink their claws into the brains of the young. No, God had shown him the way, and the time. And the time to strike was now. General Holden no longer argued with God the way he might once have when he was younger. When God had told him, repeatedly, that it was time to tear the USA in two, he had whined and bargained and tried to find another way. In the end though, one denies God's requests at one's own immortal peril. And so, though he had cried a patriot's tears at being forced to do what he had to do, in the end he had stood up tall and done the deed. That had been his test, his cross to bear. God had asked an old soldier to put an end to the country he had spent his life defending. But as God had known it would, it all turned out for the better. The CSA was born, and with it the hope that Christ's message in the world wouldn't be drowned out in the filthy muck of high tech secular humanism and pagan magic.

Yes, General Holden knew that God was at the top of his chain of command. He knew that He infinitely outranked him. And in this action, today, too, he knew he was called, knew he was just following orders. Yes, the young analysts had talked of the dangers, of the resistance they were meeting from forces they did not yet understand. Yes, they had warned of the blowback to the CSA that would come, of the danger to the commercial pleasure worlds in the astral spaces if the gatekeepers withdrew their support.

But all of that he had known already, even before they told him of it. What they didn't understand was that he wasn't playing that game, the game the war computers had worked out in every permutation they could think of. No, he was playing God's game and that wasn't a game. He wasn't going to try to put the genie back in the bottle. He was going to smash the bottle and let God deal with the genie. Let God show people there was a heaven and a hell and that the directions -for both directions- are very, very clear. There is no middle ground. He was going to bell the cat and then let the bell devour the cat. And he half smiled at that image

General Holden took his command seat. He was –though it was of course a very closely guarded secret- really quite magnificently augmented. The nanobots in his brain and elsewhere where now activated, and they and the drugs expanding his sensorium allowed him to directly interface with a number of powerful systems. The augmentations also allowed him from time to time to reach in –just a little bit- into certain people's minds and help them come to the right conclusions. He actually didn't like the augmentation functions that much, rarely used them in fact, oh well except maybe on women from time to time, God knows he wasn't a saint. Today his God and his nation needed him to be in his full war regalia, like some Patriarch of old brought back to life. Today he would track almost everything that was going on. Though all the decisions would be made by the war computers there needed to be an –augmented human- in the loop, and with General Holden in the loop, even the war computers might be in for a surprise.

Flush with the power of his command and the mind-performance drugs he smiled a stern smile to himself. He knew there was really no way to lose: he and the CSA had already made billions by offering pay-for-view of today's actions to a number of very important actors on the global power stage. And he smiled fully now -the blessed smile of the saved- for the climax in front of them and the world, would be glorious indeed for all to behold, when General Holden raised His victorious cross high above Lhasa. Today he would wield the sword of the almighty and smite the witch -that whore of Babylon- in her lair, and in doing so -God willing- he might even usher in the return of Christ himself. It was about time. Things had gotten too far out of hand. God's house needed to be put in order.

His eyes glowed and the joy/power/clarity coursed through him. All of this talk of tolerance and coexistence was dangerous nonsense. There is right and there is wrong. And if the Buddhists and the New New Age people hadn't learned from history that Might very definitely made Right, then they were in for another lesson. General Holden leaned back and closed his eyes, felt one with the world the nanobots connected him to, breathed in deeply as his sensorium expanded to connect with a vast web of information, and of agents, and of arms. He felt uplifted in the service of a cause much greater than him. He had become the arm of God, and he also, though he scarcely noticed it, had become quite engorged in a central part of his distantly receding body.

2. Red Team/Blue Team/Green Team/No Team

General Pike was happier than he had been in a very long time. It was the happiness of re-uniting and reconciling with his daughter. It was the happiness of discovering he was a part of one larger mind made up of eight smaller minds. It was a happiness that made it hard for General Pike to play the role of General Pike. But he knew he had to keep the transformation hidden. He was now the ultimate double, triple, eight-fold agent, the others knowing everything that he knew and everything that he was doing, and he in turn, knowing all about them and what they were doing. There was no point in trying to keep the Lhasa attack plans of "God's Chosen" secret, as the plans were now known, as well as he himself knew them, by Grace and Tashi, Faith and Tsewang, Ani Choedon and Aaron and also by Aaron's mother. It took all of his discipline to pretend to be the soldier he had been.

And Aaron's mother in particular didn't make it very easy for him. She was really quite attractive and attracted he was. She reminded him of his ex-wife. She was everything that he was not: spontaneous where he was rigid, sensuous where he was stern, illogical where he was logical, and forgiving, laughing and dancing, where he was unforgiving, grim, and always unflinchingly in control of himself. There she was now, in the corner of his field of vision as he tried to make sense of the pre-operation reports, cavorting quite seductively in a most inventive, rather teasing cross between a uniform and a negligee.

And yet, looking at her again now, he saw she had reverted to full uniform -cut rather short and tight it's true- but she was very much in uniform. Seeing that he was looking at her, she saluted, and then winked, rather languorously. God, how he wanted to laugh. So what if she was dead! She was the most alive thing he had known since the brief days his ex-wife and he had enjoyed, before that is, the soldiering took him over completely.

Most of all, deep down, nestled in his carefully hidden joy, Brigadier General Pike was at peace. He just wasn't worried any more. There was, it had turned out, a meaning embedded in the killing and the chaos, something deeper and enduring, and real, much more real, than the death he had been dealing in for so long. Amidst his joy, he also felt sadness that it had taken him so long to wake up. Beyond the fresh memories of the newly discovered parts of himself, he could sense he was connected with others, also waiting for him to discover them. Many of these were individuals he had killed over the years -and there were many of them- and dealing with them, would take time. But he now knew, whatever happened, that he had time, vast stretches of time, the kind that makes true patience.

As he gave the signal for his team to insert, he wondered what they would meet. He knew militarily the goal was to seize the high ground, and he prayed they would. Or rather prayed they would find some of the peace that he had found. That instead of the pumped-up mindstream conversion missions they had been sent out on, that the high ground would instead seize them. He wanted them to wake up from their warrior/boy dreams, into full humanity. He knew Tashi had warned security elements in the ETTC, the Ecoharmonium of Taiwan Tibet and China. Aaron had similarly alerted his contacts in what was left of the USA. The nun, Ani Choedon had told the monasteries to begin a great cycle of prayers, and Tsewang, poet that he was, was dashing about town warning everyone that the Crusaders were coming for Lhasa, but of course, no one believed him. His daughter Grace, under house arrest though she was now, clearly was not stopped by any physical boundaries, and he could sense her gathering her coven and their friends. Faith was very torn. Loyalty was deep in her, but a deeper loyalty to love and compassion and friendship, had awoken in her. He knew she knew there was another parallel mission for Lhasa that had been planned. She didn't know what it was, and neither did he, and this troubled him. General Holden was perhaps a better strategist than he had given him credit for. Perhaps all of this, the mission of God's Chosen, was just a feint, a diversion, a softening up for something else to come.

And then there was Aaron's mother, who was much more than just Aaron's mother, and was very much up to something, some of it at levels too deep or too high perhaps for even General Pike -connected though he was to her- to completely follow.

3. A Mudra for the Ages

They descended like so many brilliant angels, like magnesium flares infused with deity, like white phosphorus shells slowed down into some graceful revelation for all to see. They rained down into the pre-dawn awakening of Lhasa. A show of force, and beauty and awe.

But really it was all a show. The tulpa technology didn't require it, the fireworks that is. But the poets of PsychWar had had their way.

What really happened, and here the after-action report is very clear, was that -one would have to say- things did not go exactly according to plan. There were some converts of course, if that is the right word for what was done to their minds. It can be surmised these were individuals who were ripe for conversion. They had seen in their own lives the warts and imperfections of human beings practicing Buddhism, and it hadn't sat well with them. Especially now that Buddhism - Tibetan Buddhism especially- had gone so big time, had become so wealthy with the income it got from protecting the dreamlands.

But the majority of CIAs (Converted in Action) were of God's Chosen.

Some of the soldiers –God's Chosen- had been unable to arrive in Lhasa. It had been hidden from them. Some described winding up in a dark, swirling conflict zone, of which there were many around the world. Others described a desert landscape with nothing and no one to be seen.

Others must have been close as they burst out of the astral realms full of righteousness, only to find themselves powering the revolution of giant prayer wheels suspended in the sky.

Others arrived in what was clearly a monastic setting, where their pumped-up mindstreams didn't seem to have much affect on the monks, who -quite the contrary- smiled, and invited them to debate the merits and logic or lack thereof of Christianity versus Buddhism.

One reported meeting a Tibetan girl and falling in love, and wanting to do everything he could to find out who she was so he could return and ask her to marry him.

One said he met Christ, though he was dressed as a Tibetan, wearing Tibetan garb.

A few encountered protective deities, mostly in wrathful form. One or two did appear in a beneficent form offering to help, saying the Tibetans very much needed to be helped to come closer to the Dharma.

Many of the young soldiers came upon a Lhasa surrounded in concentric circles for deep miles around by inwardly glowing meditators holding hands. The meditators - reported the soldiers- seemed to be from everywhere, were of every race and age and gender. The circles, even with their mindstreams pumped to the maximum, proved completely impenetrable, though not in a hostile way. Some of the soldiers in fact found themselves welcomed in, joining hands with the others, and feeling at last, at peace.

Very few of the soldiers -when they found themselves back in their plastic cocoons in their underground chambers- would ever be much good at soldiering again.

All of this was in the after action report, though it was less after action, and closer to realtime reporting than anything else. Generals Holden and Pike both saw what was happening almost as it was happening. Neither were that surprised. General Pike pretended to be displeased, but secretly he was happy for what he knew many of the young soldiers had found. He was happy that the extended parts of himself, the other seven beings he shared a broader identity with, were also happy that somehow the word had gotten out, that somehow or other, the attack had been thwarted.

General Holden was another matter entirely. He was pumped up with rage and nanobots and drugs. He wasn't surprised at what had happened. He had spent enough time on the other side to know it was a tricky place full of surprises. He wasn't dumb. He knew that the military applications of this technology still had some kinks in it. He knew it and his clients knew it. Today was just a demonstration as far as that was concerned. No, what was boiling in his gut was that he really hadn't yet begun to fight yet. And he smiled, and felt a most pleasurable sensation in his loins.

And then she appeared in front of him, as he had suspected, hoped, that she would.

4. Who Are We to Judge

She was a half-beast. Half woman, naked, alluring, half-bird, wings of soft gold and silver. Her eyes, large and slowly blinking as they regarded him, were half human, half those of a bird, and they pulled the war-machine enmeshed General Holden in, so that he already wondered if he would have the strength to resist. He very much didn't want to resist, the human part of him that is, but he also was more than human. He had steely depths. He had deep dark scaffoldings of numbers and electrons twinned with neurons and their synapses and deeper than that still, of a force that had to be God, could not, with its power, be anything else. And so, knowing the dreamrealms allowed it, he followed her beckoning flight with his own flight. She of an earthly-unearthly beauty, he, armed to the teeth, deadly to anyone who would dare to stand in the way of the Will of God. She was a will o' the wisp whose eros made his manhood ache. Desire and sex were her mother's milk, not out of desire for seduction, but because that is what connected everything into the one body of the Great Mother. This was belonging. This drinking at the tit of life and giving life with loin and heart and love and song and story. With a brush of her wings alone, she had healed many, mostly unbeknownst to them. General Holden, with the touch of a button, had dispatched many, to their maker, or rather, to his maker, and thence of course to eternal Hell.

They alighted soon enough after flight in the inter-spaces to a calm clearing in the woods, to a small white stone chapel. And this did surprise him a bit. The bird-woman said nothing, but told him mind to mind that he should go in. He wanted very much to ravish her, then and there, to delight in her exoticism, and suck the cries of ecstasy from her bird-bones, and then perhaps to crush them, but there was something in her, some invisible strength, a force field of utter otherness, that pushed his mind away from this, and instead turned him toward the chapel door.

He entered to find a simple space. A medieval chapel really, all of the same white stone, pure and simple, with neither alter nor votive nook, nor statues of saints set about in dark corners. All there was, was a circle set in stone in the floor in the middle of the chapel, a circle made of stones of slightly different hues so that it formed the circle of a faint circular rainbow.

General Holden marched to the center and spat. "Alright Witch, I'm here. Show yourself."

And then she was in front of him, a young girl, of no more than 14, dressed modestly, as any good girl of the CSA had to be.

And it enraged him. "Don't you dare. Show yourself as you really are! I command you!"

"But this is also how we really are. We are not so simple as what your mind makes us out to be. Surely you know this General, you who are also not so simple as you pretend."

"Change. Now. Or I am leaving."

And now there was a young woman in front of him, in a long dark cloak with a hood that covered her head and hid most of her face in shadows. He thought she might be General Pike's daughter, but wasn't sure. "Is this better?" she said, "more fitting to your preconceptions of who we are?"

"Who is we? Are you not alone?"

"No, I am not alone. I am never alone. I will show some of the others, but you mustn't be afraid, we are not here to fight you, not today at least," and seven more of her sisters, all dressed similarly, though in cloaks of different hue, appeared around the circle that General Holden was standing in the center of, and for a moment the General was afraid, until he remembered who he was and what he was connected to, and then he smiled and stamped his foot and seven of his footsoldiers appeared around him, so that they formed a circle within the circle of the witches. And these weren't the young believers chosen to be part of "God's Own." No, these were real soldiers he had chosen on the basis of a different criteria, not belief so much as lack thereof or rather belief and loyalty to him. These were men who could rape as easily as kill. Men, who knew as he did, that the real world wasn't a nice place, and that nice people got nowhere without people like them to "help" as needed.

"General, we welcome you and your boys, and if it would calm their rage, and soothe their aggression, and help them to understand we are not the forces of darkness and evil you imagine, but really rather, life itself, if it would help at all, we do offer our bodies for you to enjoy and learn from," and she smiled, and her voice -her voice saying this, some quality in her voice and the way she said it- made all of them yearn to take what was being offered.

"A witch offering sex?" and he spat at the ground again, "surely you know that is the oldest trick in the book."

"It is not a trick in the book. It is the book itself. It is what writes the book. It is beauty and grace and love and yes, mystery and passion and pain."

"I'll tell you what writes the book. God writes the book and anything not written by Him is consigned to the flames. And God help us, we will consign you and all of your witches to those flames. But I don't have time for arguing metaphysics with the likes of you. Where is your leader. Is it you?"

"We have no leaders. We are all equals."

"Nonsense. Of course you do. Where is little Miss Dolly, the Dalai Lama?"

"The Dalai Lama?" and the circle of witches laughed, as only witches can laugh, laughter as beautiful as a choir of deeply alien, profoundly earthly, crystals, laughter so beautiful the soldiers began to reach for their weapons to protect themselves from succumbing to the overwhelming beauty.

"General," said the witch in front of him, "your mind is pumped up on drugs and shot through with all those military computers. It cried out loud and wide in the astral realms for witches, and so we came. But the Dalai Lama, she's not a witch, she's a nun, and we are very much not one of those!" and the witches laughed again and General Holden's rage lashed out and he roared "Shut up," and even the witches obeyed, while the men crouched just a bit lower as if ready to spring at any moment for the beautiful jugulars, semi-exposed in the cowlings before them.

***

Pangu also obeyed, or so it seemed as he -who was so careful with his starting and stopping- abruptly stopped his narrative.

"Pangu," said Tashi, "What's wrong? Are you afraid of the General, too?"

"Can a truck be afraid, Tashi? No look, things have changed, the darkness has lifted." And Tashi saw that it was so. The scenes of madness and chaos surrounding them were gone, and it was a pellucidly lucid morning and they were in the outskirts of a Lhasa he knew and loved. The air was clear and numinous, and he felt as if he were in the middle of a glowing soap bubble at the bottom of a pond of the purest water, and that if he just reached up his arms and lifted his head to the sky and embraced the forever of the Tibetan sky above them, that he would float up, ascend into some celestial awakening. And he wanted to do so, almost would have tried, but something in him kept him down, some nagging doubt, some perpetual insecurity, a worry that gnawed at his toes and lashed his ankle to the earth. But he knew that his home wasn't here, as much as he loved Lhasa, but rather was up there somewhere, and that if he had only had more courage, the door had been there for him to walk through.

He looked at Pangu, in his old farmer's guise, and felt that Pangu saw the moment pass, too. And then they both smiled. Who knows why.

"So, Pangu, I think you might not be telling me everything. What's really going on? Come on, tell me, before I rip your solar panels out and sell them for Momos!"

"Hmm," calculated Pangu, "though old it is true, they would still fetch quite a lot of momos. But Tashi, I am telling you. The story is not just a story. I've cobbled it together out of things that are real, to pass the time, it is true, but also to help you, in a way, understand what happened."

"Ok, ok, so the General is real I suppose, so tell me what happened when he met the witches?

"Well, we aren't completely sure. The General hasn't completely recovered or rather, he's changed. His body appears to have suffered a stroke and he is physically incapacitated, but he is still hooked into the drugs and the nanobots, and the military computers. In that sense, he appears to be more vigorous than ever.

"Uh oh, that doesn't sound good."

"It's a worrisome development, particularly given what he did in Lhasa," and Pangu looked carefully at Tashi as if to emphasize how significant this was, and as if to see a glimmer of remembering start to appear in Tashi's eyes.

"What he did in Lhasa, what he did in Lhasa," muttered Tashi and his head began to ache like there was some metal chick inside of it bashing its beak against a skull that was cast iron. "Pangu what exactly do you guess happened between the General and the witches, you know, after he told them to shut up."

"Well," said Pangu...

Chapter 21. The Swarming of Goodness

"I am walking in a forest with a friend who is to my left. We come to a clearing that opens up onto the view of a lake. At the edge is an illustrated stone marker. On the stone is a man with flowing hair speaking. 'This is Christianity,' my friend says. 'It is mostly based on the saying of a relatively young man.' We continue walking in a counterclockwise semicircle through the forest. We come to two illustrated stone markers at the edge of a ravine. The two stone markers are of two friends talking with each other. My friend says, 'In Tibetan Buddhism, dreams are considered important.' I can hear the two friends in the two stone markers talking with each other. One is asking the other what he dreamed. The friend replies that he dreamed of clouds. His friend asks if he saw any faces in the clouds, and if so, whose. Just as the friend begins to answer this question, I fall in absolute agony to the ground. Weeping in abject sadness, unable to stop I begin sliding down the slope into the ravine. My friend comes to help me and to console me."

-from 4 Dre ams with Holes- DHG

1. Worship and Warships

General Holden glared at the circles of witches, and his circle of loyal men glared along with him. They all had prototype weapons, fashioned by the CSA's physicists, that were supposed to function against dreamrealm beings. But he didn't give the signal for them to be used, just yet.

"Ladies, I'm going to warn you just this one time, if ever again one of the womenfolk of the CSA report being visited by you demon succubae, and is turned against her will into a scheming harlot, we will hunt you down, every last one, and make the Inquisition look like a Girl Scout slumber party." The walls of the chapel began to change, move farther out, and the rainbow circle in the floor of the chapel that separated the witches from the soldiers widened and grew dark. The men waited for the signal to attack but it did not yet come, and they, hardened though they were, were growing nervous, edgy to get the job done. But General Holden held them in place, not just by his rank, but by the force of mind control he now wielded.

"General," said the cowled woman in front of him, "it would be better for you if you do not attack us. We are not what you think. You know the rules of this place. We are as much made up of your own mind, as we are beings separate from you. Please, just look at what is coming, and think." In the wall behind her, a tall alter grew, shaped like a missile, and the General recognized it as the one from his church as a boy, the tall stone alter that kept the devil out. And he shuddered and was exuberant in equal measures as he saw it bulge, and bow out, as some mighty force began to exert its irresistible will to emerge into the light of day and have its way. And then the alter, the door, could resist no more, and it swung inexorably open, and out he walked, an almost infinitely more powerful version of General Holden. This one fully enmeshed in the sensorium-enhancing drugs, in the war-machinery linking nanobots, this one, without any doubts or hesitation, this one, with his thoughts knowing your thoughts and with his thoughts changing your thoughts to match his needs.

And they all stepped back, even the General and his men, as if that would do any good. And then he laughed and said, "Well, he certainly is a handsome devil," and then he and the newly birthed General laughed together and his men joined in. Looking around him at the witches, now withdrawn even further from the circle of his men, the black, once rainbow, circle in the floor now also widened, he spat on the floor and said, "You're fools really, believing in Mother Earth and Earth magic. It's a planet, nothing more, to be used as we need to use it. You, and the Dalai Lama and anybody who wants to are welcome to all the dreamworlds you can imagine. You can have the high ground. But we will seize the low ground, for Him, because that is rock on which everything else is built," and this is when he gave the signal to the watchers of his body back home, to proceed with the second phase of their Lhasa adventure. Perhaps it was his decision alone, or perhaps the other, more powerful General Holden had something to do with it, and perhaps the separation, the difference between the two of them was growing so inconsequential as to be moot.

Then he gave the signal to his men to kill the witches, but they were already gone, except for the witch that had been in front of him, but had moved to his side as the other general had emerged from out behind the alter, now hanging uselessly open like some busted door. He turned to her, brandishing the weapon he had always had, thinking she would disappear, too, if he tried to eliminate her. But his was a very cool rage now, and he thought it wouldn't hurt to try, having forgotten her warning, what with the arrival of this new guest. And indeed, the mind of the other General Holden, must have had a subtle, very subtle touch in pushing him to act in this way too, and so act he did, turning with a smile to plunge the shaped, astral matter charge into her breast. She did not flinch, or move away, having anticipated that this was how it would go, and offering herself, for whatever reason, but when this spirit knife -call it that- entered her chest, it was the General whose breast was pierced with horrible pain, and he doubled-over, and collapsed. The witch, quickly pulled the spirit knife out of her chest and threw it expertly at the other General Holden, the one newly emerged from behind the alter, but it flamed and disappeared before it had even halfway crossed the space between them. Knowing this power was too great for her to be able to resist for long, she quickly dropped to her knees and placed for a moment her hand on the chest of the fallen General Holden and then she fled, half woman, half-bird, wings of softest gold and silver, her large eyes blinking and filling with tears.

2. Fecund Metal

It was a most beautiful morning in Lhasa. There was something, uplifting, exhalted even in the air, even more than usual. The winter Tibetan sun was brilliant and cleansing. Snow still silked much, the powdered blessing of millions of visiting stars that had fallen in love with this world and decided to stay for a while. The Tibetans were almost feverish in their Kora and devotions this morning. Word of the triumph the night before in the Samboghakaya, the astral, dreamrealms, had gotten out, and people were thankful, and yes, a little proud and triumphant. The few who had been converted to Christianity were quickly identified, and accepted and hugged, and shown where their houses of worship could be found. Well, accepted by most. There were a few who grumbled and scoffed. But Her Holiness had made it clear in her gentle laughing way that healing must be for all, or it was for no one.

Tashi and Pangu were at the outdoor market, the old market in the Bharkor, close to the Potala. As they had anticipated, Pangu's deliveries from the village had fetched a good price, and they were both happy, happy at the commercial success, and happy, in Tashi's case, of having had this deeper layer of himself unfold and show him that he was very much not alone, not alone in a metaphysical sense, though that was true, too, but not alone in a very visceral sense. For, he felt now, really as well as he felt himself, what the other seven were doing and could remember what they had always remembered, almost as well as he could remember what it was to be Tashi. Remembering and forgetting it turned out was a very strange thing. Remember too much, and it became hard to walk. Forget too much, and it became hard to walk in a meaningful way toward one's real destination. Tashi was remembering, tasting these others just enough to be able to continue to walk, but seen from the outside, he probably seemed just a bit drunk.

It's not surprising that no one at first noticed the rivulets of silver flowing from points around the periphery of Lhasa. In a way it was like the way the meltwater beneath the glaciers in Greenland and Antarctica had not been understood -except by a few scientists of course- as harbingers of what they were, sudden dissolution and breakup into chaos and disaster. The snow, beautiful as it was, also mostly covered their trails, as did the general sense that the battle if that's what it was, of the night before, had safeguarded Lhasa, and now Tibetans could do what they loved to do most, celebrate with a mixture of prayers and food and flirting and dancing and Chang. It was probably the dogs, the Dokki, the massive Tibetan mastiffs who noticed the alien smell first and heard the subtle metallic skittering. They issued their howling alarums from all around the city and people began to look. And here and there a child, a keen-eyed grandmother, a security camera looking for something else caught track of them as they crossed a half-cleared street, scaled a wall or a house, or dived into a sewer. When the light caught them, the rivulets were beautiful, glinting not just silver, but hinting at gold and diamond, and the almost-transparency of semiprecious rainbow.

Pangu, as "well-connected" as he was, noticed it perhaps a nanosecond after the dogs. Noticed it, obtained a still from a security camera, analyzed that, and then inspected satellite imagery to arrive, a few seconds after the howling, at his conclusion. "Tashi," said Pangu, with as much urgency in his voice as he could simulate, "Military microbots are pouring in from points around Lhasa. The vectors all converge on the Potala, and my best guess is that the target is Her Holiness, the Dalai Lama." Pangu displayed the imagery he had collected.

"Kunchokkhen. How much time do we have?"

"Very little. We need to organize resistance right now with everyone we can get who is close to the Potala. We need to form a circle around it and insulate her from this."

"Can we stop them? Are they armed?"

"We may be able to slow them enough to give her a chance to flee. As to the type of weaponry they represent, I don't know."

"Ok, send out your data and conclusion to all the authorities. Flood social media with what is happening. We'll start here. Broadcast my voice and project some pictures of what's coming." Tashi was dressed in his formal work Chupah as he had been planning to head off to his office after the delivery. It made him look quite official as he climbed on Pangu's roof and began warning people, while Pangu projected holograms of the approaching microbots.

"Citizens! Tibetans! Form a circle around the Potala. Protect Her Holiness. She's under attack. Arm yourself with what you can.

When you see these things, smash them, beat them back, don't let them get to the Potala!" and it worked. Or rather it almost worked.

People had gathered quickly, as many as were up this early, and word went out and people rushed out in pajamas to take up positions. There were grandmothers and grandfathers praying with malas and prayer wheels thinking their devotion would be enough to stop the onslaught. There were children, too, -their parents unable to stop them from joining- who already with their toys had a better idea what to expect, and had indeed played games like this. People had what they had, sticks and rocks, heavy boots and kitchen utensils. Some fire brigades were hooking up hoses, and the police and militias were getting organized and organizing those around them. But there simply wasn't enough time, and of what was coming, there were far, far too many.

When the silver waves did come -of shining mercurial spiders carrying the reflections of the morning sun on their glistening backs- a shudder went through the hastily gathered crowds of defenders. It was a shudder at their beauty and inhumanity, as much as a shudder of fear at the prospect of this clash with an unknown. Buddhists though they mostly were, and sworn not to kill, no one thought they would be killing some form of life, and so there would be no hesitation, no attempt at some non-violent form of resistance. It was in fact the monks and nuns who were most aggressive, knowing that what they were offering –their bodies- were impermanent, and knowing the protection of the Dharma was a great, a very great mandate.

But the microbots were hungry. And the purpose of their existence, the whole reason for them having been called into being, was to find, and eat, the Dalai Lama, and then perhaps transform her into something else more satisfactory to their masters. They were like ants at a picnic spread near to a great colony, near several great colonies. They had the scent of food, and the pathways to that food, and the loss of a soldier or two or a thousand meant nothing to them. The 3D printers must have been in some cases printing them for months. And as smart and brave as the defenders of the Potala were, using everything at their disposal from bare hands to pots and pans, the military microbots were programmed to react faster and smarter. Where there was a physical barrier erected, they climbed over it, or self-assembled into a bridge for their fellow spiders to cross. Where somehow the crowds had managed to somewhat stop them, the spiders collective mind showed them other less protected routes to surge through. They were fast, fluid, clever, and there were millions of them.

Tashi and Pangu were at the Lukan, the Naga Temple side of the Potala. It was not so much that they had chosen this place to make their last stand, as that was where they were when the first of the shining silver microbot spiders showed up. They were so small and few at first that the threat seemed overblown. They were easily dealt with, Pangu running over a few, Tashi even, dismounted, smashing them under his heel. But then the waves and waves came and it was clear that this particular tide of metal would not be stopped. Tashi would forever become one of the iconic figures of the resistance. Waving a long "darchok" –the Tibetan prayer flag pole- back and forth he climbed up the rough lower walls of the Potala higher and higher to brush away as many of the creatures as he could. The last thing he would be able to remember was a small group of the spiders gathering around him, peering at him with red sensors, red sensors he knew were windows into a deep soul lurking behind them, a force, very much alien and irritated at his resistance. And then the spiders self-assembled into something like an arm, and powerfully thrust him off the wall and out into the air for him to drop like so much discarded animal tissue. He fell perhaps, only ten meters or so at most, but it was enough. His private battle was over.

Pangu saw this and drove to his side, seeing he was still alive though seriously hurt. Pangu and all around called for help, and eventually, in the midst of the chaos, help came and Tashi was carted away. Images of his heroic stand, one hand clutching the rough stones of the lower Potala walls, the other brandishing the darchok, knocking off the spiders creeping upwards, would go viral and insure his fame whether he survived or not. A number of Tibetans and citizens were injured and even lost their lives in their frantic defense of the Dalai Lama. But it wasn't many. They had not been the target of the spiders, because the spiders only targeted someone or something that was proving particularly effective in blocking their path.

Pangu was having some success. He had reached out to his friends for help. They had cobbled together a way to corrupt communications between the spiders. It was all encrypted, but Pangu had been playing back intercepts, and adding lines of code here and there, and the result seemed to be working. Some of the spiders around him were acting confused, moving back and forth in stutter-steps, circling endlessly on themselves. It was this success that made him a target. From amongst the swirling waves of the microbotic spiders, some turned a bright red and formed a circled around him. At one bound they leaped and covered him with their redness, making it seem as if he was bleeding from all his old truck pores. Pangu, devout practioner as he was, was well-prepared for what was to come. He was deep into his preparations for the coming transition, and also deep into connections with friends who had knowledge of what to do with the microbots. Indeed, if a truck can be said to be joyous, Pangu was joyous at his sacrifice. It was his own private Chöd, but offered in the service of Her Holiness.

And yes, there it was, the moment when there was an infinitesimal opening into the mind of the microbot swarm, and in that moment, just before his own physical dismemberment, he tried to insert a package which he and his friends hoped, might change the grim outcome to come, just a bit. And then he offered himself fully to the demons.

The video of Pangu's demise was most remarkable. It is said that it marked him forever as a hero, for another form of life at least. One moment the red spiders leaped on him, almost covering him entirely. The next moment, he fell apart, as the spiders released an almost instantaneously acting molecular debonding agent. And then little pieces of what had once been the old truck, littered the ground where he had made his last stand, and the spiders turned from red back to their mercurial silver and rejoined the surge of other demons unstoppably crawling up the Potala toward she who was calling them, irresistibly, irrevocably and irredeemably.

3. A Certain Pride, a Certain Humility

She awoke radiant. A palpable, committed, down to earth radiance. Her attendants, advisers, fellow nuns and monks, those that were awake, paused for a minute in what they were doing, or not doing, and felt a subtle, but truly seismic shift in reality itself. A few of them realized it was because the Dalai Lama had awoken, a not surprising realization as she was very much in some ways a creature of habit. She had always been a very strong nun. The regularity of her practice had proven to be such a helpful lattice for all of the many realizations on the path that had bloomed for her over her still rather short lifetime, that -in demand as her time had become- she still did not short change her devotion to practice. Today would be no different.

Waking itself was such a powerful teaching moment. The strangeness, the familiarity of it, as one quickly wrapped oneself in the cloak of a manufactured identity and assumed that that was that.

She herself loved descriptions the physicists were toying with, that matter was what was left after various waveforms –essentially dreams- interfered with each other constructively and destructively. Or some said, matter was the waste material left over from the metabolism of lighter beings. There might be something to that she had at times thought. A great organic metaphysical-physical circle of being all nourishing and being nourished by the other stages. One as dependent on the other as the other was dependent on it. Even worms, she thought, were needed to make it all turn. The Khadromas, the angels, owed them that much. Yes, the Dalai Lama loved the entry into the body. From everything and everywhere, to here and now and this. She looked at her small hands, and considered what they would be doing today.

And then she added another cloak to her being, a heavier, darker one. The security establishment of the ETTC had warned her that another attempt on her life was coming. They had encouraged her to withdraw into a less public posture until they understood the nature of the threat, and they assured her they were close. Her own advisers had advised her to accept the advice. And she had even consulted the Nechung Oracle. She was after all considered to be more than just a simple nun, though –and she sighed- to have just been a simple nun would have been more than enough. And the Nechung Oracle had writhed and whirled and shook its heavy headdress about and growled out low words indistinctly, almost un-understandable except to those trained to understand them, and he had said, "There is no duality, but one has arisen. One who is caught in the web, needs another," and they had all hemmed and hawed and said it seemed to confirm the warnings, but she had heard another message in it. And so she had said no. She would not change her public posture. She would not hide.

In addition to being an exceedingly stubborn nun, and of course the incarnation of Chenrezig -a fact she had to from time to time remind her advisers of to make sure she had some say at least in things- she also had other friends, other sources of information. It was inevitable. Sitting, gone, gone, gone beyond gone, in the clear light of the void, there were things that she could see, and even do. And today was a day that she felt well-prepared for.

***

Tashi was not feeling well. He was agitated, and a bit irritated with Pangu. "This, this isn't right. They should have protected her," said Tashi and he looked around, as if seeing Lhasa for the first time. "There's something just not right here, and you know it and you're not telling me," and he would have kicked the truck, as he had done many times in the past, but the truck wasn't there, there was only Pangu, the old farmer standing before him, looking worried. "Pangu, where's the truck? You know the village needs you!"

"Ah, yes, the truck. Well, as you have frequently noted, it was rather an old model in not optimum shape. Come sit with me, and have some tea, and I will finish what I have started, and hopefully you will have thought me a good truck, if nothing else…"

***

Know that I will guide you even in the states of sorrow,

While those who turn away, forsaking me,

Will turn their backs on all the Buddhas.

Only suffering can be the fruit of such an error.

Yet even then, my love will not forsake them,

And when their karma is exhausted, they will come to me.

Yeshe Tsogyal

1. Gloria in Excelsis

The surging uplift of translucent quicksilver flowing up the walls of the Potala was magnificent. Catching the gold and pinks of the morning Himalayan sun, it seemed a heavenly fire that would catch on to all things and purify them forever. And the world was watching. Not just General Holden, physically in a coma, but deeply enmeshed and conscious in a deeply buried web of military computers, not just James Jeffries "JJ" Wallfield III and all of the pay-for-view industrialists excited at the coming prospectus, not just the advertisers who were groaning they had not yet capitalized on this spectacle, but the world, the world that had turned to Tibet as a vision of many things, compassion foremost, but also as gatekeeper to all of the dream realms that humanity was now beginning to colonize. Quick as it all was taking place, there were hundreds of millions mesmerized by what was happening. But it was the groans and heartrending cries of the Tibetans and their fellow citizens that forever provided the soundtrack to this event. Their attempts at defense breached, they could only watch with horror as the screen showed Her Holiness the Dalai Lama, sitting in the most perfect of meditation postures, on the balcony of her private apartments, the balcony where many Dalai Lamas before her had gone out to watch the comings and going of their fellow human beings. She sat there as serene as serenity itself, while the military microbot spiders scrambled upward, accelerating their pace as they now caught scent of her exact location.

And then they were upon her. As if an ocean of mercury had dispensed a mighty circular wave to sink finally and forever an island whose independence it could no longer stomach. General Holden exulted, sending shivers through the equipment monitoring his brain, as he knew what was coming next. A quick devouring of the witch's body and out of that and the multitude of spiders, the self-assembly of a mighty silver cross that would surmount the Potala and declare once and for all that God's Kingdom had come at last.

But just as the horror of those who loved this little nun's quiet humor and joy reached its own peak, so did things not quite exactly go as programmed. The feasting of the military spiders on her little body, which should have been almost instantaneous, was taking time. The first spiders on her skin everywhere, had indeed nibbled, but then hesitated, and in fact were hesitating, were vibrating back and forth in tiny little fast gyres of indecision, and then the indecision was over. They now knew clearly, collectively, in minute detail what to do, what template to follow, and to the horror of the cabal of CSA officers who had planned this, they began to self-assemble into something completely different than that ancient Roman instrument of capital punishment.

Above the Potala there bloomed a beautiful translucent quicksilver rose, blushing with all of the colors of the rainbow. Not a rose, really, but morphing through stages that were exquisitely flower-like. Until they assumed Her Holiness's inward, distinct visualization of the mandala of Chenrezig. Not the 2-dimensional casting of what was in fact 3-dimensional, but the full sphere of the mandala, perfect in every detail. And there it stayed, fully awake and displayed above Lhasa for the world to see. For things can be changed. Nothing is inevitable. A little tweak here and a little tweak there and a radically different future emerges. And Her Holiness, from her youngest childhood, had really been an adept at visualization. Visualizations so clear and in such detail that they seemed to stand almost on their own in fully fleshed out perfection. And the mandala of Chenrezig she had always loved. Had always loved the sand mandala ceremonies, and really, she thought, this was not that different. There were moments when the deeply enmeshed meaningfulness of Dharma in all things ecstatically manifested themselves. She smiled, and shimmers of light coursed through the mandala of Chenrezig fully bloomed above the Potala, and fully displayed for all.

2. Inner and Outer

Tashi had a headache. Moreover he was having a lot of trouble opening his eyes. That is to say, when his eyes were closed he seemed to be seeing as well as when his eyes were open, and when his eyes were open, well it was some strange scene that made no sense to him at all. Basically he just wasn't sure which view was the eyes open view and which view was the eyes closed view. The best solution, especially given how much his head hurt, was just to keep his eyes closed and rest a bit, if that is, he could figure out which was which. So summoning up all of the force of will he could muster, and that wasn't very much at the moment, he firmly closed his eyes, and in doing so his eyes opened and he saw he was in what appeared to be something like a hospital room. He saw people sitting and standing around his bed, for that was where he realized he was. People who seemed familiar, friends, family perhaps, he wasn't completely sure at the moment. They did not any rate appear to be looking at him with any hint of hostility, quite the opposite in fact.

The first to speak was an eccentric looking yinchee man who smiled and said, "You're probably feeling a little disoriented about now, about what is real and what is not and trust me, as someone who has studied this question in considerable depth, and often wondered if the question is really worth asking at all in fact, I would recommend not worrying about it. Just go with the flow. And if you ever come to Boston, we can talk about it a bit, OK?" Tashi would have nodded if he knew what the hell the guy was talking about, or if he could move his head for that matter which he wasn't sure he could or not.

Next another yinchee man, a soldier of some sort, walked over and put his hand on Tashi's shoulder. "You should be proud of yourself son, you put up a good fight. Now get well soon. I don't think this is all over yet." Then he stepped back from the bed crisply, leaving Tashi with a strange desire to salute, but again, like his head, he wasn't really sure if he was able to move his arms yet or not. He moved his eyes over to the next figure in his room and saw thankfully it wasn't another strange foreigner. It was a little Tibetan nun quietly chanting prayers, the Medicine Buddha puja he thought, and was surprised that he recognized it, even if in fact he didn't. The nun realized he was looking at her and without missing a syllable, smiled and winked at him. Tashi wanted to laugh, but that hurt too much so he settled for smiling instead and was pleased that he could at least manage that.

Next to the nun was the figure of a woman cloaked mostly in blue, whose face he could not see completely clearly, but which, from what he could see, like some lover by moonlight had a most earthly/unearthly beauty to it. She moved closer to his bed, almost floating and as she came close he smelled the freshness and sanity of pine forests with brooks dancing through them. She smiled broadly and his headache disappeared. And then she began making slow passes with her hands over his body, never touching it, but as she did so he felt waves of pure lifeforce enter back into him, in an aching relief from the pain and a release back into the joys of healthy embodiment. He could feel his manhood begin to move, too, and he was most pleased it still appeared to be working, if nothing else was. Then she was done, and saying nothing but smiling broadly, she floated back from the bed, as she had seemed to float to it.

And then, over there in the corner, where there was a votive nook, he noticed there was floating another lovely yinchee woman, this one a little older, and really quite sexy, rather underdressed perhaps for Tibet, but he didn't mind that at all, though he sensed that the first yinchee man, the eccentric, was embarrassed. And she was smiling too, in all her suggestiveness, and rather than say anything instead made a gesture with her hands which opened somehow a door from somewhere else, through which stepped Dolma, his companion on some of the journey. She was wearing her blue Chupah, luminous in way that filled the whole room with a serenity that was as much felt as it was seen. She walked over to Tashi and took his hand and was quiet for a moment, regarding him with love and pride. Then she said, "Tashi-la, there comes a time, when the telling and the teller become one, when the dreamer and the dream turn out to be the same, when a story even, twists around upon itself and begins to sing of the storyteller as just one more embedded song. Some will say that disentanglement comes from cutting the bonds to everything and turning away. Others, that the only real truth lies in deeper entanglements, lies in twisting them this way and that to suit yourself. But the heart is neither this nor that, and has no boundaries printed on it. Liberation and compassion bloom together, or not at all." And then she rang the ritual bell in her hand and he woke up.

3. Upper and Lower

Tashi began the process of reassembling himself. It was a process he didn't usually notice, as it tended to happen quickly when he wasn't really paying attention. First, it wasn't so much that he gave names to things, as that he noticed there were things there, and that later if he should so try, he could probably name them. Then he began to gather around him the very loose threads of a few crucial memories of who he was, or who he was supposed to be, including his name. He realized that he was in a hospital room, and that unlike the other hospital room, which was very fast fading from his memory, this one didn't have any people floating about. He could see from the little light coming in the window that it must be either just before dawn, or perhaps just after sunset. He wasn't sure of that other thing at all, which he found a name for, time. Whenever it was, he saw, as his eyes grew accustomed to being open, that there were other people in the room. He stared almost cross-eyed at one particularly wild-looking Tibetan and then realized with a relief it was his good friend Tsewang. He let out a groan and Tsewang perked up immediately and said, "Ah, it appears our hero has awakened!"

Then a quite young yinchee woman came over to his bedside and entered his field of vision. The worry on her face in no way marred her honest beauty, seemed in fact to be a natural part of it, and he realized that he knew her, too, but couldn't at first remember why or when or what her name was. And then she said, "Tashi, I am so sorry, I didn't know this was going to happen. I didn't know this was planned, please forgive me. I truly, truly never wanted to hurt anyone!" And then she began to cry making Tashi's head hurt even more. Given that he was the one in pain he didn't quite think it was fair that she was the one crying. Tsewang came over and put his arm around the woman to comfort her, saying, "It's alright Faith we believe you. Everything turned out the way it was supposed to turn out. We all played our part. Me, you, Tashi, the Satanic mills of the C.S.A. It's OK, something new has begun."

And Tashi realized mostly who Faith was, and felt just a little jealous that his good friend should be comforting her so. And then a great deal more of what had happened came back to him, and he would have sat bolt upright, tried to sit bolt upright, but couldn't quite move very well yet, "Her Holiness...Her Holiness, is she, is she..." he managed to croak out. And then they both smiled, and most mischievously they pushed Tashi's bed over to the window, and the two of them lifted his head just enough for him to see –there- surmounting the rooftops of the other buildings, the Potala, and rising above it the most marvelous sight: a fully realized glowing sphere, pulsing gently with a living luminous blessing. It was the mandala of Chenrezig, one he knew quite well from his years as a boy at the monastery. And a thrill and a simultaneous chill went through him, "It's beautiful! So beautiful, so… I'm dead then? This is the Dewachen?"

Tsewang laughed, "With me here? Hardly! No, no such luck. Quite the opposite, you've survived and have been born again!" And they all laughed, even Tashi, weakly. And then after a bit they laid Tashi's head back on the pillow, and he felt the strongest urge to close his eyes again, knowing this time when he closed his eyes, he would actually be able to get some sleep. And he looked at Tsewang and Faith, both of them smiling and knowing he needed to sleep, and just before he closed his eyes, he saw Pangu, the old farmer, standing by the door to the room, and Pangu, too, was smiling.

4. The World Just as it Is

She thought perhaps now was the time. She understood now something of her little friends' minds, and how much they wanted to belong and to work together; how much in fact they wanted to be helpful. And she thought they could be helpful, now that they were removed from that other influence which had so misused them. And there was so much work to be done, in healing the ravages of climate change as it had affected, and was affecting the Tibetan Plateau. The roof of the world needed to be saved. The roof of the world from which so many mighty pure rivers flowed down to nourish and cleanse so many; the roof of the world, which could show the way, or at least one very good way, out of the mess they had gotten themselves into.

And so, as dawn at last came to Lhasa, she revealed for all to see the silver dorje above the sphere of the most perfect mandala, all shimmering with colors and life, also made of shining silver, and seeming also to be singing an infinity of harmonious silver songs, songs of infinite space filled with an infinity of Buddhas, all pure and in harmony with each other, a Khadroma choir of soft, healing bells; and with the dorje of her mind she cut the mandala in two, and her visualization was perfectly reflected in a dorje of the little silver beings above her, and all of it now, the great perfect spherical mandala of Chenrezig, dissolved down into rivers of silver that coursed down the sides of the Potala, as pure as any Himalayan snowmelt stream, and it all flowed out, in every direction, into the world, and this time there was no one to stop it, people watching as the silver flowed down and past them, swirling around their boots and through the streets of Lhasa and out finally into the as yet undestroyed beauty of Tibet itself.

Coda: Exodus and Invocation

The wind is full of prayers, and the rocks, too, are carved full of prayers, and the carving of prayers into rocks goes on, and the praying of the wind goes on. There are some places where the great wave of disenchantment of the world never quite reached. It climbed to the top of the Tibetan passes and was re-enchanted. It sobbed in recognition of all that it had forgotten, a world that lived: Gods and Goddesses and demigods and demons and spirits everywhere, and each and every sentient being embodied or not, a friend, a mother, in an endless telling of a story that only stopped when one awoke, and even then did not really stop so much as go on joyously, with all the connections between doing and being, clear, and freedom come as natural as mountain air.

The streams were full of prayers, and the rivers and the great grasslands; the caves were full of meditators and the bones of meditators, still sitting in meditation position, and of paintings on the cave walls, not of bison and the hunt, but of dakhinis and dharma protectors, and of mandalas, the visualization of which created a door for stepping out of this world and into the world from which it had emerged. And there were monasteries, as large as little cities themselves, where monks and nuns chanted and laughed and practiced the art and science of having the mind understand itself. And the skies, the endless skies, above the nomads and the yak were peopled by clouds that were the clouds in the mind of the people who walked below them. Clouds that taught and told and preached and sang poems and prayers. Everything was connected to everything else, as intimately as family, as closely as lover to lover, and inner was outer and outer was inner, no one being able, or wanting, to close the doors on the immensities on either side of that equation. The earth had raised high a cradle to teach all that lived upon her and with her, of their inheritance and their belonging. No cathedral of man could rival these mountains and valleys in sanctity and uplift. And when the world, finally, in great tragedy and sadness, broke into the fastness of the mountains, the secrets that had been there preserved and nurtured, flowed out into the world, and the world was changed.

Lha Gyalo! Victory to the Gods!

Pö Gyalo! Victory to Tibet!

Apologia

I'm old now. I've had a lot of lovers. I gave much of this story to
my truck, Pangu, to sing, but in truth, he was sometimes just a
vehicle, and in truth and fact much of what I learned about
events was shared by him with me. There is actually much more
to this than I have told, and though I am now tired, I have not
quite found the peace I hoped for. My prostrations and prayers
are still a bit empty, and my mind, as is the mind, races this way
and that in remembrances and in wonderings of why I did this
and not that, and why those distant events, touched me, touched
us all. And though I know all things change and come to an end,
this body certainly, I do still grieve for the earth and the trials it
is facing. I do not have the true equanimity that comes with
being truly unattached to things. I have loved too much, and
perhaps, love too much still.

Tibetan and Buddhist Glossary

Akuh Tonpa: Uncle Tonpa, a Tibetan folk hero/trickster character

Ama: mother

Amdo: one of the three main cultural regions of Tibet

Ani: a nun

Bagleb: Tibetan bread

Banden: a traditional Tibetan apron worn to by a woman to signify that she is married

Bardo: the inbetween state, as in the state after death and before rebirth

Bharkor: central square in Lhasa around the Jhokhang

Bodhisattva: a realized being who returns to work for the enlightenment of all sentient beings

Bon: the original pre-Buddhist religion of Tibet

Chak: ritual obeisance

Ch'an: Chinese for Zen

Chang: Tibetan barley beer

Chang Kan: A Tibetan beer shop

Cha ngarmo: sweet tea

Chenrezig: the Boddhistava of Compassion

Chöd: a Tibetan Buddhist practice in which one offers one self to demons and hungry ghosts as an act of compassion and to learn the ultimate emptiness of the self

Chukan: Alter room.

Chupa: traditional Tibetan dress

Churra: hard dried cheese

Chushigondro: Tibetan guerrilla group active up until 1973

Dewachen: the "Blissful Land" where good practitioners can be reborn

Dharma: the law, the rule, what underlies all things

Dolkar: White Tara

Dolma: Tara

Dorje: a ritual tool that represents the thunderbolt of enlightenment

DrakMar: Red Blood cliffs in Upper Mustang

DurTroe: Charnel grounds: where corpses are disposed of for the sky burial

Guru Rinpoche: the powerful Bodissatva who brought Buddhism to Tibet slaying demons on the way

Gyalwa Rinpoche: The Dalai Lama

Jhagoe: vulture

Jhang Thang: the empty quarter of Northern Tibet

Jhokang: A Temple near the Bharkor; one of the Holiest Temples in Tibetan Buddhism

Kaliyuga: last, and demonic, of the four yugas described in Sanskrit scriptures

Kamalasila: a scholar of the Madhyamaka school of Buddhism who was present at the great debate at Samye

Kapse: A Tibetan deep-fried pastry prepared for Losar

Kempo: an abbott, a religious teacher

Kerang debu yinbei: "How are you?" (Tibetan greeting)

Khadromas and Khadros: literally "Sky Travelers" female and male Tibetan Buddhist "angels"

Khampa: Tibetans from the Eastern Tibetan cultural region

Khatak: a white scarf offered in greeting or farewell or to an esteemed person

Khorwa: illusion

Kora: circumambulation

Kunchokkhen: a Tibetan curse

Kusho-la: Honorable teacher

Kyichu: the River of Happiness that flows through Lhasa

-la: honorific ending in Tibetan

Lharamba: PhD equivalent for a Buddhist scholar

Lhasa: literally "Place of God"

Losar: Tibetan New Year

Lungta: Tibetan prayer flags

Mani: prayer wheel

Moheyan: the Ch'an monk that presented the "instantaneous" enlightenment school at the debate at Samye

Momos: Tibetan dumplings

Nagarjuna: great Buddhist philosopher

Ngak: mantra

Ngapa: tantric lay practitioner

Norbu-lingkha: The Summer Palace

Om Mani Padme Hum: the mantra of Chenrezig

Pak: a pressed together round bar of Tsampa commonly eaten in Tibet

Palden Lhamo: protecting deity of the Gelugpa school of Tibetan Buddhism

Peu ki kup: monkey's butt

Pö: Tibet

Pöcha: Tibetan tea

Potala: The Dalai Lama's abode

Rangzen: freedom

Rinpoche: "precious one," a high teacher

Sambogagaya: middle of the three worlds between the Nirmanakaya (physical world) and the Dharmakaya

Sangha: the community of like-minded practitioners

Sarpa: new

Shendun: prayer

Shol Jhakhan: a teahouse in the old Tibetan part of Lhasa

Sky burial: as a final act of compassion a dead body is cut up and offered to the birds for their nourishment

Tashi Delek: traditional Tibetan greeting

Thanka (tanka): a traditional Tibetan Buddhist painting of Buddhas, Deities, or Mandalas, etc., used to assist a practitioner in their visualization exercises

Three Worlds: in Tibetan Buddhist metaphysics the three main types of existence

Thukpa: Tibetan noodles

Thummo: the practice of creating internal psychic fire to stay warm at high altitudes

Tinngazin: meditation

Trisong Detsen: the second of the three Dharma Kings of Tibet

Tukshezhe: thank you

Tulku: a reincarnate teacher

Tulpa: a fully realized visualization that can be seen by others beside the meditator who created this visualization

U-Tsang: Central Tibet

Vajra: thunderbolt

Vajrayana: the thunderbolt path, Tibetan Buddhism

Woma, woma: "Once Upon a Time" in Tibetan

Yinchee: foreigner

Yinchee gopse: a blonde foreigner

Yidam: a protective deity

Acknowledgements

With profound thanks to HBG and LLD and other friends who did their best to make this all palatable to the reader in the face of my abject laziness.